FINDING FRANKIE

A TUPER MYSTERY

TERESA BURRELL

SILENT THUNDER PUBLISHING

COPYRIGHT

FINDING FRANKIE
A Tuper Mystery
Copyright 2019 by
Teresa Burrell
All rights reserved.
Cover Art by Madeline Settle
Edited by LJ Sellers

ISBN: 978-1-938680-32-8
Library of Congress Control Number: 2019916134
Silent Thunder Publishing
San Diego

To Ringo, a wonderful dog and companion, whose life was cut short by a hit-and-run driver. You will always be by Tuper's side in his heart.

Acknowledgements

A special thanks to those who made this book possible.

JP
Clarissa Bartosik
Jerome Johnson
PJ Klakken
Shane Klakken
Clarice Preece

Thank you, **Donna Pennick,** for the cover photo.

My Amazing Beta Readers:

Beth Sisel Agejew
Vickie Barrier
Meli White Cardullo
Janie Greene-Livingston
Alisha Henri
Gena 'Fortner' Jeselnik
Crystal Johnson
Sheila Krueger
Lily Qualls Morales
MaryAnn Schaefer
Colleen Scott
Uma Swati
Sandy Thompson
Denise Zendel

OTHER MYSTERIES BY TERESA

CHAPTER 1

Tuper leaned against the bar in Nickels Gaming Parlour. He took a drink from his bottle of orange soda pop and set it down on the counter. The sound of screeching tires, followed by a thud and a deafening clang of metal on metal interrupted the quiet. He moved quickly for a man in his early seventies, his cowboy boots clicking on the wood floor as he strode across the room and hurried outside. Clarice, the bartender, an attractive woman in her mid-fifties ran out behind him. By the time they were outside, the vehicle had left the lot and turned the corner. They only caught a glimpse of taillight as it drove out of sight.

Tuper and Clarice ran to the body sprawled across the wet pavement. Tuper glanced around and clutched the gun in his holster. Behind them, patrons, ignoring the spring rain, poured out of Nickels to see what was going on. As one man ran past the body toward a silver Camry parked twenty feet away, he shouted, "My car!" The vehicle had been clipped as the hit-and-run driver left the lot, leaving a broken headlight and severe dents to the driver's side.

"Oh no," Tuper said, as he approached the man on the ground. "It's Squirrely."

Clarice pulled her cell phone out of her pocket and called 9-1-1. "This is the bartender from Nickels Gaming Parlour on Last Chance Gulch. We need an ambulance. There's been a hit-and-run in the parking lot."

Tuper squatted his tall, lean body down beside the man. "Squirrely," he yelled. "Talk to me." He leaned close to his face to see if he could feel his breath. He could not. Tuper shook his head, partly because of the odor that came from Squirrely's mouth and unclean body that suddenly smelled like a wet dog. Tuper knew his friend hadn't bathed in several weeks. Even when he did, Squirrely would put the same clothes back on without washing them. Tuper saw Squirrely's lips move, as if he was trying to talk. Tuper leaned in again, holding his breath to avoid the smell. Squirrely murmured.

"Just hang on," Tuper said, as he tried to decipher the words.

Squirrely murmured again, and then lay still.

"What did he say?" Clarice asked.

"It sounded like, *Give to Elba* or *Ella or Emma*. I don't know. That's all I could make out."

Clarice reached for Squirrely's wrist to check his pulse, but it was bent all the way back. A bone protruded out of the side, and blood flowed at a fairly rapid pace. She leaned across him to check the other wrist, her hair sopping up blood. "He's still breathing, but he's in bad shape."

As Tuper talked to Squirrely, his voice choked up and tears ran down his thin, rugged face. The drops followed the scar down the right side, from the corner of his eye to the bottom of his chin. Squirrely didn't answer. Tuper kept talking until he heard the sirens. The Helena Fire Department arrived within minutes. The crew was no sooner out of the truck when the ambulance from Montana Medical Transport arrived and took over.

Tuper pushed off the wet pavement to get out of their way. He stood back against the wall of the casino, feeling the rain for the first time. He felt a little weak and leaned back to brace himself, but his cowboy hat hit the wall, and he dropped his head down just slightly. He was standing there in his plaid western shirt and jeans, his silver belt buckle covered in blood, and his gray mustache still wet with tears, when Clarice approached. Her prematurely silver hair was wet, and the tips were red with blood. She hadn't noticed her bloody hair until she caught Tuper staring at her. She wiped it with her hand, only smearing the blood more.

"He's still alive, Toop. They'll get him to the hospital now."

Tuper shook his head without saying a word.

"Why would anyone want to hurt Squirrely?" Clarice asked.

"I saw him last night. He was talking crazy, then he gave me his duffel bag. He said if anything happened to him to look inside." Tuper shook his head. "He said, 'Do what you can to make things right.' Those were his exact words. I tried to get him to explain, but he wouldn't."

Two black-and-blue police cars drove into the lot.

"Hopefully, *they* can find out who hit him," Clarice said, nodding toward the cops.

"I gotta go." Tuper started to walk away, past the small crowd of gawkers. A few had gone back inside or stood under the awning near the casino.

"The cops are going to want to talk to you. We were the first on the scene."

"You talk to 'em. You know as much as I do. I'm going to see what's in that duffel bag before I talk to them."

"What should I tell them?"

"Tell 'em only what you saw. That's all you really know."

"Toop, don't get yourself mixed up in something you can't get out of."

"I ain't got stuck yet," Tuper said. "Find out where they're taking Squirrely and let me know. I want to be able to check on him."

CHAPTER 2

Ringo, a blond mutt, stuck his head out the window of a beat-up, faded-red 1978 Toyota. The dog grew more excited as Tuper came closer, spinning around joyfully at his master's approach, while apparently enjoying the rain from the open window.

"Hey, boy." Tuper patted him on his wet head and scratched behind his ears. Then Tuper walked to the back of the car, untied the rope that secured the handle to the bumper to keep the door from flying open, and opened the hatchback. Squirrely's dirty, black duffel bag was still there. Tuper was anxious to see what was inside but didn't want to do it there in the parking lot. Too many people buzzing around, not to mention the cops and the weather. Tuper was uncertain as to what he might find, and he had a feeling this wasn't the time or place.

He got in the car and sat there for a second, debating which way to go. He didn't want to drive all the way to Clancy to his cabin. It was too far and would be muddy from the rain. He didn't need to get stuck trying to go up the mountain. So instead, he drove to Clarice's house. He just needed somewhere private and dry.

A young woman, about five feet tall, with short, spiked, reddish-orange hair, answered the door. She wore jeans and hiking boots.

"Hi, Lana," Tuper said.

Lana had been living with Clarice and her sister, Mary, for a few months now. Tuper had saved Lana from a drunken cowboy trying to take advantage of her in front of Nickels casino. When Clarice discovered Lana was homeless, she took her in. Tuper and Clarice were old friends who acted more like siblings. Over the years, they had grown extremely close, but there had never been anything romantic between them. Clarice dated occasionally but hadn't developed a long-term relationship with anyone in some time. Tuper, on the other hand, had been in many long- and short-term relationships, but none that ever settled him down.

"Come on in," Lana said. "If you're looking for Clarice, she isn't here."

"I know. I just left her at Nickels."

Lana looked at the duffel bag Tuper was carrying. "Are you moving in? Because there's not much room left in this house, and I've got the sofa, so you'll have to take the floor. I'm not giving up my bed for you, old man."

Although Lana and Tuper were like fire and water, opposites in every conceivable way, she had proved to be a worthwhile asset with her exceptional computer skills. What she could do with technology was way beyond anything Tuper could have imagined. She had helped him when he was hired to find a woman's missing son. He wouldn't admit it to Lana, but Tuper was amazed at her brilliance in the tech world. Everyone over the age of three was a technological genius to him, which was evident by his continued use of a flip phone. He didn't know enough about computers to fully appreciate that her skill set went way beyond the average person's. She had tried to explain to him that she was a *hacker*, but he still didn't quite get it. To him, it was as if she were speaking a foreign language.

Tuper, on the other hand, brought seventy years of experience to the table and seemed to know everyone in the state of Montana. If he couldn't get something done, he usually knew someone who could. When asked where he got information, his response was, "I know a guy."

Although Tuper admired Lana's skill set, he was often bothered by her incessant talking. He had told her on more than one occasion, "It only takes one word to say *yes* or *no*." Together, they were an odd couple but very effective.

"No, I ain't movin' in," Tuper said. "This bag belongs to Squirrely. And don't call me old man."

"Okay, Pops."

Tuper shook his head, walked into the dining area, and set the duffel bag on the table.

"Seriously?" Lana gave him a look. "That thing is filthy. I know Clarice wouldn't want it on her table."

"I'll wipe it off when I'm done." Tuper started to open the bag. They both knew he wouldn't clean the table.

"Why do you have Squirrely's belongings? That's probably everything he owns in that one bag, and you have it. Why is that?"

"Squirrely's in the hospital."

Before he could say anything more, Lana started asking more questions. "What? Why? What happened? Is he okay?"

"If you'll stop jabberin' for a durn minute, I'll tell you."

Lana touched her index finger to her thumb and moved

7

them across her lips in a zipping motion. She sat still, waiting for his explanation.

"Squirrely was hit by a car this morning."

Lana waited to hear more, but that's all Tuper said. Finally, she couldn't stand it any longer and asked, "What do you mean 'he was hit by a car?' How bad is he? Is he going to live?"

"Dunno. He's unconscious."

"Who did it?"

"Don't know."

"Is he going to be okay?"

"Don't know."

"What do you know?"

"I know he was hit by a car, and he's in the hospital."

"Why aren't you there?"

"'Cause I need to know what's in this here duffel bag first."

Tuper unzipped the bag and pulled back the panels so he could see inside.

"Holy moly!" Lana said. "Those are hundred-dollar bills. There must be thousands in there. Where did Squirrely get all this cash? He lives in the back of Humpty's Bar. Heck, most of the time he lives on the street. How could he have all this money?" Her eyes widened. "You don't suppose he stole it from the bar, do you? Squirrely doesn't seem like that kind of guy, but he had to have gotten it somewhere. It's not like he could've been saving it all his life. He doesn't even have money for shoes."

"He don't need shoes. I already gave him some from that cowboy friend of yours."

The night Tuper saved Lana, he took the assaulter's cowboy boots and gave them to Squirrely.

"That's not what I mean. How could a guy have all this cash and live the way he does?" Lana started pacing around the room, but she didn't stop talking. "He must've gotten it somewhere recently. We need to find out where. What are you going to do with the money? That's probably why he was hit by the car. Someone is after him, and I bet it's about the money. It's always about the money. Why are people so greedy?"

Tuper shook his head at her chatter. He removed the cash from the bag, creating a huge pile on the table, as he searched for anything that might offer an explanation. He removed a stainless steel .38-caliber revolver with a satin finish and a black handle. When he checked it to see if it was loaded, he found all five chambers empty. He laid the gun on the table. The words *Ruger SP101* were etched across the two-and-a-quarter-inch barrel. Underneath, it read *.38 Special Cal.* Below the cylinder, on the frame, was the serial number. He watched Lana as she started to jot down the information from the gun, and her wide eyes as she was distracted by another item in the bag—an old newspaper, still folded like it had not been opened. He removed it and handed it to Lana.

"What's this?" she asked.

"Looks like a newspaper to me."

"I see that." She stared at the paper more closely. "It's dated May 4, 1994. That's twenty-five years ago, almost to the date. That's strange. Why would Squirrely have an unread paper from that long ago?" She examined the paper more closely. "It looks like it was opened and refolded. But why would he have saved it?"

"Beats me." Tuper put the gun and the cash back in the bag.

Lana held out the paper. "What do you want me to do with this? Can I read it? Maybe there's something about missing money. It must have something to do with the money. Why else would it be in there?"

"Can you talk and read at the same time?" Tuper asked.

"I don't think so."

"Good. Then read the paper."

Lana scowled at him.

Tuper looked out the window. "The rain has let up. I'm going to see how Squirrely's doin'." He closed the bag, picked it up, and stuck the bag behind the sofa.

"Are you leaving that here?"

"My car doesn't lock."

"You're not afraid I'm going to steal it and take off?" Lana asked.

"Are you?"

"No, of course not."

"We're good then," Tuper said and walked out.

CHAPTER 3

Lana retrieved the Lysol and a clean rag from the cabinet in the laundry room. She wet the rag, then sprayed the table with the disinfectant. When she was satisfied it was clean, she sat down on the sofa with the newspaper and began to peruse it for articles that might be significant. She was surprised by how thick it was. She flipped through the paper, counting the pages: twenty-six. By today's standards, it looked like a Sunday paper instead of Wednesday's, without the extra ads.

The paper was dated May 4, 1994 and was published by the *Independent Record* in Helena, Montana. Lana quickly checked online and found the company was still in business. The newspaper was almost as old as she was. She remembered what her life was like back then. Her family had seemed so happy. She couldn't help but wonder when it all started to go wrong. *That's not true,* she thought. She knew exactly when it started. She slipped into her Scarlett O'Hara mood, which she seemed to do more and more these days. *I'll think about that tomorrow.* She pushed the memories of her family out of her mind and continued to read. She had no idea what she was looking for but hoped she would know when she saw it.

In the top left corner, it read *Cloudy with rain possible, high of 63 and low of 40.* Lana checked the weather app on her phone and found not much had changed in twenty-five years. She wondered if the winter in 1994 had been as long and cold as this year. She started to check online, then stopped. She was getting off task. It was highly unlikely that Squirrely kept the paper because of the weather.

The main headline read *Armored Truck Trial, Guard Thought Robbery a Joke.* Lana read through the article. Five men had been involved in planning the holdup, but no money had actually been taken. Lana opened a Word doc and entered the names of the men listed in the heist. She would check them later.

The next headline was *LD Barn Burn,* and the blaze appeared to have started accidently with a controlled fire and strong winds. The owner, Mike Linderman, went to the property the morning before to make sure the fire was out, but he apparently didn't check carefully enough. Smoldering dead grass and old hay seemed to have ignited a railroad tie near the barn, and gusty winds had done the rest. Lana saw no connection to Squirrely, but her imagination allowed her to create a whole scenario that could involve him. She typed *Mike Linderman* in her Word doc along with the headline and moved on.

Boy, 3, Lost...and Found. The boy had been missing for four hours and was discovered about a mile and a half from his home. She didn't know how old Squirrely was, but he definitely seemed too old to be the lost boy and not likely his father either. It was hard to tell how old homeless people were. They all looked aged to her, even the young ones. She recorded the information anyway.

The next headline read *Doctors Unlikely to Copy Kevorkian*. Not knowing who Kevorkian was, she read the article and discovered he was a physician who was acquitted for an assisted suicide of a man with Lou Gehrig's disease. She thought it highly unlikely that had anything to do with Squirrely or the money he was carrying around. Nor did she think the articles about the last chance to see an eclipse this century or the Rolling Stones tour were what she was looking for. But she couldn't be absolutely sure. She knew little about Squirrely's background and didn't even know his real name. She made a note to find out what Tuper knew. It might help her narrow things down.

Lana sighed. She had only gone through the front page and had already created hours of research for herself.

Tuper sat in the waiting room at St. Peter's Hospital where Squirrely had been admitted. Two middle-aged women sat a few seats away. One couldn't stop crying, the other trying to console her. A man came in, carrying two cups of coffee. The sobbing woman shook her head, and the other took the coffee. Tuper surmised from their conversation that the crying woman's husband had been in a car accident and was in pretty bad shape.

No one was in the waiting room for Squirrely, and Tuper didn't expect anyone would show up. Squirrely didn't have much family. His father had been gone for more than a decade. He had a sister who lived in Nevada, but Tuper didn't know how to reach her. Squirrely's parents had been living in

Nevada with their daughter until his father passed away and his mother, Norma, moved back to Great Falls, where she had friends. Squirrely checked on her whenever he could get transportation to Great Falls. But Tuper didn't have a phone number for her or he would have called. He wasn't even certain Squirrely's mom had a phone. He did know where she lived because he had taken Squirrely there many times over the years, but Great Falls was a good hour and a half away. Making contact would have to wait until he had more information about Squirrely's condition. Tuper had little to report and wasn't sure what good it would do anyway. He didn't know if Norma would even come to the hospital to see Squirrely. His mother was a cantankerous old woman who didn't seem to care about anyone but herself. Squirrely's father had been just the opposite. Tuper had only met him once but found him to be a loving and thoughtful man with a great sense of humor. It was a wonder he had stayed with the old woman for so many years, but they had celebrated their fiftieth wedding anniversary. The old man would've shown up in a heartbeat if he knew his son was in trouble. Tuper didn't expect that of Squirrely's mother.

The only other person Tuper might expect to see was Sean, the big Irishman who owned Humpty's bar. Squirrely spent most nights on the streets, but when it was too cold, Sean let him sleep in the back room of the bar as long as he didn't drink the alcohol. Sean allowed him to have one beer and one shot of Jack Daniels for "keeping an eye" on the place. Squirrely never broke the rule. At first, Sean had counted the beer and marked the Jack Daniel's bottle, as well as a few others, every so often but soon stopped when he never found anything missing.

Squirrely was an odd man. He didn't seem all that bright

and didn't talk much about himself, but he loved to gossip about others. He knew a lot of people but, with the exception of Sean and Tuper, wasn't close to any of them. He got his nickname because he was easily distracted and had a hard time sitting still. He had an annoying habit of saying *yeh* with almost every sentence he spoke. The word almost clicked when he said it, sounding more like *yuck*, but Tuper would be glad to hear a *yeh* from him right now.

A tall, balding man wearing scrubs came into the waiting room and looked around. "Anyone here for someone known as…" He looked down at the paperwork again. "Squirrely?"

Tuper stood up. "He's my friend."

"Come with me, please."

Tuper followed the doctor to the Intensive Care Unit station, where he asked a nurse to take down some information.

"What's his real name?" the doctor asked Tuper.

"Frank, I think."

"Do you know his last name?"

"I've heard it, but I can't recall right now."

"Does he have any family?"

"His mother lives in Great Falls, and he has a sister in Nevada. That's it as far as I know. No one here in town."

"I don't suppose you have contact information for either of them."

"Nope."

"Do you know Frank's address?"

"He doesn't have one. Lives on the streets most the time."

"Anything else you can tell me about him? Medical history maybe?"

"Not really. I've known him about fifteen years, but he don't talk much about himself. I don't think he ever went to the hospital in that time. Never knew him to be sick much, except with a cold or something."

When the doctor appeared to be done with his questions, Tuper asked, "How is he?"

"I can't tell you much because you're not family, but he survived the surgeries. He's not conscious, and when he wakes up, he's going to be in some pain."

"But he will wake up?"

"I believe so, but I can't be certain, and I have no idea when that might be."

"Can I see him?"

"Sure, as soon as he's brought in here."

When the doctor walked away, the nurse led Tuper to a room in the ICU.

"You can wait here. They're bringing him up now."

Tuper sat down on the only chair and waited. About ten minutes later, two men in scrubs wheeled Squirrely's bed in and hooked him up to an IV stand and a couple of monitors. They talked to each other, then left without saying anything to Tuper.

Squirrely had a cast on his right arm. The whole right side of his face was swollen and bruised. The left side and his left arm were covered in bandages.

"You're a mess, Squirrely," Tuper said, not expecting an answer. "You better pull through this. And what's with all that money in the duffel bag?" Squirrely lay there unconscious, but Tuper continued to talk. "You're a crazy SOB, you know that? I wish you'd a told me what was in that bag yesterday. Maybe I'd a kept a better eye on ya."

The one-sided conversation went on for a few more minutes, until Tuper's phone rang.

"Hey, Pops, are you at the hospital?" Lana asked.

"Yeah."

"How's Squirrely? Is he going to be okay?"

Tuper shook his head. Lana never asked a question and waited for an answer. She usually threw out two or three more before she stopped talking. "He's still unconscious, and he's pretty bandaged up."

"What did they do? Did he have surgery? What's his prognosis?"

"Don't know. Don't know. Don't know."

"What do you mean you don't know? Did you ask the doctor, or at least a nurse?"

"They won't tell me anything because I'm not family."

"Why didn't you tell them you were his father, or brother, or something? They wouldn't have known the difference."

"Didn't know I had to. I don't spend much time in these hospitals."

"Never mind. I'll find out."

"You going to chop into the hospital records?"

"It's hack, Pops, not chop."

"You can do that?"

"If I can get into banks and police programs, I can certainly get into hospital records. I'll call you back when I know something."

CHAPTER 4

Tuper's phone rang, and a photo of Lana showed up on the screen. Tuper had fussed at Lana the first time she tried to tell him how to use his phone. It made him feel stupid, not knowing what some four-year-old might know. But he liked that he could see who was calling, so he let her set it up. She had tried to get him to buy a smart phone, but that was going too far. All he needed was to be able to call someone when he wanted to and to receive calls. He didn't need the dang thing to make coffee, or whatever else it could do.

Before Tuper could say hello, Lana said, "Squirrely had a distal radius fracture that they had to set, and they put a cast brace on it to keep it immobile."

"He had a what?"

"A broken wrist with a temporary cast."

"Why didn't you just say that?"

"Because that's not what the record says."

"What else did it say?"

"Multiple contusions and abrasions on his face, arms, and legs," Lana said, then added, "He has bruises and scrapes."

"I can see that. Anything else?"

"He has a basal skull fracture, which they're monitoring. His chart says it may require surgery if it begins to show excessive leakage of cerebrospinal fluid. There are concerns about internal bleeding, which they are also monitoring closely. What is Squirrely's real name?" Lana switched topics without a break in her thoughts.

"Frank something."

"That's not much help. I've been reading this newspaper to figure out how it's connected to Squirrely and the money, but I can't do much without his real name."

"Maybe the paper's not connected."

"Why would he have a twenty-five-year-old newspaper if it didn't mean something to him? The man barely has a full set of clothes, but he kept a newspaper for twenty-five years. It has to be important, and there must be something that will tell us why he kept it."

"You have a point. I'll get you Squirrely's name."

"And anything else you can about him. His birthdate, any old addresses, family, where he went to school. Did he grow up here in Montana? Does he have relatives here?"

"I think he's from around Roy originally, but I'm not sure." Tuper told Lana about Squirrely's mother and sister. "That's all I know."

"Well, Pops, you need to find out more information if you want my help."

"Right. And I suppose there's no point in staying here. I have no idea when Squirrely will wake up, and I'm starting to feel a little caged. I'll see what I can find out."

"I'll keep checking the hospital records, and I'll let you know if there are any changes."

"You'll be able to tell that?"

"As long as the hospital updates the information, I can."

∿

The rain had stopped completely by the time Tuper drove to Humpty's to see Sean. The small dive bar in East Helena was located on a side street next to a boat shop that had been closed for fifteen-plus years. The tavern had an old sign that lit up, but the "t" had been burned out for years, so it read *Hump_y's*. Only the locals went there, and not many of them. Tuper often wondered how Sean was able to keep the place open. He was certain the owner made more on the house's take from the backroom poker games than on alcohol sales, and the games were only once a week. The bar held six small tables with chairs, two slot machines, and the only working jukebox in town. The same songs had been on it for as long as Tuper could remember—a mix of Irish tunes and old country. A step back in time, which was probably why the old locals kept coming back. It was unusual to find a patron under sixty, unless they accidently wandered in. Even then, they didn't stay long and seldom returned.

Sean, a large Irishman in his early fifties with red hair and a beer belly, stood behind the counter drying a glass. He had inherited the bar from his father some ten years ago and had taken a liking to Squirrely. Tuper wasn't sure why.

"Hi, Toop," Sean said, as Tuper walked up. "How's the *craic?*" That was Sean's usual greeting when anyone entered the bar. It had taken Tuper about a year to learn that it just meant "How's it going?"

"Not bad," Tuper said.

"It's a fierce winter we had. Glad to have it over." Sean set down the glass. "If you're looking for Squirrely, he's not here."

"I know. That's why I'm here. Squirrely's in the hospital."

Sean looked up. "That's a fret," he said, with audible concern in his voice. "What happened?"

"Hit-and-run in front of Nickels. It looked like they were aiming for him."

"That's crazy. Why would anyone want to hurt Squirrely?"

"I was hoping you might help with that. Has he been acting strange at all?"

"You know Squirrely. He's always a little...well...squirrely. You're talking to him about something, and all of a sudden he's on to something else. His mind never seems to be on the same page as anyone else's, but I haven't noticed anything out of the ordinary."

"Have you seen him spending time with anyone?"

"No, I don't think so." Sean glanced at the other end of the bar where the only two patrons were sitting, both older men with scruffy gray beards. "Excuse me." He walked to the other end, picked up two bottles of Miller Lite on his way over, and popped them open. He set them down in front of the men and picked up some cash.

"Gotta take care of the boys," he said, putting the money in the register.

Tuper gave him a nod and asked, "Have you had any new customers coming in here?"

"Mostly the regulars that have been with me for years. Occasionally, someone new will wander in, but most of them don't come back." Sean thought for a minute. "There were two guys in here night before last that I hadn't seen before, but they didn't come in together. The second one came in after the first had already left. It was odd having two strangers in the same night. It doesn't happen often."

"Was Squirrely here?"

"Not at first, but he came in before the first guy left."

"Did Squirrely talk to him?"

"I think he did. I remember when Squirrely came in. The guy waved for him to come to his table."

"Did he go?"

"He was walking over, but I'm not sure if he got side-tracked along the way. I was serving a customer, so I stopped watching them. The man left shortly after that."

"And Squirrely? Did you see him later?"

"No, come to think of it, I haven't seen him since."

"So, you don't know if Squirrely talked to the second guy?"

"I'm pretty sure he didn't. He was already gone by then."

"What did the guys look like?"

"The first one was short and heavyset, about sixty or sixty-five, I'd say. The other was younger, maybe thirty-five or forty, tall and muscular. He didn't fit in here at all."

"Did you talk to either of them?"

"Yeah, I welcomed each as they came in. And since they were new, I made sure they knew it was a cash-only bar. I tried to strike up a conversation, but they didn't have much to say. The older guy said he was just passing through on his way to North Dakota, which didn't make much sense because this bar isn't on the way to anything. You pretty much need to be looking for it to find it."

"Did you talk to the first guy after that?"

"No."

"What about the second guy?"

"Just got him a second round of drinks, which was also strange."

"How's that?"

"All he was drinking was bottled water. It's a good thing he didn't stay too long because I only had three bottles and he bought two of them. I didn't try to talk to him because he seemed to want to be left alone. You know me. I like to talk and joke with the customers, but some just want to drink, and I'm not going to bug them. As you can see, I can't afford to run off any paying customers." He chuckled.

"How long have you known Squirrely?"

"Over fifteen years. He started coming in here when my *oul fella* still owned the place."

Tuper knew *oul fella* was the term Sean used for his father. It was an Irish thing. "So, your father knew him too?"

"He's the one who started letting him stay in the back room when the weather got fierce, but he didn't stay much in the early days, only when it was really bad. Squirrely doesn't like to be caged much, but the older he gets, the more he takes to the shelter."

"Do you know his last name?"

"It's Finnigan. He's an Irish lad. I expect that's partly why my *oul fella* took him in."

"Do you know anything else about his background? I'm aware that his mother lives in Great Falls, and he has a sister in Nevada, but that's about all I know."

"I met his mother once. She's a crotchety old woman. I don't care to see her twice."

"I know what you mean." Tuper smiled. "Do you happen to know Squirrely's birthday?"

"I can't help you there." Sean sighed. "Are the cops looking for the guy who hit him?"

"They are, but they don't have much to go on. I don't know how much time or money they're willing to put into a crime against a homeless guy."

"But you're looking too, right?"

"You know I'll do what I can for Squirrely. Thanks for your help."

As Tuper walked away, Sean said, as he always did, "May the road rise up to meet you."

CHAPTER 5

L ana sat at her computer, looking for information about Frank Finnigan. She tried Frank, Frankie, Francis, but there were just too many to narrow down. She needed a middle name or at least an initial, or a birthday or something before she could do much more. She started researching the names of the people she had collected from articles on the first page, hoping one would connect her to Frank Finnigan.

When that didn't lead her anywhere, she decided to delve back into the newspaper. She still had twenty-five pages to search through. The first article was about a famous children's book author-illustrator, Richard Scarry, who had passed away. Lana remembered those books from when she was young. She loved the character Lowly Worm.

Lana added Richard Scarry to her list, even though she was certain she wouldn't find a connection. She also added John Wayne Gacy, who lost his appeal to block his execution for the murder of thirty-three young men and boys. The article titled *Social Security Bonuses Criticized* didn't produce any viable names, nor did the one about closing military bases. She also took no notes for the probable cause found in the Woody Allen case or the Songbird being taken off the threatened extinction list. Even though many of the articles didn't seem to have any value for her, she still had to read every article to make certain.

The next news item was intriguing; at least it involved money. The headline read *Fugitive Executive Duped Many*. It was about a businessman, Miller Bozeman, who molded an engineering firm in St. Louis into a hot investment, then absconded with millions of dollars, changed his name, and moved to South Carolina. He supposedly made a visit to New York and mysteriously *died*. Unfortunately for him, he hadn't died, but was caught and would stand trial. Lana was curious about what happened to him after he was arrested and wondered why a man who seemingly had a happy life had left his family and fled. *Had he planned it all along? Or had something gone wrong?* She certainly understood running away. She knew that all too well.

The remainder of the page was a weather report. Finally, something she could skip.

Lana returned to her computer to see what else she could find out about Bozeman, hoping for the name Finnigan to appear. The money Squirrely had was chump change compared to what Bozeman ran away with, but at least there was news that was about money.

Lana googled *Miller Bozeman* to see what happened after the scandal. She discovered that when he was caught, his wife was living with him. She had claimed that her husband was dead when she was initially approached by the FBI, then she was arrested for her part in the deception. Their son, Christopher Bozeman, was later charged with conspiracy to commit bankruptcy fraud for helping to hide furniture, rugs, and other valuables. Later that year, both parents pled guilty to fraud. The plea deal included dropping the charges against their son.

A snarky smile crossed her lips as she thought about her own family. Lana felt sorry for Christopher, but at least his parents came through for him in the end. She knew how easy it was to learn bad things from your parents. She was living proof of that. She started to feel anxious and shook it off. She had found no connection to Frank, aka Squirrely, and it was time to move on.

She opened the paper again to page three. She glanced through an article about bison finding greener pastures in West Yellowstone and one about retired federal workers suing the state for illegal taxation of their pensions. The short exposé about the man who killed his half-brother with an ax was likely not related, but Lana noted the names of the men involved and would run them later when she had more information about Squirrely.

The rest of the page was made up of Mother's Day ads, and page four was primarily local political stuff and a Doonesbury cartoon. Page five was much of the same with a lot of ads aimed at Mother's Day sales. Page six dealt with Israel, Syria, and South Africa. Squirrely didn't strike her as an international kind of guy. She glanced through the articles and moved on. Page seven was a full-page ad for the grand opening of Helena County Market. Lana couldn't remember a store with that name, so she googled it and found it had closed in July of 2005.

Page eight had articles about Garth Brooks, Tonya Harding, and the upcoming Rolling Stones tour—all not Squirrely material. An explosives threat in a Helena store and a missing diabetic teen required further investigation, but neither led her to Squirrely.

Lana felt frustrated. She was only a third of the way through the paper and had nothing really promising. She hoped it would jump out at her when she saw it. Whatever it was, it had to be important enough to keep the paper for twenty-five years, something big.

She skipped pages nine, ten, and eleven because they were all about sports news. Unless she found out Squirrely was a sports fanatic or gambler, she wasn't going to waste her time. She did the same with page twelve, which covered the stock market.

Lana read through her notes and decided to revisit the article about the three-year-old lost boy. He had disappeared from his home, then was found four hours later, over a mile away. There were lots of theories about what happened, but the most likely was that the child had been kidnapped and then let go for whatever reason. No one was ever charged or convicted of a crime. The parents were investigated by the Department of Public Health and Human Services, but the boy was placed back with them after the investigation. Lana knew all too well that some people just shouldn't be allowed to raise children. She didn't know if the boy's parents fell in that category, but she hoped not. Children deserved to have parents who loved them and put them above their own selfish needs. She had decided long ago that she would never have children. From the upbringing she'd had, she was sure she wouldn't know how to raise them properly.

Lana shook her head and got back on task. The lost boy would be twenty-eight now, an age at which he could be Squirrely's son or grandson. Lana pursued that line of thought, but never found any possible connection. Another dead end.

She was starting to get bored with this whole thing and hated all the personal stuff it brought up for her. It also made her think she needed to check her old Hotmail. She'd had the account for years and occasionally got an email from an old friend. She liked getting messages from them, but she never answered for fear the account might have been hacked. It had once felt like that address was her home, especially after she moved to cyberspace. She had been completely homeless for a while, but now Clarice had taken her in. She liked living here, but she knew it was temporary. She would have to move on eventually. That's why she had to check that email—because it was the one *he* had too. She needed to know if he was getting too close. He couldn't resist playing with her mind and scaring her if he could. She stopped for a second, took a deep breath, then opened the folder. She perused the list of messages, discarding all the junk, until she saw the first email from him.

—*I see you've been busy. Good work.*

She knew that was a bluff. She hadn't done anything that he would know to be her cyber signature. She continued down the list. The second one read:

—*I'm leaving the country for a business trip. Want to go along? I can pick you up on the way.*

Lana slammed her laptop closed. Shaking, she stood up to pace, telling herself to calm down. But he could push her buttons from thousands of miles away. *Why did she always let him get to her?*

CHAPTER 6

Tuper drove to Great Falls alone. He pulled up in front of the assisted living home where Squirrely's mother lived. Light rain fell as he walked across the parking lot. He liked the rain, but it had been three days of wet, and he was ready for a break. He took off his hat and shook it, walked inside, and checked in at the front desk.

"I'm here to see Norma Finnigan."

"She should be in the dining area." The man behind the desk stood up. "I'll take you to her." He walked out of the cubicle and around to where Tuper waited. "If you take her out of here, you need to let us know. Are you related?"

"No, just a friend."

The man raised an eyebrow and looked as though he was about to say something, but then stopped. Tuper suspected the employee couldn't believe anyone would visit her unless it was a familial obligation.

"Is she still as cantankerous as ever?" Tuper asked.

The man smiled. "All of our residents are wonderful people."

"Yeah, I bet," Tuper mumbled.

They walked into the dining area, and the man led Tuper toward the back, where a woman sat at a table with a man in a wheelchair. The rest of the tables had four people.

"The residents always sit in the same place. They don't have to, but they choose to, and they can be like little children if anyone takes their seat. If someone moves out, you'll see a shift if other residents have been waiting to sit near their friends. No one is fighting to get to the table with Norma."

"But she's not alone, at least someone is sitting with her."

"He's deaf. Have fun." The man smiled and left.

Tuper sat down in one of the empty chairs. "Hello, Norma."

"Who are you?" she said irritably.

"My name is Tuper. I'm a friend of Squ ... your son, Frank."

"Why ain't he here? He too busy to come see his own ma?"

"No, ma'am. He's had an accident, and he's in the hospital."

"I guess he ain't coming to see me then."

She didn't ask how her son was or what had happened to him, but Tuper wasn't surprised that her concern was about herself. He had never met a more selfish woman in his life.

"Not today. He's still unconscious."

"Tell him to come see me when he's better."

"I'll do that. But now I'm trying to find out who hurt him, and I need a little information from you. What's his middle name?"

A server came by with a cart of juices, milk, and coffee. "What would you like to drink, Norma?" she asked.

"Cranberry juice, if it's any good. None of that Kool-Aid you try to pass off as juice."

"It's not Kool-Aid, Norma." She poured a glass and set it down.

Norma took a sip and made a face. "That's awful. It's half water."

Tuper noticed the juice looked too light in color to be undiluted, but he had a feeling that it wouldn't matter to Norma. She would complain anyway.

The server gave the man in the wheelchair a cup of coffee and offered Tuper a drink, which he declined, so she moved on to the next table.

"You're smart to turn it down," Norma said. "Everything is awful here."

"Sorry to hear that." After a few seconds, he asked again, "What is Frank's middle name?"

"Francis, named after his father, the lazy bum."

Tuper wasn't sure which one she was calling a lazy bum— her son or her deceased husband. "His name is Frank Francis Finnigan?"

"No," she scowled. "His full name is Harold Francis Finnigan, Jr. His father was senior. I never liked the name. I wanted to name him Russell Howard after my father, but Harold wouldn't have any part of it. I would've done it anyway if he hadn't been there when I filled out the birth certificate. I started calling him Frank, and after a while, everyone was doing it."

"When's his birthday?" Tuper wondered if she would remember it—not because her memory was going. In fact, she was very sharp. He just wasn't sure she cared enough about Squirrely to remember his birthday.

"The twenty-sixth of September."

"What year?"

"Every year," she said with a snarl. "It doesn't change."

Tuper didn't know if she was being sarcastic, or if she was that dumb. He chose to believe the latter.

"What year was he born?"

"1951."

"In Roy?"

"In Lewistown."

The server brought two plates of food and set them down in front of the old man and Norma.

"What *is* this?" Norma asked.

"It's beef, green beans, and rice," she said and hurried away.

The old man began to eat. Norma pushed the food around on her plate, poking at the green beans. "They're hard." She put a piece of meat in her mouth and immediately spat it back onto her plate. "That's awful."

"It's pretty tough," an old woman sitting at the table next to them muttered, as she chewed. "And the green beans aren't cooked. Nothing unusual."

"Where did Frank grow up?" Tuper asked.

"That kid never did grow up, but we lived in Roy mostly. We moved to Great Falls after he and his sister graduated from high school. Frank tagged along. I finally had to kick him out."

"What did he do when he left home?"

"He said he joined the military, but I don't know if I believe him," Norma said. "What does it matter?"

"I'm just trying to get some information that might help me help him."

"There ain't much to tell. He was a sweet little boy, but a no-good teenager, and he ain't no better now."

Tuper was certain what her answer would be, but he asked

anyway, for Squirrely's sake. "Would you like me to take you to see him?"

"No," she shot back. "It wouldn't do any good if he's unconscious anyway. You can bring him here when he's better."

CHAPTER 7

Tuper called Lana immediately after he left Norma in Great Falls.

"Hi, Pops. What did you learn? Anything important?"

Tuper waited until she stopped asking questions and for a second or two after to make sure she was done.

When he didn't answer right away, she asked, "Are you there? Why aren't you talking to me?"

"Just waitin' for you to stop gabbin'. Are you done now?"

"Yup." She made a loud smacking noise with the P-sound on the end, mocking Tuper.

"Squirrely's name is Harold Francis Finnigan, Jr., and he was born on September 26, 1951 in Lewistown. He lived in Roy until after high school when the family moved to Great Falls. He may or may not have been in the military. That's about all I got."

"Not bad, old man."

"I'm going to the hospital to see Squirrely. Do you know if anything has changed?"

"Let me check." For a few minutes, the only noise was the

clicking of Lana's keyboard. Then she said, "Nothing new listed except the latest blood pressure numbers. They're still pretty low. It doesn't look like there have been any changes to his condition."

"I'll swing by there and make sure. Then I'll stop by Clarice's. Tell her she can make me supper if she wants."

"I'm sure she'll be glad to hear that."

Squirrely looked the same as when Tuper had left him. He sat beside his bed and reached for a place that didn't have a bandage or cast. His left shoulder seemed okay. Tuper laid his hand on it, and the blanket fell, revealing a tattoo of an eagle, a globe, and an anchor. The words around it were blurred. Tears rolled down Tuper's cheeks. He swallowed. He hated that he had become so emotional the last few years, crying at the drop of a hat. He had always been quick to tears, but the older he got, the worse it became.

"You're gonna come out of this, Squirrely," he said out loud. "And I'll find the jerk who did it to you, or I'll die tryin'. That's a promise." Tuper paused. "I saw your mother today. She's somethin' else. I know you didn't have it very good growin' up with that woman. It's a good thing you had your dad. I know from what you've said about him, that he was a really good guy." Tuper blew his nose and took a deep breath. "I wish you could tell me what that money and that newspaper are about. You sure got me wonderin', and you got Lana goin' too. She'll keep diggin' until she finds an explanation. It's drivin' her a little crazy, which I don't mind sayin' is kinda funny."

Tuper stopped talking and sat there with his friend. The

only sound in the room was the occasional beep from Squir-rely's vitals machine. There was nothing more to say. After a few minutes, he took out his phone and called Lana.

"Squirrely was in the Marine Corps."

"How do you know? Is he awake? Did you ask him? When did he serve?"

"He has a tattoo with the Marine Corps emblem."

"That doesn't prove anything."

"It may not prove it, but that's where I'd start lookin' if you're checking for a military record."

Lana was anxious to get on her computer to see what she could find out about Harold Francis Finnigan, Jr. She started with the easy stuff, using legal search engines, but before long she was hacking into birth, school, and criminal records. It was all so easy. When she was first learning the skill, she thought she would never master it, but now, most of the time, it wasn't even a challenge. She almost wished the tech compa-nies would come up with something more difficult. Too many other people could do it as well, and she knew how dangerous that was. She thought of herself as a *white-hat hacker* because she didn't use her skill to commit crimes or do damage to anyone, but there were plenty of others who hacked for illegal purposes.

Within a few hours, Lana knew more about Squirrely than he probably knew about himself. She couldn't find regular school records because data hadn't been entered online back that far. But she did learn from newspaper articles that he was a member of Future Farmers of America and had raised a prize pig. Much to her surprise, she discovered he had been champion of the debate team. He won first place in the regionals and took second in the state of Montana.

Lana started running the newspaper names she had found so far, doing a cursory check to see if Frank's name showed up anywhere. She didn't have to look very far before she found that Miller Bozeman, who committed the million-dollar fraud, had used the alias John Finnigan.

She set that aside and continued through the newspaper, hoping for something obvious that would send her in the right direction. Most of the articles weren't much help. Lana didn't think the Navy wanting more combat women or the flawed steel components in submarines could possibly connect to Squirrely, but she would come back to them if she found something in his background that led her there.

Pages fifteen and sixteen had articles about local awards, plus two obituaries, two funeral services, and thirteen state deaths. Lana jotted them all down. She would check later for a connection.

The article on page seventeen really annoyed her: *Accept Women as Equals, Bar Advised.* The state bureau had made recommendations to the bar association regarding sexual harassment, gender bias, and lack of respect accorded females in the legal profession. *What was taking them so long?* Lana wondered if anything had really changed as a result of the recommendations. She wanted to follow up with more research, but she had to get back on track. She kept perusing, looking for clues.

Page eighteen was filled with the TV guide, a few comic strips, the day's horoscope, and some advice column called *Dear Abby* that Lana found rather comical. She skipped the next page because it had more comics, the crossword puzzle, and two articles on how to treat cancer.

The next three pages were classified ads, which seemed like an insurmountable task if what she needed was in there. She decided if she didn't find what she was looking for elsewhere, she would come back to them. She also skipped the health-related articles on AIDS, emergency contraceptives, and the health care reform bill. *That fight never seems to stop,* she thought.

The last four pages were all ads, so she returned to her research on the most promising article—the St. Louis fraud with Miller Bozeman. She needed to find out everything she could about Bozeman and why he used the name Finnigan. She was able to get the con man's full name and birthdate just by googling it. Lana knew from experience that when people chose an alias, instead of picking something totally unrelated to them, they often chose someone they knew. Maybe they didn't even realize it, but they picked names that were in their unconscious mind.

Lana's first attempt was to find a familial connection, so she hacked into the biggest ancestry site she knew. She was always amazed at the information she received from the site or where it led her. It didn't take long to find a whole line of Finnigans in Bozeman's wife's family tree. Bozeman's mother-in-law was born a Finnigan.

CHAPTER 8

L ana was deep into the net when Clarice came in, carrying two bags of groceries.

"Are you off work already?" Lana asked.

"Yeah, it's late."

Lana glanced at her laptop. "I guess the time got away from me."

"What are you working on?"

"Squirrely stuff. I'm trying to find something that might lead us to the guy who ran him down."

"How can you do that on the computer? Do you have a license plate number for the car or something?"

"No." Lana wanted to tell her about the bag with the money and the newspaper, but it wasn't her place. She never told anything she wasn't sure should be shared. She had learned at a very young age to keep secrets. Her whole life was a secret. Besides, Tuper would tell Clarice if he wanted her to know.

"How is Squirrely?" Clarice asked. "Have you heard?"

"Tuper's at the hospital with him now, but I haven't talked

to him in a while. I checked the hospital records a little bit ago, and there hasn't been any change. He's still unconscious, and he's pretty beat up. His blood pressure is still low, and there's a concern that he may need brain surgery. Oh, and he wants you to make him dinner—Tuper, that is, not Squirrely."

Lana realized she used the word *dinner* instead of *supper*, like Tuper had. If she wanted to fit in, she needed to be more careful about using local colloquialisms. She knew that certain words could be a tell-tale sign about where she was from.

"Of course, he does." Clarice set the bag of groceries on the counter.

"Do you have more in the car?" Lana asked, starting to stand. "I'll get them."

"No, that was it."

After a knock on the door, Tuper walked in. "You should keep that door locked. You never know who might just wander in."

"I can see that," Clarice said. "I'll have supper ready in about half an hour."

"Nice of you to invite me."

"She didn't," Lana teased. "She just said it would be ready. That doesn't mean she wants you to stay and eat."

"You be careful, Agony, or you may be the one not getting any supper."

Tuper had started calling her Agony shortly after they met. She, in turn, called him Pops. Over time, they both seemed to have adapted to the nicknames. They both had strong, diverse opinions about most things, but their skills complemented one another. Tuper seemed to know everyone in the state of Montana and had a persuasive way of getting things done. Lana, on the other hand, obtained her information by peering into people's lives without them knowing it. Together they made a good team.

"How's Squirrely?" Clarice asked, interrupting their banter.

"I don't know. The doctors are just waiting for him to wake up." Tuper sat down at the table, removed his cowboy hat, and placed it on the chair next to him.

"Did you tell Clarice about the duffel bag?" Tuper asked Lana.

"I figured that was your place to tell."

"What duffel bag?" Clarice asked.

Tuper walked over to the sofa and fetched the bag. He started to set it on the table when Lana said sternly, "Put it on the chair. That thing is dirty. I already spent half the morning sterilizing the tabletop."

Tuper did what she asked and opened the duffel.

"What the heck?" Clarice exclaimed. "Where did that come from?"

"Squirrely."

"How much is in there?"

"Don't know. Haven't counted it." He looked at Lana. "Have you?"

"No, I've been too busy following up with the newspaper."

"What newspaper?" Clarice asked.

Lana told her how old the paper was and how she had spent the day researching the articles. "I haven't found anything yet that connects Squirrely, except that one guy involved in corporate fraud used an alias that is the same as Squirrely's surname."

"Finnigan?" Clarice said.

Both Tuper's and Lana's heads spun around, and they glared at Clarice.

"You knew Squirrely's last name?" Lana asked.

"Yeah, he told me one day."

"Why didn't you tell me?" Tuper added.

"You didn't ask." Clarice shrugged. "Do you think the newspaper and the money have something to do with Squirrely being run down?"

"It must," Lana cut in. "It's too big a coincidence that Squirrely gave Tuper a bag to guard with thousands of dollars, an old newspaper, and a gun—then the next day someone plows him down."

"There was a gun too?" Clarice scowled.

"Yep." Tuper said.

Lana's eyes brightened. "I wrote down the make and model earlier, but what's the serial number? Maybe I can track it."

Tuper removed the revolver from the bag and looked for a number. "It's right there, but these old eyes can't read it."

Clarice grabbed a pad of paper and pen off the counter and said, "Let me see it."

Tuper laid the gun on the table, and Clarice wrote down the number. She handed the paper to Lana, who typed the number into a search field on her laptop. Tuper took the note back and stuck it into his pocket.

"How much money do you think is there?" Clarice asked.

"Over ten thousand," Tuper said.

"You think?"

"Yep. They're mostly hundreds."

"Why don't you just count it?" Lana piped in between clicks of her keyboard.

Clarice looked at Tuper. He just shrugged, so she went to the backroom and came out with a towel and spread it on the table. Tuper dumped the cash on the towel, and they both started making stacks of $1000. When they finished, they had thirteen stacks, plus another three hundred and thirty-three dollars. "That's odd," Clarice noted.

"Depends on where it came from," Tuper said.

"Sounds like a three-way split to me," Lana said. "If you divide $40,000 three ways, you get $13,333, with an extra dollar. Or maybe it was $80,000 split six ways."

"Do you suppose Squirrely meant the money when he said to give it to Elba?" Clarice asked.

"What?" Lana asked. "Who's Elba? I thought you didn't know about the money until you opened the bag. Did Squirrely tell you something about the money?"

"Before Squirrely was taken to the hospital, he said, 'Give to Elba,'" Tuper explained. "That's the best I could make out. He might have said Ella or Emma, or who knows what. And I don't even know if he was talking about the money. It may not even be important."

"Or it may be very important, Pops. I'll keep watching for a similar name when I'm researching. Who knows? It might lead us to his assailant." Lana tuned out their voices and went back to work, mumbling something about having to look through everything again with Elba in mind.

Tuper and Clarice continued to play around with different scenarios for the amount of money until Lana spoke again. "Did you know the NRA has a list of guns with their serial numbers on their website? The problem is that different manufacturers could have used the same serial number, so it's easy to make a mistake using their charts, especially if the guns are similar."

"How does that help us?" Tuper asked.

"I'll tell you," Lana said.

"No doubt," Tuper mumbled.

"From the maker's marks on this gun, we know it's a Ruger SP101 .38 caliber revolver, so we just need to trace the serial number with Ruger as the manufacturer."

"That's amazing," Clarice said. "How do you find that stuff?"

"Anyone can do it. I just used Google. There are other sites that also provide charts and information that will help find out a weapon's manufacturer. I ran the serial number and found which guns fit that number. Apparently, you can find the make, model, and value of the gun with just a simple search. But we need other information, like who owned it and where it has been. That's a whole different kind of search, and it won't be easy."

"Can't you just hack into some law enforcement site and run a trace?"

"It's not quite that easy. I'm not sure if I can get into the right place to get the information we need. Some of it is controlled by the feds, but I'll keep at it."

"See what you can find out, and I'll do the same," Tuper said.

"What are you going to do?" Lana asked.

"I know a guy."

CHAPTER 9

Tuper sat at a small table next to the window in
Firetower Coffee, watching people dash through the
rain as they moved across the parking lot. The unique coffee
shop in downtown Helena wasn't the kind of place he
would've ordinarily frequented, but he had been there once
before to meet his friend, Deputy Sheriff Johnson. The café
was filled with rock-music memorabilia, guitars hanging from
the ceiling, and pictures of the Beatles as well as other rock
stars Tuper didn't recognize. He preferred a more country
atmosphere, and he wasn't into fancy coffees and teas. But
this was convenient for his friend, and he'd been informed
that the coffee was the best in town, not that he cared. Tuper
ordered tea before he sat down.

A county sheriff vehicle pulled up and parked outside. A
tall, older man with gray, protruding brow ridges and a Clark
Gable mustache exited the car and walked in. He glanced at
Tuper and nodded, then stopped at the counter.

"Clarissa, a cup of coffee, please."

"Coming right up," the young waitress with bright pink hair said.

The deputy waved to a man behind the counter. "Hi, Nord." Then he walked toward Tuper and took a seat across from him. He reached over to shake Tuper's hand. "Nice to see you, Toop."

"Thanks for coming, Johnson."

"Always. So how goes the war?"

"I'm still standing, but my friend, Squirrely, is not. A car plowed him down in front of Nickel's casino this morning."

"I heard about that, but I thought he was a homeless transient without any ID. I had no idea he was a friend of yours."

The waitress walked up and set the steaming coffee cup in front of the deputy. "Can I get you anything else?" she asked. Johnson shook his head, so she turned to Tuper.

"I'm good," he said.

"You sure?" Johnson asked. "I'm buying."

"No, thanks." When the waitress left, Tuper continued, "Squirrely is homeless, but he has lived in Helena for years. I contacted the detective on the case and gave him his real name. I doubt if it'll help them find his assailant though."

"And you need a favor from me?"

"It's a big one."

"What is it?"

"I have a gun I'd like traced."

Johnson sighed. "Is it connected to the hit-and-run?" he asked. "Never mind, don't tell me."

"Don't know for sure."

"Toop, I owe you big time, and I'd like to help, but I don't think I can pull this one off. All law enforcement gun traces go through ATF now. The National Tracing Center in Martinsburg, West Virginia handles everything. They're the only ones allowed to run a trace." Johnson shifted uncomfortably. "If I gave them the information and submitted a request, I'd need a helluva cover story for my boss. Unless that gun is connected to a case I'm working on, I can't do it. They'd have my hide."

"I understand. I don't want you losing your job over it, especially since I'm not sure it even means anything."

Johnson sipped his coffee. "I'm sorry, Toop. Is there anything else I can do?"

"Do you know if they have any leads on who hit Squirrely?"

"From what I understand, there are no witnesses except the victim and a guy from the bar who saw the tail of the vehicle and reported it as likely a dark pickup."

Tuper tipped his head to one side. "That was me. I only got a glimpse as it turned the corner."

"And your friend is still unconscious, right?"

"No change there."

"I'll do what I can to keep an eye on the case for you. They don't have much to go on, so if you have other information you want to share, it might be helpful. I know the detective on the case. He's a good guy."

Tuper couldn't see how telling him about the bag could help—without getting Squirrely in trouble. He had a bad feeling that the money hadn't come through any legal means and that finding the assailant wouldn't change what already happened. Although, he was suddenly concerned the person might try again.

Tuper and Johnson walked out together.

"Try to stay dry," Johnson said.

"Will do."

They exchanged goodbyes, and Tuper drove to the hospital. Squirrely was lying in the bed still hooked up to the machines.

"Anything new, Rhonda?" he asked the nurse who was checking his vitals. She was the same one who'd been there earlier in the afternoon. She had been friendly and helpful and didn't ask if he was related. She just answered his questions.

"No change."

"You've been here a while?" Tuper asked. "How much longer do you have?"

"My shift started at two this afternoon. I'll be here until eleven, and I'll be back tomorrow."

"Has anyone else been in to see him?"

"Only a detective, but he just looked at him and asked about his condition. He asked me to put a note in the file about giving him a call if there was any change."

"Thanks." Tuper sat down in the chair next to Squirrely's bed. It made him feel better to know Squirrely was safe for the night. He would see to that. He wasn't concerned about getting sleep himself, since he got little anyway. Most of the time, he slept in an armchair, so tonight would be no different.

Tuper had just dozed off when Squirrely's vital-signs monitor started beeping. The machines went off so often that he wouldn't have paid much attention, except this one was louder and lasted much longer. Two nurses dashed into the room, and one shut it off. They were followed by a doctor and an orderly. Tuper was asked to leave, so he waited outside the room, unsure of what was going on. He kept checking his watch and wondering. It seemed like hours before anyone came out, but he knew it was closer to thirty minutes. Several people left, while others came in. Still not knowing, Tuper waited in the hallway. Suddenly, Squirrely was wheeled past him and down the hallway.

When he was out of sight, Tuper checked at the desk and was told, "His blood pressure dropped. He has internal bleeding, and they're prepping him for surgery. It'll be a while, so you may want to go home and get some rest."

CHAPTER 10

L ana checked the time on her computer: *1:09 a.m.* She was tired, but she liked working in the wee hours of the morning because it was quiet and she could concentrate. No one was around to interrupt her. Clarice was working a rare closing-shift at Nickel's. Her sister, Mary, was spending the night at her boyfriend's house, and Tuper had left to go *who knew where,* which meant he was probably with one of his lady friends.

The web was quieter too, and she was less likely to get caught if she hacked into sites when no one was active in them. She looked at her list of names to research. At the top, she added Elba, the name Tuper thought he heard Squirrely whisper, then decided to start with the obituaries.

The first one was for a seventy-three-year-old doctor from Pennsylvania who had resided in Helena for quite a while. He died in his home state after a short bout with cancer. Lana researched each name in the obituary but found no connection to Squirrely.

The second obit was for a sixty-year-old man named

Alfred Short Bull who died after a short time in the hospital. No further explanation of his death was given, and no relatives were listed. But the obit mentioned he had served in the U.S. Air Force and noted the funeral arrangements. Lana found it a little odd and kind of sad. She felt bad for Alfred Short Bull and wondered if he had anyone in his life who had cared for him. Had anyone shown for his funeral services? The same could happen to her if she were to die. Now she had Tuper, Clarice, and Mary, but they didn't really know her. If they did, would they still care about her? She shook it off and went back to work.

Alfred Short Bull was tough to track, but she found he was born in Fort Yates, North Dakota. His military record showed he fought for seven months in the Korean War, lost an arm in battle, and was given an honorable discharge after a year of service. What little she found did not lead her to an Irishman named Frank Finnigan, nor anyone named Elba.

Lana heard the key turn in the lock on the front door. She checked the time: *2:32 a.m.* Clarice was home.

"How was your shift?" Lana asked.

"Fairly busy for a Sunday night, until about ten, then it died. I had most of the clean-up done before closing, so I got out of there pretty quick. Have you heard from Tuper?"

"Not since he left here after supper."

"I hate to do this to you, Lana, but I need you to open tomorrow morning. We're short staffed, and I don't think I can make it."

"Whatever you need. Now that I have a bike, I can ride there on my own," Lana said.

"It's too dark and dangerous," Clarice countered, then added, "and wet."

"I have a light on my bike, I know my way around now, and the rain is supposed to stop tonight. I'll be fine."

"I've already arranged with Tuper to pick you up and take you."

"He doesn't mind?"

"He's always up before the chickens anyway. You just have to see that he gets breakfast when you get there."

Clarice said goodnight and left the room. Lana had one more thing she wanted to check before she stopped researching, even though she had to get up in just a few hours.

Clarice had gotten Lana a job at Nickel's and taught her how to tend bar. It wasn't anything permanent or full time, but she was able to fill in shifts whenever she was needed. She didn't particularly like being a bartender, but it was income she needed. Besides, it helped Clarice, who managed the bar. Clarice had been kind enough to take her in, and Lana wanted to pay her back any way she could. Whatever money she made for the week, she gave a third of it to Clarice. She tried to give her half, but Clarice insisted that was too much. Sometimes, Lana only worked a shift or two. Only once did she earn a full week of pay. So, her checks didn't amount to much, but she also used her tips to help buy food.

The work was awful, dealing with a bunch of drunks, many of whom thought they had a right to flirt with the bartenders—after all, wasn't that what the tips were for? Clarice had warned her it would be tough, but she'd had confidence that Lana could hold her own. She based that on the night they met, when Lana kicked a guy in the groin with her hiking boot after he grabbed her butt. When she was hired, she was told not to get physical, but she didn't have to take their guff either.

Lana continued to research the obituaries. The thirteen

state deaths listed for that day included a man named Patrick Gallagher, forty-four, from Roy, Montana, the cause of death not stated. The location caught Lana's attention because Squirrely had grown up there. She checked the population and found it only had 108 residents. It had 163 in the 2000 census, so it had lost some. She didn't bother to check what the population was in the 1960s and 70s, other than to see it was never a thriving metropolis. Small enough that everyone had to know everyone else. The question was whether Squirrely and Patrick had lived there at the same time. If Patrick had also grown up in Roy, they would've had to go to the same schools together. They were less than a year apart in age. Lana had already checked the system and found that the high school currently had sixteen students in grades nine through twelve. The middle school had six students, and the elementary had only eighteen. She expected the numbers weren't a whole lot different when Squirrely was there.

Lana's plan was to hack into the school district records to see if the boys had attended school together. She thought it might help her gain some insight into Squirrely as well. But when she got into the school's mainframe, she hit a dead end. The information in the program only went back ten years. She needed to see the physical records. Which meant she had to convince Tuper to drive her to Roy.

Lana shut down her computer and went to bed.

Tuper didn't leave the hospital; instead, he stayed in the waiting room, dozing occasionally, until Squirrely's surgery was done. The doctor came out and explained the surgical process, but Tuper didn't really understand or even hear anything—until the doc said, "The surgery went well. He's heavily sedated. Why don't you go home and get some rest?"

Tuper checked his watch: *5:38 a.m.* He stumbled out to his car and started toward Nickels casino to get something to eat, when he remembered he was supposed to pick up Lana and take her to work. He turned around and drove to Clarice's house. He was getting hungry, and since Clarice wouldn't be at the bar, he would have to count on Lana to fix him something. He wasn't sure he could trust her cooking.

He called Lana and told her about Squirrely's condition on the way to her house.

"Is he okay? What did they do? Where was he bleeding? Was it his brain, or his stomach, or what?"

"I don't know, Agony. I just know his blood pressure dropped real low, and they had to go inside and fix it."

"What happens now?"

"The doctor said all we can do is wait. The surgery went well, but we can't expect him to awaken for a while. I'll go back this afternoon and see how he's doing."

"Are you okay?" Lana asked.

"Nope. I'm tired and hungry. Can you fix me something to eat?"

"Sure. I'll make it at Nickels when we get there."

"Are you sure you know how to cook?"

"How hard can it be?"

"Oh boy." Tuper sighed.

As soon as Lana got set up at the bar, she made breakfast for Tuper, which he hated to admit was pretty good. She told him what she had learned the night before and suggested they take a trip to Roy.

"I looked it up on Google Maps," Lana said. "It's less than a four-hour trip, even as slow as you drive, Pops."

"I know where Roy, Montana is."

Lana continued to make her case. "We need to check out this Patrick Gallagher guy. Don't you think it's more than a coincidence that his obit was in the paper Squirrely was carrying around? I'm guessing that's why he had it. This guy is around the same age and seems to have been living in Roy the same time as Squirrely. I haven't found anything else in the paper that connects to him, so it's really all we've got. Don't you think? Unless you have something else you're holding back. By the way, I haven't found Elba yet. I don't think Elba is even a person's name. Elba is an island in Italy best known as the place where Napoleon was exiled in the early 1800s, but I don't think that's what Squirrely was talking about. Although, if you want to send me there, I'd be glad to check the place out."

"Okay." He put his hands up in a gesture to stop. "Okay, Agony, please stop talking. I'll drive you there."

"You can't drive to Elba. I told you it's an island in Italy. Besides you have to cross an ocean."

"I meant to Roy, you nutcase, but only if you promise to not talk all the way. Not one word."

Lana smiled. "I don't know if I can keep that promise, but I'll only say things that are important."

"Like that's gonna happen." Tuper shook his head. "It's gonna be a long trip."

"I can leave here shortly. Clarice won't need me after my relief comes in. And I'll bring my laptop with me. I can look up stuff as we go. You need me."

Tuper knew he would regret it. He already did, but at least there wasn't a chance of falling asleep on the drive since she would chatter all the way in spite of their deal. He got up from his barstool and started to walk away.

"Where are you going?" Lana asked.

"To the back room to take a nap on the sofa. Wake me up when you're ready to leave for Roy."

CHAPTER 11

They weren't out of Helena's city limits before Lana fell asleep. Tuper smiled. *That's when she's at her best,* he thought. He liked the quiet, and he still had Ringo to keep him company on the long trek. The rain had finally let up, and the sun was shining. He relaxed and enjoyed the ride until about halfway when Lana woke up and started chatting.

"So much for a peaceful ride, eh Ringo?"

Lana frowned, and Ringo stuck his head up front in response to his name. She patted the dog, who hung out for a few minutes, then lay down in the backseat.

For miles Lana watched the scenery with fascination, remarking occasionally about the wide-open spaces, the fields and cows, and the obvious lack of concrete. Shortly before they reached Roy, Lana checked Squirrely's hospital records. It took some time because she kept losing the internet, but she finally got it. "He's doing fine."

"Who?"

"Squirrely. I knew you were worried, so I checked. His

blood pressure is higher than it has been since he was admitted, and his other vitals are good as well. He's still not awake."

"Thanks," Tuper muttered.

When they arrived, Lana commented on the size of the town. She couldn't remember ever being in a place so small. It had a main street with a bar on each end, plus a general store, post office, tire shop, and a church.

Just as they started up Main Street, Lana pointed and said, "Will you look at that?"

"What?" Tuper said.

"Pull over. I have to see that."

Tuper stopped and Lana jumped out. "It's just an old phone booth," Tuper called out.

"I know. I've just never seen a real one before. Not like that one." Lana opened the door and examined the booth, and then returned to the car. "There's no phone in it." She sounded a little disappointed.

"No kidding."

They drove on and soon found the school on a side street. Both the elementary and high school were not only on the same lot, they were in the same building.

Lana checked the time. "It's not quite noon, the school should be open. Let's go there first."

"It's your dog and pony show," Tuper said.

"Any idea how we're going to get information from them? It's not like I can get inside and hack their computer. It wouldn't do any good anyway since they're living in the nineteenth century, when nothing was computerized."

"Wasn't it your idea to come here?"

"Yeah, but you're the one with the *hands-on* experience. I thought you might have a brilliant idea."

"We'll schmooze them. Use a little country charm."

"That's your brilliant plan?"

"You got a better one?"

Tuper let Ringo out, poured some water in a dish, and set it by the car. Then they walked inside the brick building to a small hallway with two doors on each side.

"This looks like something out of a 1950s movie," Lana said. "Nothing like the schools I attended."

"I don't expect it's changed much in the last fifty years," Tuper said, glancing in the only office with an open door.

Inside, they found an older woman chastising a student worker who was standing behind a long counter. The student wore a long braid down her back and gave them a quick smile. She probably hoped the company would stop the older woman, whose face appeared to be frozen in permanent disapproval.

"I have an idea," Lana whispered. "You work on the old lady. I'll take the student."

"Humpf," Tuper grumbled, approaching the counter anyway. He waited until the woman stopped bellowing.

"What can I do for you?" she asked in an irritating voice. Then before he could answer, she softened it. "Sorry, sir. May I help you?"

"I'm looking for a friend who went to school here. He graduated around 1969. I was in the Marine Corps with him, and we're having a reunion in a few weeks." Tuper felt guilty saying he was a veteran when he wasn't, but he needed a cover. "I'm hoping to get a little information that might lead to his whereabouts today. I'd also like to get a photo from back then to use at the reunion, just for kicks. Do you still have school records from that long ago?"

"We do, but they wouldn't be easy to access. They're all in storage, and that would be a lot of file boxes ago. What's his name? Maybe I remember him. I've been working here for nearly forty-five years."

"Frank Finnigan."

"I don't remember the name, but I started here in '72, so I guess I just missed him. Sorry I can't help. If you'll excuse me, I have a meeting." She turned to the petite student, "Connie, don't leave the office until I return."

"Yes, ma'am."

Lana watched the young girl. There was something fascinating about her. She had a dainty nose and full lips—a natural, country beauty that would have likely been considered *plain-Jane* in the city. How different things were here, she thought. When the older woman left, Lana approached the student. "She really lit into you. Are you okay, Connie?"

"Yeah, I'm used to it. She goes off at least once a day. No biggie."

"How long have you lived here?"

"Born and raised. Well, I was born in the hospital in Lewistown, but I've lived in Roy all my life."

"I expect you know everyone in town."

"All one hundred and eight people." She laughed. "Make that one hundred and nine. The Bernsteds had a baby last week."

"Wow, I can't imagine living in a town where everyone knows everyone. Is it like one big family?"

"Sort of, but sometimes it's a pain. You can't get away with much because someone will surely tell your parents. Everyone knows everything about everybody, and I mean *everything*."

The comment sparked Lana's interest. "Has anyone lived here more than fifty years?"

"Lots of people. The kids seem to leave shortly after graduation, but some of the older folks have been here all their lives. We're talking eighty, ninety years."

"So, if I wanted information about someone from fifty years ago, who would I talk to?"

"That's easy. Bella Younger is the town gossip. I heard she's been that way all her life. She just turned seventy-five." Connie looked up at the clock. "I'm sure she's in the bar by now. Just buy her a drink, and she'll tell you anything you want."

"What does she look like?"

"She has short, curly, cinnamon-colored hair with gray roots. She dyes it, but she only goes about every three months, so by the time she gets back to the beauty shop, the gray has snuck through. She looks like she's due to go again real soon. At least, she did when I saw her last Wednesday, so unless she has already gone to the beauty parlor, she'll be showing plenty of gray. She's a little heavyset and uses a walker sometimes, but most of the time, she's fine without it. She needs it more when she leaves the bar than when she goes in. The place won't be that crowded so you'll be able to spot her."

"Which bar?"

"The Legion. Go out front to Davis Street, then go left one block to Second. Make another left, go three blocks to Main, and it'll be on the corner. You can't miss it."

"Thanks, Connie, you've been a lot of help."

"My pleasure. It's always nice to see a new face in town." She paused. "If you don't find what you're looking for and you need to get into those old school files, we can do that. It'll just take some time and a little lifting of old boxes. And I can get one of my brothers to help if we need it."

"I just might take you up on that."

CHAPTER 12

B ella Younger was seated alone at a table near the
entrance, and two men sat at the counter. The only
other person in the place was the bartender.

Tuper stopped at Bella's table and asked, "The food any
good here?"

"Best in town. Course that ain't saying much, but you can't
go wrong with a burger and fries." She smiled, then asked,
"Where are you from?"

"Missoula mostly," Tuper lied.

"What are you doing in Roy? Are you lost?"

Tuper gave her a charming smile. "No, just lookin' for a
friend."

"Will I do?"

Lana chuckled. The old lady was flirting with Tuper. From
what she'd observed, Bella was too old for Pops. He usually
had younger women latching onto him. Lana couldn't quite
understand the attraction, but accepted that, in his own way,
he could be sort of charming.

"Let's see about that," Tuper said. "Mind if we join you?"

He started to sit before she could say no. "I'll even buy you a drink."

"By all means, join me."

"I'm Tuper, and this is—"

"His granddaughter," Lana interrupted. "Pops may not look old enough to be my grandpa, but he is, and a great one too. I'm Lana. Thanks for letting us sit with you."

"I'm Bella," the woman said. "So, who's the friend you're looking for?"

"Frank Finnigan."

"That goes back a ways. He left here a long time ago, right after high school. He had a sister a year or two older than him. Her name was Marlys. My younger brother dated her in high school. Frank was dating a girl named Amber, and they would double date. I think it was mostly because Frank's father let them use his car if they went together. A 1965 yellow Mustang. He wanted to make sure my brother and Marlys weren't left alone. As it turned out, *that* wasn't the couple that was the problem. Amber and Frank were the ones that needed watching. Marlys left after high school and went to college in Helena, I think. My brother stayed here and worked the fields with my dad."

The bartender, a man in his late sixties, walked up to the table, and Bella said, "This is Tuper and Lana. Don is the owner." They all shook hands. "They're looking for Frank Finnigan. Do you remember him?"

"I remember Harold Finnigan. Frank must've been one of his kids. He lived over on Davis, near the school. Nice fella, but he left a few years after I came here."

"That's the one," Bella said.

"What can I get you this morning?" Don asked Tuper.

"We'll have a couple of burgers, one with an extra meat

patty, two sodas, orange if you have it, and whatever Bella is drinking."

Lana spoke up. "No orange soda for me. I'll have black coffee, please."

As Don walked away, Bella asked, "You ever been to Roy before?"

"Nope," Tuper said.

"How do you know Frank?"

"We were in the Marines together. We're trying to round up some of the guys for a little reunion."

"So, that's why she couldn't find him," Bella said. "He joined the military. I expect his mama had something to do with that."

"Who couldn't find him?" Tuper asked.

Lana was typing something on her phone. Tuper thought it was rude to be texting when people were talking. Besides, she needed to be listening in case he missed something. He gave her a dirty look, but she ignored him. He had no control over her. He could've just as well left her home.

"His girlfriend Amber," Bella said. "She tried to find him but couldn't. Now, I don't know for a hundred percent, but Amber got pregnant, and I'm pretty sure Frank was the father. Mama Finnigan tried to pay her off. She wanted Amber to give up the kid, maybe even get an abortion, although Mama Finnigan was Catholic and didn't believe in abortions. The rumor is she tried anyway." Bella leaned back and shrugged. "But who knows how much of that was just talk. She may not have gone that far. But that woman was a real bear, so it's hard to say what all she done. I know for a hundred percent that Amber got pregnant because she had the kid. But she said she never could find Frank."

"He never said anything about having a kid," Tuper commented.

"No one was ever sure if Frank even knew. The rumor has it that when Amber went looking for Frank, his mama found out and intervened. It was quite the scandal in this small town. Gave the folks something to talk about for nearly a year. Once the baby was born, it all settled down."

"Does Amber still live here?" Lana asked. Tuper was surprised she was even listening.

"No, she left right after the boy was born. Her mother said she married a guy from Lewistown, and they were living in Grass Range. I'm not sure I ever believed that story. Amber's father passed away some time after that, and her mother moved to Arizona to live with her other daughter. I lost track of them after that."

"Do you know who Amber supposedly married?" Lana asked.

"I don't know the name, sorry. I'm not sure they ever gave one."

"What was Amber's family name?"

"Carlton."

"What did she name the boy?"

"Clarence Francis. She called him Frankie."

So, Lana was paying attention, Tuper thought. Then she went back to typing and swiping on her phone. He hated all the gadgets in the world now. Life was much simpler a short time ago.

Don brought over the drinks. "Burgers will be up in a second."

Bella continued to tell stories about when they were young. Some included the Finnigans and the Carltons, others were just fun things she remembered about small-town living.

Just as Don walked up with the hamburgers, Tuper asked, "Do you know someone named Patrick Gallagher?" The plate clanged as it hit the table. The noise startled Lana, who caught an anguished look on Don's face. He hurried away.

"How could you know about him?" Bella's voice sounded edgy. She quickly added, "He didn't come to Roy until after Frank left."

Lana spoke up. "We don't know anything about him. When Pops started looking for Frank, I did a little internet research. The first thing was to run the obituaries to see if Frank was still alive. Patrick was one of the people from this area whose death was listed. There were others, but I don't have the list with me. I remembered his name because it's the name of a movie star I really like." Lana paused and put her finger to her lips. "Wait a minute, the actor's name is Peter, not Patrick. Yeah, Peter Gallagher. Oh well, he still reminded me of him. He starred in a movie called *Mr. Deeds*. And in one called *While You Were Sleeping*. I love that movie. Of course, it also stars Sandra Bullock, and I love her. Don't you?"

"I'm not sure which movie star you're talking about, but I do like Sandra Bullock." Bella spoke calmly, more so than she had earlier, and seemed deliberate, almost cold now. "So, you already know Patrick Gallagher is dead. It happened twenty-five years ago."

"How?"

"I don't remember." Bella picked up her bourbon and swigged it down. "I need to get going. It was nice meeting you folks."

Lana and Tuper were both certain she didn't really think meeting them had been "nice." Something about Patrick Gallagher had spooked her ... and the bartender.

CHAPTER 13

"That was rude," Tuper said shaking his head, and wondering how kids could spend so much time on the phone.

"Her leaving like that, I know."

"No, you texting on that smart phone thingy. You kids need to learn to communicate."

"You're giving me a lecture on communication?" Lana scoffed. "You never talk about anything. I have to pull it out of you."

"Humpf."

"Besides, I was taking notes. I didn't see you writing down any of the names and information she gave us."

"Didn't need to." He tapped his finger on the side of his head. "It's all up here."

"Sure it is, Pops."

Tuper pulled the extra meat patty off to save for Ringo, then they ate their hamburgers, paid the bill, and left. Neither spoke about Squirrely until they were in the car. Finally, Tuper said, "I think we hit a nerve."

"Yeah, with both Bella and the bartender," Lana said.

"You saw that too? I thought that plate was gonna break the way it hit that table."

"And he couldn't wait to get away. But how can Patrick Gallagher's death have anything to do with Squirrely? They were not in Roy at the same time, unless Bella didn't tell us the truth. Why do you think she would lie about it? Maybe the biggest scandal wasn't a pregnant girl. Maybe they robbed a bank or something. That would explain the money. Maybe others were involved too, and one found out Squirrely is alive and tried to kill him. And how did Patrick die? Maybe whoever is after Squirrely killed Patrick. Bella has to know the cause of death. That woman has a memory like an elephant. She remembered details about everything else, and she knew Patrick was dead, but didn't remember how he died? There's definitely something wrong here."

Tuper shook his head. "You're getting carried away."

"You don't think there's something wrong? Bella remembered the type of car Frank's father drove forty-five years ago, even the color, and she can't remember how Patrick died twenty-five years ago. That's sketchy."

"I agree. I just don't believe we should jump to murder and robbery without a little more information."

"Maybe not, but they're hiding something."

"Just because Patrick's not connected to Squirrely don't mean this town don't have secrets. I just don't want to get off task and not find what we're looking for. We can't even be sure Squirrely's hit-and-run had anything to do with his bag of money."

Lana tilted her head and glared. "Seriously? That's just too big a coincidence. And you must think so too, or we wouldn't be here."

"I suppose."

"So, what now, Sherlock?"

"We passed another bar on the way into town. It's right up the street. I think we should go ask a few more questions."

"Good idea. You and Ringo do that. I'll go back to the school and see if Connie really will help me look through the old files. It sure would be a lot easier if they would come into the twenty-first century and get the information online. I hope the grumpy old woman is gone or I may not get anywhere." Lana rambled on for the entire two blocks they drove to the school. "Come get me when you're done. If I don't get anywhere and can't get information, I'll walk to the bar." Tuper drove away.

Lana peeked in the front door to see if Connie was alone. When she didn't see the old woman, she approached the counter.

"Hi, Connie."

"Oh, hi. You're back. I was just about to leave. Did you want to see the records?"

"Yes, if that's possible."

"Sure, it's not like they're top secret or anything, but if we go right now, I won't have to explain anything to Mrs. Emma Tate. Come on, I'll take you. Then I'll come back, check out, and join you."

"Her name is Emma?"

"Yeah, why?"

"Nothing. I just like the name." Lana smiled. "Too nice a name for such a grumpy woman."

They walked to a locked room at the end of the hallway. Connie opened the door and let Lana inside. The large storage closet had no windows and file boxes stacked five high.

"That's a lot of boxes," Lana said.

"It could be worse. In fact, it was. The last five years of information was entered directly into the computer, so there are no physical records for that period. We actually destroyed the ten years before that, after we got them entered in the program. We're working our way back, but it's a slow process." Connie coughed. "It's a little dusty in here, but why don't you just look around and see where you want to start. There is some organization to it." She pointed to the boxes on the left. "Those are the first records we have. I'm not sure when the school opened, but those are from the early 1900s. Not much in them. What years are you looking for?"

"Late sixties, early seventies, I think."

"That's going to be somewhere over there." Connie pointed to a row of boxes about five stacks deep. "But those years are toward the back. I won't be long." She dashed out.

Lana felt overwhelmed. She opened a box marked *1981-82, High School, Freshman* just to see how they were set up. The folders were in alphabetical order. The first was for a student named James Anderson with a thin file that contained his progress reports, extracurricular activities, attendance, and very little else. William Bain, on the other hand, had a much thicker folder that included a slew of disciplinary forms. She had to look at each piece of paper to see what it was about. Had the information been digital, she could've done a word search. Computers were so much easier. She wondered how anyone managed without them.

Lana was still learning her way around the system when Connie returned with a thin, lanky boy about the same age.

"This is my twin brother, Martin. He volunteered to help."

"Sure, I did." He gave Connie a sarcastic look, then turned

to Lana. "Really, I don't mind helping. What do you need me to do?"

Martin moved the first three stacks of boxes out of the way. The fourth stack was labeled *1965-67 Freshman-Sophomore.*

"I'll need to look through all of those, but I'd like to start with the bottom one," Lana said. "Those must have been small classes because they fit in one box."

Lana opened the box and discovered that the tab for Freshman contained four folders, and the one for Sophomore only three, each with a class list. She took a photo of both lists. The freshman class had three boys and a girl: *Amber Carlton, the name Bella had mentioned.* Lana made a mental note to copy her file as well, if she had time.

"Those classes are really small," Lana said.

Connie laughed. "We had a class once that had only one student in it. He was on the *Johnny Carson Show* with a girl from another state who was also the only one in her class. That's Roy, Montana's biggest claim to fame."

Lana pulled out Harold Francis Finnigan's folder for his freshman year. She took a photo of the front, which featured a picture of a freckle-faced kid with messy, curly hair in need of a trim. She wanted to spend time looking through the file, but she didn't want to hold up Connie and her brother, so she quickly thumbed through and took photos of anything that might be of interest. Then she photographed Amber's file, as well as the other student, Karl Haberman.

She did the same with the next three boxes, which also contained two classes in each one. By the last box, the class sizes had gotten bigger. The junior class had gained a new student named Patrick Gallagher. Lana snapped photos of all his files. *Why did Bella lie about when Patrick came to town?*

CHAPTER 14

Tuper parked in front of the bar next to an old pickup, the only vehicle in the tiny lot. The building needed paint and the windows needed washing. Above the door was a sign that read, *The Bar.* Tuper and Ringo stepped out of his old Toyota and approached the door. Tuper smelled a strong scent of urine, probably from the guys who left the bar drunk and couldn't wait any longer. He had seen that many times. Tuper went inside, with Ringo at his heels. He soon realized the bar was in complete contrast to the first one. The Legion bar had been light and airy and smelled like home cooking. This one was small, and dark, and smelled like a mixture of beer and sweat.

Four men sat at the counter. Tuper walked up with Ringo at his side and took a seat where the bar curved, giving him a good vantage point to see all of the patrons. He was also close enough to talk to them. When he ordered an orange soda, an old guy with a white beard mumbled, "We got a dry one here."

"I'm sure he's got his reasons," a young man in a red cap said. "Leave 'em alone."

"It's just a little early for me," Tuper said, "and I've got a long drive ahead."

"Where you from?" Red Cap asked.

"Missoula."

"That *is* a long way. What brings you here?"

"I'm trying to find a buddy from the Marine Corps who grew up here."

"Does this guy have a name?"

"Harold Francis Finnigan. He went by Frank."

"I knew Frankie," White Beard cut in. "We grew up together."

"Really?" Tuper picked up his orange soda, walked over to the man, and extended his hand. "I'm Tuper."

"Karl," the man said, giving him a shake. "Nice dog."

"Thanks. Do you have any idea where Frankie might be now?"

"None. He left here right after graduation, and I haven't seen him since. His whole family left. Apparently, you've seen him since I have."

"Do you know if he kept in touch with anyone else in town?"

"His girlfriend maybe, but she doesn't live here anymore. Don't know where she moved to. Other than her, I was the closest to him. And I never heard a word from him once he left town. So, I'd say no."

"I guess he could've gone anywhere after he left the Corps," Tuper said. "Looks like I hit a dead end." Curious about what Squirrely had been like when he was young and hoping it would lead to something helpful, Tuper continued to ask questions about his childhood. "What kind of a kid was Frankie?"

"He was a good friend, always had my back. He got me out of a lot of scrapes."

"Did you know his sister?"

"Everyone in this town knows everyone," Karl said. "Marlys was a couple years older than us, and she was always supposed to be watching Frankie, but it was really the other way around. By the time they were teenagers, Frankie was protecting her."

"Did she need protecting?"

"Sometimes. She was a beautiful girl, and all the guys were after her."

"Did Frankie play sports?"

"He would have. I mean, our classes were so small, we never had enough for a team. My older brother had a home-gym set, and Frankie and I used to work out on it. He was relentless, always trying to buff up. By the time we were seniors, he looked pretty good."

"I know he was in good shape in the Corps," Tuper ad-libbed. "Did you know his parents?"

"Certainly. His father was the best. He would take us fishing and hunting, and sometimes we'd just go camping. He was a busy guy, but he always seemed to make time for us kids. But Frankie's mother didn't seem to care what he did as long as he didn't embarrass her. She paid a lot more attention to her daughter. Frankie didn't seem to mind too much because he had his dad. He worshipped that man, wanted to grow up to be just like him he often said. His dad was in the Marines too. I suppose that's why he joined."

Tuper sipped his soda. After a few minutes, he said, "There's another guy I was curious about."

"Who's that?" Karl asked.

"Patrick Gallagher. Remember him?"

The two men who hadn't said anything suddenly stood up. One gave Tuper a long, lingering look before they walked out.

Karl said, "Who are you?"

"I told you, the name's Tuper."

"Are you a cop?"

"No, I'm just looking for my friend."

"And what does he have to do with Gallagher?"

"Nothing, as far as I know."

"Leave it that way. I think you've asked enough questions."

CHAPTER 15

W hen Tuper picked up Lana at the school, Ringo jumped in the backseat, and they started the long trip back to Helena. Tuper was pleased when Lana immediately opened her laptop and started to work. He thought he wouldn't have to listen to her constant chatter, but the reprieve didn't last long. They hadn't even reached Lewistown, only a half an hour away, before she asked, "Did you learn anything at the other bar?"

"Yup."

She waited for a couple of seconds, then asked, "What did you learn, Pops?"

"No one in that town wants to talk about Patrick Gallagher."

"Why do you say that?"

"I was told to quit asking questions. But I guess it don't matter much if Squirrely didn't even know him." Tuper checked his rearview mirror.

"But he did," Lana said excitedly. "Bella lied. She said Patrick didn't get there until after Squirrely left town, but I saw the records. Patrick came to Roy partway into his junior year and was in the same class. So, even if Squirrely left right after graduation, he and Patrick went to school together for well over a year."

"Did you read Patrick's file?"

"No, but I took photos of everything they had on him for both his junior and senior years. The folder wasn't that big, but I'm uploading the photos onto my laptop, which is something I can do without the internet. All I have to do is connect my phone to my laptop. When I try to do anything else around this town, I keep losing the signal and it's irritating." She spat the words, then more calmly said, "I shot all four years of Squirrely's files. Since the class was so small, I took pictures of the other students too."

"Good work, Agony," Tuper said, almost regretting it the minute the praise came out of his mouth.

"Thanks, Pops. I knew you needed me. You do, you know? Well, I know you do, even if you don't. I can help you with this."

Tuper glanced in his mirror at a dark sedan, and so did Lana.

"Are we being followed?" she asked, sliding down in her seat.

"Good move," Tuper said, unsnapping his holster, freeing his pistol.

"Who is it?"

"I don't know yet. Maybe it's some local yokels making sure we leave." He didn't want to worry Lana, but he would've expected a pickup, not a black sedan, from someone they had riled up in Roy.

"If that's the case, they shouldn't follow too long. I'll just stay down for a while if that's okay with you."

"Something you want to tell me, Agony?" It wasn't the first time Lana had ducked down when she thought someone was following them.

"No, not today."

Tuper let it go and continued south on US-191 until he reached the US-12 junction, where he turned toward Helena. It was getting dark and harder to tell if they were being tailed. When he had another open stretch, he accelerated as fast as the old '78 Toyota would go. He barely got it up to eighty, and for many drivers in Montana, that was a slow speed. The sedan behind them kept up. "Can you check the hospital and see if there is any change in Squirrely?"

"Sure." She sounded happy for the distraction. The WiFi signal got better the closer they got to Helena, so a few minutes later, she said, "It looks like the doctor came in a short time ago and made a few notes. Squirrely's still unconscious, but he seems stable. Recovery from surgery uneventful. That's it."

"Thanks," Tuper said. "Did you get everything downloaded onto your computer?"

"Actually, you say *uploading* when you're putting something on. *Downloading* when you're taking it off, but that doesn't matter. Yes, it's done." She perused the information she had gained, giving Tuper a running monologue. "Squirrely was a freshman in 1965 and 66. He got mostly A's and B's on his progress reports, but a note says he was shy and needed to participate more in class. Good school attendance, only missed two days as a freshman. Member of FFA. That's about it for that year." She paused. "Dang!" she exclaimed, making Tuper jump.

"What did you find?"

"Nothing. I just realized I should've looked at the old yearbooks. I might've found something different. Oh well, too late now. We didn't really have time anyway, since you were asking questions that got us run out of town."

"We didn't get run out," Tuper said, checking his mirror.

"They're still there, aren't they?"

"I don't know, but I think so."

"How will you shake them? It's not like you can outrun them in this death trap."

"Don't be making fun of Ringo's car, or I'll send you to the backseat and bring him up here with me." Ringo's head appeared at his shoulder. Tuper reached over and patted Ringo on the head. "It'll be easier to get rid of them once we get to town—unless they decide to start shootin' or something before then."

When Lana didn't laugh, it concerned him. He didn't really expect those Roy characters to shoot at them, but he had no idea who might be after Agony or what they might do.

"Let's see if there's anything exciting in Squirrely's sophomore year." Lana sighed.

"What's wrong?"

"I'm just a little frustrated because some of the photos aren't as clear as I'd like." She continued to look at each page.

"So? Are you finding anything interesting?" Tuper finally asked after a few minutes of silence.

"Squirrely took a woodshop class, joined the debate team, and played Atticus Finch in the school play, *To Kill a Mockingbird*. That's pretty impressive. He must've had quite the way with words in high school. He's still clever, but I would've never pegged him for an orator. We already knew that he won second place in the regionals on the debate team, so he had to have been pretty good. I wonder if he said 'Yeh' before every sentence back then." She was quiet for a few more minutes. "It doesn't show that he participated in any sports in high school."

"That's what his friend, Karl, said. But he worked out in Karl's home gym a lot."

"Yeah, Karl was the other student who graduated with Frank, Amber, and Patrick. I photographed his stuff too. It seems they all had a lot of the same disciplinary slips. I haven't read them yet, but I noticed the subject matter."

Lana continued to flip through the photos, squinting sometimes to read and occasionally checking the side mirror to see if they still had company. She couldn't tell for certain, and she noticed Tuper watching closely too. "Squirrely's grades were about the same that year, mostly A's and B's, except for the C's in P.E." She pulled up his next records on her computer, getting proficient at finding her way through the documents and knowing what to skip. "Junior year, more debate, and drama star. This time he played Mark Twain in a one-man show. Good attendance and grades about the same. Not much to report."

Ringo stuck his nose over the seat and into Lana's cheek. She squealed before she realized it was the dog.

"You okay?" Tuper asked.

"Yeah, just a little jumpy, I guess." She turned back to her laptop. "This is interesting. In his senior year, things changed somewhat."

"How?"

"He went to the regional debates, so maybe they distracted him from the rest of his studies, but his grades really dropped. The first semester he had all B's except for an A in drama, but in the last semester, his academic marks were all D's. He also had three discipline slips. That's three more than he had all the rest of his high school days."

"What were the problems?"

"One was for using the school bus as a party ride and driving it to a remote area for a big celebration. Fifteen kids were involved, so most of the high school, or at least the cool kids, I presume. But Squirrely was the driver, so he got into more trouble than the rest." She looked at the next screen. "He also put a wet, sticky varnish on a teacher's seat. Someone else was involved, but Squirrely wouldn't rat on him or her. The third one is a one-day suspension for Squirrely and two other boys, including a referral."

"What was the referral for?"

"It doesn't say, but it looks like it has something to do with MHP. What is MHP?" Lana continued to chatter as she searched the internet for MHP. "It could stand for 'mobile home park,' but that's not likely. There's MHP Real Estate, but that's in New York." She continued to bang away on her keyboard. "There's MHP Salud, a program that helps Latino communities." She paused for just a few seconds. "Nevermind, that's only been around for thirty-five years. Mhp Pudding Mix, is probably not it. Uh, huh! That's it, I bet."

Tuper was silent for a few seconds. "Agony," he said sternly, "what is it?"

"Montana Highway Patrol. I bet that's it."

"If it was the highway patrol, then it had to do with traffic law," Tuper said.

"Like maybe a drunk driving, or car accident, or some criminal activity on the highway. Whatever it was, they had trouble with the law, but there's no reason stated on the form for the referral."

"How can they give a referral with no reason? Isn't there a spot for it on the form?"

Lana turned the computer toward him. "Look, there's the

line, and it had something written, but it's been blocked out. See the solid black bar? That's where it should be. Why would they block it out? I suppose if they realized it wasn't true, they might have done that because they didn't want to tarnish the boys' reputations."

"Why—"

Lana interrupted Tuper. "Why wouldn't they just remove the referral if that was the case? No, there's something sketchy about that whole thing."

"Who are the other boys?"

"Karl Haberman and Patrick Gallagher."

"Are Karl and Patrick's names on the list for the party bus?"

Lana flipped back a couple of photos. "Yes, and so is Amber Carlton's."

They were quiet for a few minutes while Lana tapped away at her keyboard. Then she spoke. "What do you suppose happened to Squirrely in his senior year?" Before Tuper could answer, she said, "Lots of things could have, I suppose. Maybe it was end-of-school boredom, or too much time on the debate trail, or too much time with Amber Carlton. Or ..." Her eyes widened like they did whenever she thought she was really onto something. "Maybe it was all about Patrick Gallagher."

Tuper didn't respond.

Lana started through another set of photos. "Patrick has eighteen disciplinary slips."

"That's a lot."

"And he still got straight A's."

"That's unusual."

"He must've been a smart kid to pull that off, especially since he missed a lot of school and was tardy for many of his classes. Three of the disciplinary slips are for ditching school and two are for excessive tardiness."

"What are the others about?"

"Two are for complaints from girls for harassment, but nothing physical or creepy. He would call them names like Gorgeous, Precious, or Stunning. I guess too much of anything can be annoying. In addition to the party bus and the suspension with Karl and Squirrely, Patrick got caught putting a stink bomb in the girls' bathroom. Oh, and he was in two fights."

"Were either of the fights with Squirrely?"

"No, but one was with Karl."

"What else?"

"The rest are suspected violations that were never proved. Someone put Saran Wrap on the toilet seat in the teachers' restroom, and he was the prime suspect. The same with the goldfish in the water cooler in the teachers' lounge, and Vaseline on the office door handles." Lana chuckled at the pranks. "He was nothing if not creative."

Lana continued to work. Just as Tuper began to enjoy the peace and quiet, Lana blurted, "I found an Emma."

"What's an *emma*?"

"The grumpy receptionist at the school. Her name is Emma. You know, Elba, Emma, what Squirrely said. Maybe he said Emma. Anyway, I'll check her out later, but what if she was Squirrely's Emma?"

"Yeah, what if?" Tuper thought it was a stretch, but it wouldn't be the first time Lana discovered something that seemed pretty far-fetched. She could run with it. He couldn't stop her anyway, even if he wanted to.

CHAPTER 16

W hen Tuper stopped at the first light in Helena, he
looked in the rearview mirror to check for the black
sedan, but it was too dark to tell the color of any vehicles
behind him. He had started watching headlights a while back
when he thought he could still see the sedan, but he wasn't
certain it was even the same car. To be safe, he slowly pulled
away from the intersection, allowing cars to pass and
watching to see if anyone lingered. Nothing was obvious. He
made a right turn into a gas station and waited. A black car
drove past and turned into the Taco Bell. When it pulled into
the drive-through, Tuper drove away.

He was in familiar territory now and was certain he could
lose a tail—if he had one—simply by driving through neigh-
borhoods. So he did.

"What are you doing?" Lana asked.

"Makin' sure no one is going home with us."

"I don't think anyone is there."

"Me either. Just bein' careful."

It was soon evident they had no one following, so Tuper

drove to Clarice's. When they walked in, Clarice said, "Just in time for supper."

"Good. I'm starving," Lana said.

"I just came from the hospital," Clarice continued. "Squirrely's doing about the same. He didn't even stir. I talked to the nurse, and she told me his vital signs are good and his blood pressure is back to normal. Sit down and eat, and you can tell me what you two learned today."

Tuper ate in silence while Lana reported what they had discovered. "I still have some files from the school to go through. I haven't touched Amber's yet, but I will right after I finish dinner." *Dang!* She'd said 'dinner' again. No one seemed to notice, but if she wanted to blend in, she needed to be more careful.

After they ate, Lana offered to help clean up, but Clarice insisted she get back to work, so Lana sat at the table across from Tuper and delved into Amber's school records. They weren't much different than Squirrely's: good attendance, but her grades were consistently average with only an occasional A in some nonsense elective. Nothing in her folder was of any help. Lana went back to Patrick's file.

"Patrick Gallagher transferred from Helena in his junior year. There's a note in the file that pegged him as a *troubled child*. That's all it says though, no explanation."

"So, he was a problem in his previous school as well," Tuper said.

"Looks like it. I need to see his record in Helena. I wonder if that high school has their records computerized," she mumbled. "It's a bigger town, so let's hope they're a little more up to date. I feel like I'm working in the 1800s here."

Tuper shook his head as she continued to babble. Then she got quiet for nearly half an hour.

"Gazinga!" Lana shouted, startling both Clarice and Tuper. "I'm in."

No one said anything for a few minutes. They had learned that the hard part was the break in, and now it would only be a few minutes before Lana started spouting information. It didn't take long. "Patrick had attendance problems, as well as tardiness, but his grades were excellent." Lana knew what it was like not to be challenged in school. She had always been the first one done with her work, looking around for something else to do. She had usually spent the time searching the internet. "I can relate," Lana said. "Here's something. He had five discipline problems in his sophomore year and was kicked out of school a month early. But they gave him credit for the year because of his excellent grades."

A minute later, Lana laughed out loud.

"What's so funny?" Clarice asked.

"Patrick created a fake student named John Thornton," Lana said, still laughing. "He used him whenever he needed a witness to a minor problem. John signed up for tennis and track, had a class schedule, and applied to colleges. Other students adopted him as their friend as well, whenever they needed him. He had been a fake student for two years before his name came up once too often." She laughed again. "The principal caught on and announced John's death at an assembly. Patrick and his friends had a memorial for him in the gym after school, with a coffin and pallbearers and the whole thing. The photos depict a gym full of students attending the service. They even dedicated a page in the yearbook to him."

"Is that why Patrick was suspended?"

"No, there were missing funds from the Poetry Club, over a thousand dollars. The investigation initially pointed the finger at John Thornton, but since he had just *died*, the blame fell on Patrick. He claimed innocence to the end, but his family was given the option of paying the funds back and leaving the school district or prosecution. They moved to Roy, which probably felt like prosecution to a teenager like Patrick."

Lana continued to search through the Helena school files, but she didn't come up with anything else that seemed helpful. She jotted down the names of Patrick's parents and a few of his close friends for further research later. "I think I have everything I can get from here," she said.

Tuper sighed. "Someone tried to kill Squirrely. It has to be something more serious than missing school funds or funny high school pranks."

"Where do you go from here?" Clarice asked.

"Hopefully, I have enough information to track Patrick from high school to his death. Or maybe from his death backward to his time in Roy. We don't even know how he died, which might tell us a lot. I'll start there." Without taking a breath, Lana went on. "And we need to see if we can find out what happened to Amber. Do you think Squirrely knew Amber was pregnant? Maybe he doesn't even know he has a son. Do you think he would want to know? I'm not sure if I would. Sometimes it's better not to know stuff, but that's hard for me. When I see something, I need to check it out. I get too curious, and sometimes I discover things I wish I didn't know. Then I can't unknow them."

Tuper looked at Lana, waiting for her to stop talking.

But she didn't. "It's going to be harder to trace Amber if

she got married and changed her name. Same with her son, if she changed his name. But, at least, I have something to start with." Lana realized Tuper and Clarice were both staring at her. She shrugged. "You asked where we go from here. So, I was telling you what I plan to do. How about you, Pops?"

"I'm going to the hospital where it's quiet."

CHAPTER 17

L ana was tired, but the house was quiet, and she was
more anxious to get answers than sleep, so she fired up
her laptop and went back to work. She liked roaming the web
late at night. Less activity meant less chance of being caught.
She didn't worry much about that anymore, except on a few
sites she avoided because she knew she was being watched.
On the rest of the web, dark and otherwise, she had free reign.

Lana had already retrieved the birthdates from the school
records, which would help in her search for Amber and
Patrick. She then pulled their birth certificates and jotted down
the parents' names and verified them with the school records.
The names were all the same, nothing suspicious there. She
would use the parents' names later for further investigation.

She began with the hunt for Amber, expecting to find a
different last name somewhere along the line, especially since
Amber had supposedly married after she left town. Lana
checked for a marriage certificate for Amber Carlton in the
five years following her graduation. She checked Fergus

County, then spread out, county by county, until she had exhausted the entire state—but found nothing. So much for the rumored marriage to the guy in Grass Range.

Lana verified the death of Amber's father and followed her mother's trail to Sierra Vista, Arizona. Sometimes it was so easy getting the information she needed. The mother lived for nine years with her daughter, Erica, at the same address, then moved into an assisted living facility and died within a year. Amber's sister appeared to still live in the same residence. Lana had a phone number that she would try if she needed to, although there was no guarantee the sister would tell her anything. It was possible Amber went with her mother to Arizona, but Lana couldn't find a digital trail for her in that state. No driver's license and no medical records that she could find.

Lana went back to Amber's time in Roy and commenced looking for a birth certificate for Amber's son. She found nothing. No record of Amber Carlton ever giving birth. It was possible she had married prior to the birth, and the child was recorded under the father's name, but there was no birth by a woman named Amber in the vicinity. Lana decided to widen her search later.

She moved on to school records for the supposed son, Clarence Francis Carlton. She found nothing in Fergus County and nothing in the area around Sierra Vista, Arizona. It would take weeks to check every school district in the state, so she moved on to medical records but came up with the same result.

The Department of Motor Vehicles was a little easier because she could check for the entire state in one spot, but she couldn't find a driver's license or ID for Amber Carlton that fit the right age and description. Lana exhausted the search in both Montana and Arizona.

She switched her concentration to Patrick and discovered he was born in Kalispell, Montana. His parents, James and Mary Lou, moved to Helena before Patrick started elementary school. His father was a car salesman for Grimes Motors and appeared to make a good living. Patrick's mother was a stay-at-home mom. They lived on the good side of town and continued to climb the social ladder. James Gallagher also participated in local politics. It was a major step down when they moved to Roy, but James continued to sell cars in Lewistown at Imperial Motors and soon became the general manager. They built a new home in Roy, the best in town. By Roy standards, they were affluent.

Patrick was not educated beyond high school, had a sporadic janitorial work history, and had been arrested several times. But his file showed no convictions beyond a drunk driving charge. Lana followed a trail for Patrick that took him from Roy to Great Falls, then to Billings and Butte, before it brought him back to Helena. However, his driver's license history stopped at Roy. There was no record of an address change or a renewed license after high school, which probably explained why he was listed in the newspaper as being from Roy.

Lana was frustrated because her gut told her there was a greater connection between Squirrely and Patrick, but it wasn't anything she could see in their digital footprints. Maybe she needed to follow Squirrely's background for a while and see where it led. But before she did, she wanted more information about Patrick's death. His obituary had been minimal, and he should've been listed as a resident of Helena.

Patrick's death certificate was easy to find, and the cause was listed as *heart failure*. Not satisfied with the information, Lana continued to poke around. She hacked into the mortuary listed for the funeral arrangements, but there were no records for twenty-five years ago. *Damn!* It was so much easier researching current information. People had social media records, blogs, and public details for every facet of their lives, including photographs and connections to everyone around them. She could really get to know a person by all the information available, but that wasn't true for twenty-five years ago.

She picked up her phone and called Tuper. When it took four rings before he answered, Lana realized it was nearly two a.m.

"What is it?" Tuper grumbled.

"Are you awake?" Lana asked.

"I am now."

"Good. I think there's something suspicious about Patrick's death."

"What?"

"His death certificate says he died of heart failure."

"So?"

"So, everyone dies of heart failure. It's not like he was old like you, Pops. He was young. What caused the heart failure? And why the cover up?"

"What cover up?"

"Aren't you listening? The cause of death. Why wouldn't it be listed on his death certificate? Who would have that kind of influence to keep the real cause of death from being stated on the certificate? Or who had the ability to change it—if it had been there? It would have to be someone pretty powerful, don't you think?"

"I think you're getting carried away."

"Patrick was a nobody, a petty criminal. Who would care about him?"

"Maybe that's the problem," Tuper said. "*Nobody* cared, so whoever signed the death certificate took the easy road."

"Maybe, but I still think there's more to it than that."

"And what would you like me to do about it at this hour?"

"Nothing. Are you still at the hospital?"

"Yup. I've been sleeping in the chair next to Squirrely. No change yet."

"Sorry to bug you," Lana said.

"What mortuary did he use?" Tuper asked.

"Wolfe & Son Funeral Services. They're still in business. It seems to have the same family ownership as it did twenty-five years ago."

"I know the place. I'll see what I can find out tomorrow."

"What are you going to do?"

"I know a guy."

CHAPTER 18

The old neon sign in front of the building read *Wolfe &*
Son Funeral Services, with an extra space after *Son.* Tuper
remembered when the sign was new. Now it was outdated
and dingy, just like the building. Richard Wolfe had started
this business when he was thirty years old. He had two young
boys at the time and decided to add *& Son* to the company
name in the hope that at least one of his boys would join the
business eventually. If they both did, he'd left room to add the
"s." His oldest son became a mortician and joined forces with
his father, but Richard never got the chance to make the word
plural because his youngest had been killed in the Gulf War
before he could choose a career.

Tuper parked in the lot, thinking about the many times
he'd been there because of lost loved ones. The older he got,
the more time he seemed to spend there. He had lost so many
friends over the years, and he wondered, as he often did, why
he was still around. He certainly hadn't been spared because
of his good, clean living.

When Tuper walked in, the young girl at the front desk greeted him with a smile.

"I'm here to see Richard. He's expecting me. The name's Tuper."

"Right this way." The girl stood up, but before she could take a step, a tall, lanky, gray-haired man stepped out of a nearby office.

"Hey, Toop. Come on in. Nice to see you. I hope you're not here because you lost someone close to you."

"No, that's not it."

They shook hands and walked into Richard's office.

"Have a seat."

Tuper put his hat on the chair next to him as he sat down. "It's hard to believe you're still working the business."

"Oh, I don't do much anymore, but it keeps me off the streets and out of the bars." Richard chuckled. "I had my eighty-third birthday last month. Each year, I take on a little less. My son pretty much runs things these days. Thanks to you, he's around here to do so. And other family members help too. That was my granddaughter out front. She started college this year, and it's a good part-time job for her." He swatted the air as if to move on. "What brings you here?"

"I need your help."

"You know I'll do whatever I can, my friend."

"I don't know if you remember my friend Squirrely. He's done a lot of handyman work for me over the last ten years. He mostly lives on the streets and needs the work, so I use him when I can."

"No, I don't recall ever meeting him."

"He was hit by a car a few days ago and is unconscious in the hospital. The driver took off, and I've been trying to find out who ran him down."

"Are the cops investigating?"

"As far as I know, but they don't seem to be having much luck."

"How does this involve me?" Richard asked.

"I know this may sound strange, but I came across something in Squirrely's stuff that led me to a guy who died twenty-five years ago. I have reason to believe he may be connected to Squirrely's hit-and-run. He was one of your clients. The cause of death was listed as *heart failure.*"

"I'm still not sure how I can help."

"Is it unusual to list heart failure on a death certificate?"

"They used to do it a lot more way back in the day, especially when they didn't really know the cause of death. Now, you mostly see it when the person dies of congestive heart failure, and it will read that way. I take it that wasn't the case."

"No, it just said heart failure. I'd like you to tell me if there was anything unusual that you can remember about the guy. Not that you would remember him, with the many bodies that have been through here, but I would appreciate it if you could check your files for me."

"What's his name and what year did he die?"

"Patrick Gallagher, early May of 1994."

"That is a while back." Richard stood and went to the door. "Brianna, will you please get me a file from the archive room." He gave her the name and date, then sat back down.

Tuper noticed Richard had slowed down quite a bit from the last time he had seen him. He hoped his health was good, not that Richard would complain. They had known each other for more than a half century. The two of them had spent a lot of time hunting and fishing together when they were much younger. They'd gone ice fishing once when Richard's boys were eight and ten years old. The older boy fell in the ice hole, and Tuper had saved him, nearly killing himself doing it.

They reminisced about the good old days until Brianna returned with a file and handed it to her grandfather. "Sorry I took so long. It would be so much faster if we put the files in a digital program, Grandpa."

"I hear you," Richard said, smiling at Brianna as she left. "She's been wanting to enter all the data onto the computer, but I've been resisting it. I guess there's not really any good reason not to. It would alleviate the storage problem we're having, and it would give Brianna more work. I think she gets bored sometimes."

Richard stopped talking and started reading the file. He flipped through the first few pages, then said, "I remember this body, and I remember questioning the cause of death."

"Why?"

He flipped to the last page in the file. "I always kept my own notes when I found something curious, in case the issue came up later. It has only happened a few times, but when it did, I was sure glad I had written things down." He was silent for a few minutes while he read what he had written twenty-five years ago. "This body was covered with bruises, scrapes, and cuts, and he had several broken bones. At least one rib was broken and his left femur too." Richard read further. "I also have a note that I overheard a family member say something about a hit-and-run."

"What was said exactly?"

"I don't know. That's all my note said. At least an accident explained the condition of the body. But it wasn't my place to question the doctor who signed the death certificate. I figured the police probably had all the information they needed."

CHAPTER 19

"Wow! Patrick was murdered," Lana said. "That sure changes things, and it makes a lot more sense." She sat on the sofa with her laptop. Clarice was at the other end, petting Caspar, her white fluffy dog.

"That's a big leap. We don't know he was murdered," Tuper said from his armchair a few feet away. "It could've been an accident, or a drunk driver, or lots of other possible explanations."

"It could be, but most likely it wasn't," Lana argued. "Someone killed Patrick twenty-five years ago, then tried to kill Squirrely in the same manner. It can't be a coincidence. We just need to figure out what the men had in common besides living in Roy, Montana. Something happened with the two of them that kept them connected."

Clarice spoke. "But why now? Why after all this time would they go after Squirrely?"

"Something must have happened that brought their attention to him," Lana said. "Squirrely's been living on the streets for a long time. Maybe they just didn't know where he was. Has Squirrely been in the news lately?"

"What are you talking about?" Tuper asked.

"Did he do something heroic or noticeable that made the news? Something that the killers might have seen. Maybe they saw him on a YouTube video rescuing someone from a burning building or giving CPR to a car accident victim. Maybe he pulled a little kid out of the lake so he or she didn't drown. So, after looking for him all these years, they found him and went after him." Lana shook her head. "Just because he was unlucky enough to save a kid from drowning."

"I'm pretty sure Squirrely hasn't been in a YouTube thingy," Tuper said dryly. "So, let's get back to the facts. We still don't know if Squirrely's accident had anything to do with Patrick."

"The facts are that Squirrely had a newspaper with Patrick's death in it. Why else would he have that paper?" Lana's eyes widened, as they did when she had a light-bulb moment. "Maybe that was not the reason he had the paper. Maybe it was something else that made him keep it. Or maybe he didn't keep the paper, maybe he just got it from someone. But I don't know what else it could be in the contents. I've looked through every article, and I didn't find anything. But I didn't check out everyone because I stopped when I found Patrick. I'll start over and do more research on the other names I ran across in the articles. And I'll check for an Elba. Maybe I'll find a connection between something else and Patrick that would explain a lot."

"You done jabberin'?" Tuper asked when she finally stopped talking.

"Probably not."

"Well, take a break. You're wearin' me out."

Lana started to say something and stopped, then she clicked a few computer keys and a phone rang.

"What are—"

Lana raised her finger to her lips, asking for silence.

"Hello." A woman's voice came from the laptop speaker.

"Hello." Lana made her own voice sound much older. "Is this Erica Carlton?"

"It's Erica Wilson. I haven't been Carlton for many, many years. Who is this?"

"Bella Younger from Roy, Montana. Do you remember me?"

"Of course, I do. Is everything okay?"

"Yes, it's fine. I'm working on a fifty-year school reunion. We're doing it for five classes. There's just not enough of us to make it work any other way."

"That's a good idea. When are you going to have it?"

"Toward the end of the summer. We haven't picked the date yet, but we will soon. Right now, I'm gathering information so we can send invitations when we firm up everything. I wanted to verify your address and get an email contact if you have one. I don't use email myself, but some high school students are going to help with that sort of thing." Lana confirmed the mailing address she'd found online and obtained her email address. "Thank you. We're also looking for your sister Amber. I don't have information about her. Do you have her address?"

She was silent for a few seconds, then Erica said, "That wouldn't be possible."

"Oh no, she hasn't passed, has she?"

"No, nothing like that."

"Is she not well?"

Another pause. "She hasn't been well for years. She lives in

Clancy, but I'm sure she wouldn't go. Maybe if I decide to go, I could bring her with me. We'll see."

"How long has she lived in Clancy?"

"Many years."

"Do you have an address so I can send her the information?"

"There's no need. I'll see that she gets it. I better go now. It was nice talking to you, Bella." The woman hung up.

"I'll be darned," Tuper said.

"Isn't that where your cabin is?" Lana asked.

"Yup. She's living in my backyard."

"But we still don't have a location. We're not even sure what her last name is." Lana typed a few words on her keyboard. "Clancy's population is 1,661. If half are men, that still leaves over eight-hundred people to sort through. Of course, we can narrow it by age." Lana read something else online. "According to the 2010 census, 7.8% of the Clancy population is over sixty-five, so that means there are approximately sixty-two females in Clancy over the age of sixty-five. I guess it won't be that hard after all."

Tuper shook his head. "It's a small town. I'll find her."

CHAPTER 20

Tuper drove the twelve miles from Helena to Clancy, where he'd lived for over two decades. Yet he knew more people in Helena than he did here. His cabin was far enough from town that he didn't frequent the businesses that often, except to play poker. And he had to go to the nearby town of Montana City for that because there weren't any casinos with poker tables in Clancy. But if Amber were a poker player, he would know her. He drove to Chubby's Diner and took out the folder Lana had given him. Inside, he took a seat at the counter, where he could see the cook through a large cutout in the wall.

Within seconds, he was greeted by the owner, Randy, a tall, leggy man with a big, gray mustache. "Well, I'll be. I haven't seen you all winter. Are you just coming home for spring cleaning?" Randy joked.

"Too much snow and too dang cold for me this year."

"You're getting soft, Toop. You used to love the cold."

"Just gettin' old."

A man stood up from the counter, laid cash down, and said, "See you later, Randy."

"Take care, Milton."

Tuper and Randy joked back and forth for a few minutes, then Randy carried out a plate of eggs, potatoes, and bacon. He set it down in front of Tuper. "Here, I just made this by mistake. And lucky for you, the bacon was ordered crisp."

It wasn't the first time Randy had used that excuse to give Tuper food. Randy had told him many years ago that if he was ever hungry he should just come by. He wouldn't need to ask for food.

Two more patrons left the restaurant, and Randy acknowledged each one, calling them by name.

"You're a good man, Randy," Tuper said, as he ate his breakfast.

"So, what brings you into town?"

"Lookin' for someone. You know just about everyone in Clancy, don't you?"

"If they eat, I know 'em."

"I'm looking for a woman…"

"You're always looking for a woman, Toop, so what else is new?"

Tuper smiled. "You can't have too many of those, but this is different. You remember my friend, Squirrely?"

"Sure, I know him. He's been in here when he stayed at your cabin over the years."

"He got hit by a car a couple of days ago, and he's in pretty bad shape. The driver took off, and I'm trying to find who did it."

"I'm sorry to hear that. Squirrely's a nice guy, a little odd, but a nice guy just the same. Who's the woman you're looking for?"

"Amber Carlton. From what I understand, she's lived here for years."

"I don't recognize the name. What does she look like?"

"Don't know for sure, but she'd be about sixty-five years old. The only information I have is nearly fifty years old. That was her maiden name, so if she married, it could be different." Tuper opened the folder and removed two photos, handing the first one to Randy. "This is Amber in high school."

"Pretty girl."

He gave him the second photo, still in awe about what Lana could do with that laptop of hers. "This is a computerized version of what she could look like now."

"She's not familiar."

"I don't know how well those programs work, so maybe it doesn't even look like her."

"But you think she's living here in Clancy."

"That much I know. The source of the information seems reliable."

"Then someone in town ought to know her," Randy said. "I'll ask around. Can I keep these?"

"Yup. Call me if you learn anything." Tuper stood, reached into his pocket, and pulled out his wallet.

"Go. Your money's no good here."

"Thanks, Randy. Nice to see you again."

Tuper's next stop was St. John Mission. He hesitated before he walked into the reception area, then took a deep breath and asked to see the priest.

"Did hell freeze over?" Father Maher said when he came out to greet him.

"Hello, Jimmy ... er, Father."

"I'll always be Jimmy to you, Tuper. Come, walk with me. I was just headed over to the church."

"Inside?" Tuper acted alarmed. "You're not afraid it'll combust?"

"No, God is stronger than you, Toop."

"It wasn't God I was concerned about. It's the other one."

"God's stronger than him too."

As they started through the hallway, Tuper commented, "I heard you were sick. How you doing?"

"The old ticker doesn't work like it used to, but I guess God's not done with me yet. He brought me back from this last round. They're still letting me perform all the masses here, but next time it happens, I expect to be put out to pasture." He paused when they reached the steps. "I'm guessing you didn't stop by to check on my health. What can I do for you?"

Tuper told him about Amber Carlton and showed him the photos.

"I know the names of all my parishioners, and there is no one named Amber anything. As for the photos, I don't recognize that woman. If she's a church-goer, it must be the Methodist congregation down the street."

"I'll check it out, but I don't know anyone there. I'm not sure how much information I'll get."

"Try it. If you don't have any luck, let me know. I can ask the pastor a few questions."

Tuper walked into the office at the Clancy United Methodist Church and was pleased to find someone. A middle-aged woman sat behind a large oak desk, looking a bit frazzled.

"Good morning," Tuper said.

"Good morning," the woman answered, but not like she meant it.

He wondered if she was having a bad day or if she just had a sour personality. "It's a beautiful day, almost as beautiful as you are."

She looked up, her face a mixture of surprise and disbelief. "Thanks," she grumbled.

He decided this woman needed a better story than the truth. "My name is Tuper Carlton, and I could use your help."

"With what?"

"I'm trying to find my missing sister. Our mother is dying, and she'd like to see her."

The woman's tone mellowed. "I'm sorry about your mother."

"I haven't seen my sister in a very long time. I recently discovered she was living here in Clancy, but I don't know where. She's been estranged from the family for many years. The reasons are complicated, and she certainly isn't entirely to blame, but things have changed and I'm sure she'd want to know what's going on. It's my mother's dying wish to see her one last time. I think Amber would regret not getting a chance to make amends. At least, she needs to have that option."

"So, how can I help?"

"I want to know if she attends this church. Do you have a roster of your parishioners?"

"We do."

"Could you check to see if she's on it?"

The woman hesitated. "I'm not sure I could give you any information even if she is a member."

"I'm not asking for personal information. If you could check to see if you even have an Amber Carlton, or an Amber with another last name. She was still young and single the last time I saw her so she may have married and have a different last name. If I knew she was a member, at least I'd know I'm looking in the right place. If she's not, I won't bother you again. I don't have much time to find her, and if she's not here, then I can move on and try elsewhere."

The woman nodded, but didn't respond as she typed something on her keyboard. A few minutes later, she looked up. "I'm sorry. I don't find anyone named Amber who has been a member of this church in the last ten years." She looked disappointed.

"Thanks for trying." Tuper pulled out the photos and showed her the young Amber. "This is what she looked like the last time I saw her." He explained about the computer-generated photo. "This is what she supposedly looks like now." He watched for a glimmer of recognition but saw none.

The woman shook her head. "Sorry."

CHAPTER 21

Clarice and Mary were both at work, and Tuper was in Clancy looking for Amber. That gave Lana the chance to delve into her research without any interruptions.

She started with the fraud article. Something about that particular scenario didn't seem right. Maybe because it was the only news that dealt with money, but for some reason Lana thought it might be connected to Squirrely. She traced Miller Bozeman, and his aliases, to his birth and did the same with his wife. But she found no names or situations that might lead her to Squirrely, other than the Finnigan in his wife's family. Lana worked a long time on that line of Finnigans but there was no apparent connection to Squirrely's family. Bozeman's son, Christopher, was adopted, but nothing appeared untoward in that either. Lana looked up every name, checked backgrounds, and ran every peripheral character against Patrick and Squirrely and didn't uncover a link. Nor did she find an Elba, or Emma, or anything similar.

Lana had gathered a long list of names that she intended to research for a connection to Squirrely, Patrick, or the town of

Roy, Montana. She still believed the newspaper was the clue to solving the puzzle. But the research would take a long time. Some of it she could set in motion and check back on later, but the rest of it had to be checked piece by piece. She discovered obscure things, such as a man who had purchased a piece of real estate had gone to the same church as Frank's mother, and that Patrick Gallagher had a cousin who was a big Woody Allen fan, hardly the kind of information that mattered.

Lana made a second list of everyone who seemed even remotely connected to Squirrely. For each of those, she set up a Google alert so if anything was posted online, a message would be sent to her Google email. She didn't expect to get much, but it was a handy tool that took very little time and could alert her of anything new those people were involved in. The only drawback was that with common names she would get alerts about others. Still, it was worth it.

Lana remembered that Squirrely, Karl, and Patrick had been in some kind of trouble in high school that was seemingly swept under the rug—the referral dealing with the Montana Highway Patrol. The issue was big enough to warrant a school suspension, but then nothing was done. And why was the basis for the referral blocked out of the school records?

It took Lana several hours to hack into the county records, only to find they hadn't entered old information back that far.

She moved on to Karl Haberman and discovered he was born in the Lewistown hospital and had lived in Roy until right after graduation. Then he seemed to vanish for a couple of years. Lana checked military records but found none that showed Karl was in the service at that time. She could find no trace of where he went for those years—no DMV records with another address, no hospital admissions, no marital filings, or credit cards. He just disappeared for two years. She was deep into her research when the door opened and Clarice walked in.

"Are you off work already?" Lana asked.

"I had the early shift today, and it's after three."

"I didn't realize it was that late. I've been working on this Squirrely thing all day."

"Found anything yet?"

Lana told her about Karl's disappearance.

"Maybe he was traveling or something. Lots of kids do that after high school. They just want to get away for a while."

"But you'd think I'd be able to find some trace of him during that time."

"What if he went to Europe or Australia or anywhere out of the country?"

"Wouldn't he use credit cards?" Lana asked.

"He could have bought travelers' checks. That's what people used to do. That's what my aunt did when she went to Europe in the sixties. She never used a credit card."

"I guess, but where would he buy them? Wouldn't there be a record of that?"

"You purchase them from a bank."

"I suppose I would need to know which bank, and even then, I don't think I could find the transaction. I suppose he could've joined a rodeo, or a circus, or something. If they paid him cash, there'd be no record. Or maybe he was homeless, or mooching off a relative. I guess there are lots of possibilities. I just hate dead ends and missing pieces."

Clarice left the room, and Lana returned to searching for Karl. He showed up again when he joined the Navy in 1971. The rest was fairly easy. He'd been stationed in China Lake for several years and married a local woman. They had their first child, a boy, when Karl was twenty-eight. Their second son was born in Sasebo, Japan. From there, the Navy sent him to Jacksonville, Florida and then Corpus Christi, Texas. Karl remained in Texas until his wife passed away a year earlier, at which time he returned to Roy.

Lana turned her attention to Patrick Gallagher's death, starting with a simple Google search. It was so much easier perusing the newspapers online than it was handling the printed version. She was glad to be alive during this computer age. She could only imagine how exciting it would be ten or twenty years from now.

She glanced through every newspaper in the county and surrounding area, but the only hit-and-run reported was an old woman crossing the street in Montana City. There were seventeen car accidents, but none seemed to be connected to Patrick. None of the hospitals had a patient by the name of Patrick Gallagher, but she did find a John Doe admitted to St. Peter's, who had multiple contusions, two broken ribs, and a broken femur. She was surprised at what she found next. She called Tuper.

"Pops, you're not going to believe this." Before he could ask, she told him about the John Doe. "Your undertaker friend said Patrick had bruises and scrapes, a broken rib, and a broken femur. John Doe has to be Patrick. What are the chances that two guys were hurt in the same area, during the same time frame, with the same injuries?"

"Not much chance, but what good does it do us?"

"That's just it. That's the good part. You aren't going to believe what else I found." This time she waited for him to ask.

"Okay, Agony, what else?"

"They lost him."

"What do you mean, they lost him?"

"John Doe disappeared from the hospital. Left. Departed. Evaporated. Escaped. They don't know if he walked away, which was highly unlikely since he was unconscious. I suppose he could've woken up and walked out, but it seems more likely that someone stole him."

CHAPTER 22

Tuper drove to Beca's house on East Custer. She had
several acres of empty land and didn't mind Tuper
parking his old pickup there when he needed to. They hadn't
been an item for several years, but had remained friends,
occasionally with benefits. Tuper didn't go inside when he
arrived. He parked his Toyota, and he and Ringo got in his
pickup and headed south.

If Amber still had a job, she could easily live in Clancy and
work in Montana City. For that matter, she could work in
Helena, but searching every possible workplace in the larger
city would be an impossible task. Besides, she was past sixty-
five and probably no longer worked. Tuper had to concentrate on finding someone who knew her. Not many businesses in Clancy existed where people might congregate, but
he went to each one and asked if anyone knew Amber. He
struck out.

He continued the same process all the way to Montana
City, where he finally reached Papa Ray's Casino, a place he
was all too familiar with. He frequented it often since it was

the only casino in the area that had poker, and that was only on Thursdays and Saturdays. The place looked more like a large bar with a few slot machines and poker tables than it did a casino. Even though it smelled of stale beer, this was Tuper's hangout, his *Cheers*, and he was greeted as such when he walked in.

"Hello, Tuper." The short, heavyset bartender had cue ball eyes and a goatee. "What are you doing here on a Tuesday? There's no poker today."

"I'm looking for a woman."

"Of course, you are."

"Not that kind."

"You have a type?" The bartender raised an eyebrow.

Tuper told him about Squirrely, who the bartender knew from visits to the casino with Tuper.

"Sorry to hear that," the bartender said. "So, who are you looking for?"

"A woman named Amber, about sixty-five. Her last name might be Carlton."

"Sorry, I don't know her, and I'd remember if I met anyone with that name."

"Why's that?"

"My ex-wife's name is Amber, but it can't be her 'cause she won't be sixty-five for another fifteen years. Unless you're not certain of the age. I haven't seen Amber in a while, so she could've aged, I guess."

"No, this Amber is definitely older."

Tuper felt like he had done all he could for one day. Hopefully, he would get a call from Father Jimmy or from his friend, Randy, at Chubby's Diner about a sighting of Amber. In the meantime, he decided to check on his home since he was so close. Tuper lived in a small cabin in the Elkhorn

Mountains, only a few miles from Clancy. He called it a cabin, but it was no more than a shack. And even though it held most of his possessions, he didn't stay there much, except in the summer months. He was getting too old to handle the cold winters. It was a one-room cabin with an outhouse. It had one window that hadn't been cleaned in more than twenty years, a bed, a wood stove, a table with two chairs, a large armchair, and a water pump. The walls weren't insulated, and in places the wind blew right through. But it was quiet and peaceful and had everything nature offered. It had served him well over the years, especially when he needed to be alone.

He hadn't been home in months, mostly because the winter had been so rough he couldn't make it up the mountain. Even now, he could see snow on the peaks, but much of the bottom three quarters had melted. He passed a clearing outside of Clancy and turned left in front of Elkhorn Care Center. He followed the pavement for about five miles, then the road turned to gravel. Even though the sun was shining, the dirt roads were still muddy. Too muddy. He was glad he had his pickup. It needed new tires, but his Toyota would never have made it through the mud. He hoped the truck could.

The more Tuper climbed the mountain, the more excited Ringo became. The dog turned around and around in the passenger seat until Tuper reached over and rolled down his window. Ringo stuck his head out and reveled in the mountain air, unfazed by the tumultuous bumps and rough ride. They bounced along the bumpy, curvy road, climbing the mountain through the mass of fir trees.

The higher he drove, the more mud he encountered. About two miles up the mountain, Tuper tried to maneuver through a muddier-than-usual spot. He veered to the right, slightly off the main tracks created by other vehicles, still staying on the road. But he couldn't keep out of the thick muck, and before he knew it, he was stuck. He couldn't move forward. He tried reverse, but that failed too. After one more attempt, he stopped—before he dug himself in deeper. He got out of the truck and gathered up what branches he could find, placing them in front and back of his rear tires. Tuper tried to roll forward again. After several attempts, the mud let go and he drove on.

Everything seemed harder these days, he thought. *Maybe I'm getting too old for this kind of living. I may have to think about selling.*

Once free, he continued upward for another two miles, then started to look for his turnoff. It was easy to see in the daylight, but if he missed it, maneuvering a turn-around without driving too far would be a challenge. He made the turn and drove about sixty feet through the muddy potholes up to the cabin. He always marveled at his dilapidated home, even with the tools, car parts, and other junk surrounding it. It was the only property he had ever owned, and he was proud of it. *I really need to get that junk cleaned up,* he thought. But he'd had the same thought every spring, and it only got worse each year instead of better.

Tuper stepped out of the truck and looked around, breathing in the cool, mountain air. Ringo dashed out too and darted across the yard. He bounced around the yard, sniffing and exploring, then ran around the corner toward the old outhouse with the crescent moon window.

Tuper approached the cabin with his gun drawn and carefully opened the unlocked, squeaky door. It wouldn't be the first time he returned home to find someone or something in his home. Once it was a bear. He didn't have to shoot it, but he was glad he was armed. On several occasions, he'd found travelers who had needed to get out of the cold. But today, the cabin was clear, and the evening sun lit up the twelve-by-sixteen-foot room, exposing the emptiness. The space was cold and dreary, but it was home. For Tuper, that meant he was surrounded by wildlife and nature. If he could, he would live here year around and just fish and hunt. But that wasn't the hand he was dealt. He was too old to stand the weather, and too many other things drew him to town.

Tuper sat there for a while with his door open, watching the rabbits and squirrels scurry around. He loved the birds that drank from the creek running between the trees not more than a hundred feet from his front door. *Nope, I ain't giving this up yet.*

The sun was starting to set, and Tuper realized he already had to leave this quiet place of solitude and get back to his search for Amber. Besides, he had to get back to town before dark since his headlights were only sporadic at best. He started back down the hill.

Tuper reached the bottom and passed the Elkhorn Care Center. He was about to pull onto the highway when he realized he hadn't checked the center for Amber's employment. He turned around and pulled into the lot.

He approached the desk where an African-American woman in her mid-forties was seated. "May I help you?" she asked.

"I'm looking for Amber Carlton."

She stared at Tuper for a few seconds, then surprised him with her response. "Do you know her?"

CHAPTER 23

Tuper was taken aback for a second. Even though he had asked for Amber, he was surprised to find she was actually there. He had initially decided to go with the dying-mother story, but instead he just said, "It's been a very long time."

"I see that." The receptionist read something on her computer. "No one has been here in years. Are you a relative?"

"Brother."

The woman stood up. "Right this way." She led him down a hallway to a living area with square tables and chairs, a television, and several sofas. There was a large fireplace at one end with a flame going.

"Isn't it a little warm for the fireplace?" Tuper asked.

"These people are always cold. They feel warmer when it's lit, so we have it on most of the time."

They walked toward the sofa near the fireplace, where a woman sat alone clutching an old black-and-white teddy bear with big patches of worn fur. The matted bear had a red heart hand-sewed on his chest with crude, black stitches. Tuper wondered how long she had had the bear.

"Amber?" the receptionist said.

The old woman looked up. "Yes."

"There's someone here to see you."

A smile crossed her face. "Really?"

"Really. I'll leave you two alone." Before she left, she leaned down to Amber and asked, "What's your last name?"

"Carlton," Amber said.

The receptionist turned to Tuper. "She has some good days and some bad days. Today is good."

When the receptionist left, Tuper sat on the sofa next to Amber. Tuper was surprised at how much she resembled their computer-generated photo. He would've been able to pick her out of a crowd. "How you doing, Amber?"

"Who are you?"

"My name is Tuper. I'm a friend of Squ … uh, Frankie's."

Her eyes lit up, and her face became very animated. "Where is he? Is he here?"

"No, he's not here. I'm sure he would be if he could, but he can't travel right now."

"My baby, my poor baby." She rocked from side to side.

Tuper suddenly realized she must have thought he meant her son, Frankie, not Squirrely. He didn't want to upset this poor woman. She obviously had some mental problems, but he didn't know to what extent. He didn't want to do more damage, and he wasn't sure talking to her would do any good. How much of what she said could he even believe? He decided to go with the truth. "I'm sorry, I meant Frank Finnigan. He's my friend."

Confusion flooded her face. "Does he have my son?"

"No, I'm afraid not."

"Frankie loves me," she said with a smile. Just as quickly it left her face. "She ruined everything."

"Who did?"

"Amber."

"Amber ruined everything?" Tuper asked, a little confused.

"Yes."

"Aren't you Amber?"

"Yes, I guess I am. I ruined everything." She paused. "Frankie loves me."

"Yes, I'm sure Frankie loves you." Tuper didn't know what else to say, but he wanted to focus on the father, not the son. "You knew Frank from high school, right?"

"Yes, he was my beau. He was so handsome and smart. He was way smarter than me. He got good grades. He was so smart. Too smart for me. Did you know he was a debate champion?"

"Yes, I heard that. What else did he do in high school?"

"We dated. He took me to dances, and once we went to the rodeo."

As long as she was making sense and confirming things he already knew, Tuper figured she'd be okay answering questions. He hoped she would remember something that might help. "It sounds like you had a lot of fun. Who was Frank's best friend in Roy?"

"Karl Haberman. They were best friends since they were about five years old. They stayed really tight until ..." She stopped, and a painful look crossed her face.

"Until what?"

"I don't know." She shrugged, and her face was calm again.

"Did Frank ever get in trouble in high school?"

She chuckled. "A few times. I shouldn't tell those stories. Frank might not like it."

"He told me he borrowed the school bus once, and you all had a big party."

The corners of her mouth turned up. "Yeah, he did that. We all did it, but Frank was the driver, so he got in more trouble than the rest of us. They couldn't do too much since the whole school was involved."

"Everyone?"

"All but three or four students who were too afraid, but they couldn't suspend us all or they wouldn't have gotten any school funding. It's always about the money."

She seemed so coherent. "Do you remember Patrick Gallagher?"

Her eyes opened wide and she wrapped her arms around the teddy bear pulling it tight to her chest with her wrists crossed. She clenched her fists and let out a blood-curdling scream, followed by a steady stream of the same line over and over again. "It's all Amber's fault. It's all Amber's fault."

A caretaker hurried over and spoke to Amber, trying to calm her down.

"I didn't mean to upset her," Tuper said. "I'm her brother, and it has been a long time since I've seen Amber. Until today, I didn't know where she was."

Amber continued to repeat the words, "It's all Amber's fault," but she wasn't screaming anymore. Within a few seconds, she was muttering the words.

"It's not your fault," the caretaker said and then turned to Tuper. "She does this sometimes."

Tuper tried to talk to her again, but she just kept repeating the same thing over and over, while picking at a spot on her blouse.

"She was so coherent a while ago. Now she doesn't seem to even hear what I say."

"That's the way it works. You may want to try again another day."

"Tomorrow?"

"Yes, but come early. She's better in the morning."

CHAPTER 24

L ana closed her laptop, too excited to sit. She paced the house waiting for Tuper. After he'd called with the new information, she'd immediately hacked into the rehab center's system. By the time Tuper returned from Clancy, she was anxious to tell him what she had found. He knocked on the door, Lana opened it, and before he was inside, she started to enlighten him about what she had learned.

"Amber has been at that facility since June of 1994. Doesn't that seem odd? The newspaper Squirrely had was for May 1994. The next month, she moved, or was moved, to the Elkhorn Care Center in Clancy. That seems like more than a coincidence to me. Don't you think?" Without giving Tuper a chance to answer, she kept talking. "Before Amber moved there, she was in an assisted living facility in Kalispell. And prior to that, she was in a mental institution in Missoula. I haven't been able to get into the hospital records yet, but I will. I need to know why she was admitted, but she must've improved because she went to a lesser-care facility after that. But then—"

"Slow down," Tuper interrupted, as he walked into the kitchen with Lana close behind. "You're wearing me out."

"Then she moved to Clancy around the same time Patrick was killed. Something must've happened that made her move. The events must be connected."

"Maybe it's a coincidence. It was a month later when she checked into the Clancy facility, right?" He removed his hat, put it on a chair, and took the seat next to it.

Lana sat down in front of her computer. "Right. She didn't check into Clancy for nearly a month, but she left Kalispell on May 2, 1994. That's the same day Patrick died. Maybe she killed him on her way to her new home."

"The woman I saw today doesn't seem capable ..." Tuper shook his head. "But that was twenty-five years ago. What kind of a facility was she at in Kalispell?"

"It had two parts. One was assisted living at its minimum, which is where she was for several years, but then in 1992, she moved to the other side, which required way more care. It houses a lot of Alzheimer's patients and people with other mental disabilities."

"Can you tell how she left there? Did someone check her out?"

"That's the interesting part. Her rent was paid for the month of May, and there's no record of her giving notice. It appears that one day she was just gone."

"So, she must have had help."

"It seems so. I've checked the records for visitors, but there's nothing in the computer. If they even kept records, they must've been on paper. They have updated all their incident reports back as far as 1985, which is when they opened. Or maybe they started with computers back then, but either way, they have all the residents on file, each with their own account. There's a lot of other stuff too, like menus and social activities, but no visitor logs until January of 2002." Lana was even more animated than usual and no longer reading from her monitor. "Maybe it was because of 9-11. Lots of things changed because of the terrorist attacks. Security heightened everywhere, you know."

"I know."

"And I can't tell where she was during that month of May. If she was at someone's house, there's no way I can find out. If she went to another facility or was at a hospital, it should be listed in her Elkhorn file, which it is not. If she was in a facility under another name, it would be likely impossible to figure it out. And what good would that do us anyway if she was in a hospital or something? She could have even been in the hospital under a different name. I don't know why she would do that, but it's possible. Isn't it?" Lana looked up but kept talking. "I guess if we want to know who checked her out, we'll have to drive to Kalispell. How far is that?" Lana started typing on her laptop.

"About four hours," Tuper said.

"Three and a half if you take Highway 83 through the forest," Lana said.

"So, why'd you ask?"

Lana ignored his question. "Have you been there?"

"Yup."

"Of course, you've been there. Is there anywhere in Montana you haven't been?"

"Not that I can think of."

"What are you driving? Do you have Ringo's car or that old pickup?"

"I have the car. Why?"

"Because I'm not riding all the way to Kalispell in that

pickup. That old junker would never make it. Besides, it's very uncomfortable. You can feel every pebble in the road."

"It don't matter what I'm driven' 'cuz *we* aren't going anywhere. And we'll need more information before I'm makin' that trip."

"I'll keep looking, but you're right. That was twenty-five years ago. What are the chances someone who worked at the facility back then would still be there now? And even if they were, they might not remember anything about it." Without a pause, Lana changed topics. "I think we need to dig deeper into the incident Squirrely, Patrick, and Karl got into with the Montana Highway Patrol. I can't find out anything more online, but I have a gut feeling that it's somehow connected. It just doesn't make sense that they all got into trouble, got suspended, and then they all disappeared for a couple of years."

"What do you mean disappeared?"

"Karl went somewhere for two years, and I can't trace his tracks at all. Patrick and Squirrely suddenly left town too. It's like they were all running away."

"Isn't that what most high school kids do after graduation?"

"Some go to college, some join the military, and some go to work, but this was different. Besides, that's not the way it works in Roy, Montana. Most of the kids stay pretty close to home at first, then after a few years they start to drift away."

"It's not that odd," Tuper said. "It was really only Karl who disappeared, and that could be anything. Squirrely joined the Marines, and Patrick moved to Great Falls, right?"

"I don't know for sure when Patrick moved to Great Falls. I know he was there a few years later when he changed his mailing address, but I can't tell where he was for the first few years after high school."

"No employment records?"

"None I can find. Nor did he claim any income on tax returns in those years."

"You can see tax returns?" Tuper asked in an incredulous tone.

Lana waved her had dismissively. "They're easy."

CHAPTER 25

After spending another night in the chair near Squirrely's bed, Tuper left the hospital and drove to Clarice's house. He had decided to make another trip to Roy to see if he could find out what kind of trouble Squirrely, Patrick, and Karl had gotten into. Maybe it was nothing, but the incident nagged at him, and that usually meant he would have to find out. Lana wanted to go along, and even though Tuper didn't relish the thought of her round-trip chattering, she did have a good instinct for getting information.

Lana was dressed and eager to go when he arrived. "Good morning, Pops," she said as he walked in.

"Mornin', Agony. I see you're ready to go."

"I'm anxious to get some answers."

"I'm hungry," Tuper said. "Let me fix a peanut butter and jelly sandwich. I'll take it with me, and we'll be on the way."

"I'll do it," Lana said. "It'll be faster."

Lana made the sandwich, put it on a paper towel, and handed it to Tuper. They walked out, and Ringo ran up to her.

Lana bent down, petted him, then climbed in the front seat of the car, laptop in hand. "I love road trips."

Tuper let Ringo in the backseat, then got in. "Please keep the chatter to a minimum. I'm tired and don't need to listen to you all day."

"Right, Pops." Less than two minutes later, Lana asked, "Where'd you stay last night?"

Tuper frowned and didn't answer the question.

"Did you go to your cabin?"

"No."

"I know you didn't stay at Louise's."

"How do you know that?"

"Because you were hungry this morning. Louise always makes you breakfast. I know that because you're never hungry when you stay there. So, where'd you stay? Do you have a new squeeze?"

"That's none of your business, but for your information, I was at the hospital with Squirrely."

Lana couldn't care less where Tuper stayed, but she did enjoy irritating him. And she found it amazing that an old guy like him had so many women at his beck and call. She was even more impressed by his loyalty to his friend. "Have you stayed at the hospital every night since he's been there?"

"Most of them."

Lana opened her laptop and started to work. After about half an hour, she asked, "Don't you find it odd that there's no record of Amber's baby being born? I mean nothing. Even if the baby was stillborn, there would've been a record. Two in fact, a birth and a death certificate. I found neither."

"Maybe she was never pregnant."

"I thought about that, but why would Bella say so? She seemed pretty certain. No, I think there's more to it than that, and I'd like another crack at Bella if she'll talk to me. She loves to talk, so I think she will. And she liked you. I bet she'd tell you anything if you bought her a few drinks."

"You pimping me out now?"

"Whatever it takes to get the job done, Pops. So, what's the plan? Are you going to try to find out what those boys did that was covered up?"

"I don't know for sure that anything was covered up. It probably wasn't anything that big, and someone just made it go away."

"But you think it's more than that, don't you? Otherwise, you wouldn't be trying so hard. I think so too. Whatever this whole thing is about started back in high school, and we'll soon find someone who can tell us what happened. It's too bad Squirrely isn't conscious. He could probably answer all our questions. But then why didn't he tell you anything when he gave you the duffel bag?" She stared at Tuper. "He didn't tell you anything, did he? Are you holding out on me?"

"Of course not. What would I have to gain by that? I told you everything I know. He just asked me to keep the bag and said if anything happened to him to do what I can to make things right."

"That didn't trigger you to ask what he meant?"

"No, I figured he'd tell me if he wanted me to know, or I'd know when I opened the bag."

"How's that working for you?"

"Humpf."

"How will you find out what you need?" Lana asked.

"I'm meeting with a guy named Jack Russell who—"

Lana laughed. "Is that really his name?"

"Afraid so. He's a retired state trooper who lives in Lewistown. We're stopping there before we go to Roy."

"Do you know him?" She quickly shook her head. "Of course, you do. You know everyone in Montana."

"No, I don't know the guy. He's a friend of a friend, and he's willing to tell me what he knows."

"Does he know anything?"

"I guess we'll find out."

Lana continued to chatter most of the way to Lewistown. When they got to Jack Russell's house, she wanted to go inside with Tuper, but he insisted on going in alone.

Tuper was only gone about twenty minutes. When he returned, he got in the car and drove off without saying a word.

"Well, did you learn anything new?"

"Nope."

"That's it? Nothing?"

"The guy was just a rookie and should've been on the call when whatever happened happened, but he was out sick that day. His partner refused to talk about it and told him the less he knew, the better."

"So, something went down, and it was covered up."

"Looks that way. We just don't know what."

"Maybe the *what* isn't so important. Maybe it's just that someone was powerful enough to keep those kids from being prosecuted."

Tuper started to agree, but she added, "Or maybe it was something so horrible they couldn't let it come out. I bet someone was killed, and those boys had something to do with it. Or maybe they were witnesses to the murder, and that's why they're dead now. Well, Squirrely's not dead, but someone tried to kill him." She paused for just a second. "Except Karl. He's not dead, and no one has tried to kill him. Or maybe they have, and we just don't know about it. Do you think Karl is in danger? Maybe we should warn him." Another brief pause. "Or maybe Karl is the one who killed Patrick and tried to kill Squirrely."

"Agony! Please stick to what we know."

They were nearly to Roy when Lana asked, "Who are we going to question besides Bella?"

"Who said we're talking to Bella?"

"I'm going to talk to her, whether you do or not," Lana said. "I want to know more about Amber and that baby."

"How do you think that'll help?"

"I don't know, but something just doesn't add up for me."

"Fine, you talk to Bella. I'll see if I can get anything more out of Karl, if I can find him."

"And warn him? You better warn him."

"And what should I warn him about?" Tuper asked. "I guess I could say, 'Remember those two guys you knew fifty years ago? Well, one of them died twenty-five years ago, and the other is in the hospital. So, watch your back because twenty-five years from now, you could be next.' How does that sound?"

"When you put it that way …"

CHAPTER 26

L ana walked into the Legion bar. It was earlier than the last time they stopped in, and the place had a few more customers. Four men were at the counter, a couple sat at a table, and Bella was by herself in her usual spot.

"Good morning, Bella," Lana said.

"Mornin'," she responded coolly.

Lana sat down without an invitation. She was pretty certain she wouldn't get anything from Bella without giving something in return. She counted on the old woman's need to gossip. She needed to offer something juicy, and the truth just might work. "Look, I know that last time we upset you with our questions about Patrick, and I apologize for that. I won't ask anything more about him. But we weren't entirely honest either. There's more to the story."

Bella stared at Lana without comment.

"The whole truth is that someone tried to kill Frank Finnigan, and Pops is trying to figure out why. I just want to help him because he's so worried. He's afraid they might try again."

"What? Someone tried to kill him? Why?"

"That's what we're trying to find out."

Bella's voice softened. "I'm sorry to hear that. But I have no idea who that might be. It's been nearly fifty years since I saw him. I don't know what I could tell you that would help."

"I don't know either, but if I can learn what really happened here in Roy back then, it might lead us to a breakthrough."

"What do you need to know?"

"For starters, Amber's pregnancy was a big deal, right?"

"That's right. It was a bit of a scandal because Frank had left without anyone knowing where he was. Plus, everyone liked Amber. She was a pretty girl, not too bright, but very sweet. Some people were mad at Frank, others were convinced he didn't know or he wouldn't have left. There was even some talk that Frank wasn't the father. Everyone took sides for a while. There's not much to do in this small town, so it gave folks something to babble about."

"Are you absolutely sure Amber was pregnant?"

"Of course, I'm sure. We all watched as she got plump as a partridge. She was definitely pregnant. I remember when she started into labor. Her parents took her to the hospital, and a few days later she returned not pregnant anymore."

"So, you saw her right after she returned from the hospital?"

"Yes, I brought her some homemade muffins. I knew she was having a rough time because she couldn't find Frank, and I hoped it would cheer her up to know others cared. Besides, I've always liked babies, and I wanted to see the little guy."

"And you saw him?"

"Yes, but not that day. I saw a photo though. She had a polaroid of him. He had some complications and had to stay in the hospital a little longer."

"How long?"

"Just one more day. They went back and brought him home, and I saw him then. Amber's mother thought he looked sick, so after a few hours, she took him back to the hospital. I thought he looked fine, but what did I know? I had never been around babies. Amber left the next day. I think I'm the only one in Roy who ever even saw a photo of little Frankie, much less the little guy himself."

"Did Amber tell you she was leaving?"

"Yeah, she said she was moving to Grass Range." Bella wrinkled her brow.

"What's wrong? Did you remember something?"

"I thought it was odd that she had no crib or baby things in the house. I know she and her parents didn't have a lot of money, but they weren't dirt-poor either. A couple of months earlier, I wanted to have a baby shower for her, but she said she didn't want one."

"Did you ask her about not having anything for the baby?"

"No, I didn't want to embarrass her. And I figured since she was leaving, she didn't want to move a bunch of stuff. Maybe she planned to get everything when she got to her new home."

"Do you know what day Amber's baby was born?"

"Yes, I do."

Lana was surprised, but this woman seemed to remember the strangest details. "When was it?"

"It was two days before Thanksgiving 1969. I was with her when she started into labor. Amber came home on Black Friday. The baby would've been three days old."

Bella was being so cooperative and seemed to be soaking up the newest scandal, so Lana pushed a little further. "Something happened in Frank's senior year where he got into trouble. You seem to have your hand on the town pulse, so if anyone knew, I figure it would be you. Do you know what I'm talking about?"

"You mean when Frank stole the school bus and the whole school had a party? Everyone knows about that."

"No, this was something else. I'm not sure what, but the police were involved."

Bella looked pensive for a few seconds. "I remember a state trooper came here, and the word was that he called three boys out of class and spoke to them one at a time. It was Frank, Karl, and one other boy."

"Bella, I already know the other boy was Patrick."

She nodded. "Everyone just figured it was something Patrick had done."

"Why's that?"

"Because so much had changed since he came to town. All the girls loved him at first, but he was such a player. He was the reason my brother and Marlys broke up, and they weren't the only couple he destroyed."

"Did the state trooper ever return?"

"He came back a few days later and spoke to the principal. Then he talked to the boys again, and that was it. It was all over, whatever it was."

"And the town never learned what had happened?"

"No. It was the best-kept secret in Roy. I dare say, the only secret ever kept in Roy."

Tuper found Karl Haberman at the same bar and the same barstool where he'd sat a few days earlier. Tuper wondered if Karl would sit somewhere else if someone was in his seat, or if he'd ask the patron to move. Or maybe he left the bar if his seat was taken. Tuper had spent time in small towns, and there were a lot of similarities among locals.

"Hi, Karl," Tuper said, approaching him.

"What do you want?" Karl didn't look in his direction.

"I want to come clean with you because I think you ought to know the truth."

"That would be a welcome change."

"Frank Finnigan is in the hospital fighting for his life."

Karl's shoulders drooped, and he swallowed hard.

"Someone tried to kill him, and I'm trying to find out who and why. I know you were close friends once, and I was hoping you could help."

"I haven't seen Frank in nearly fifty years."

"I know."

"You think it has something to do with his childhood?" Karl asked.

"I do."

Karl swiveled his chair and looked at Tuper. "Why, after all these years, would anyone want to hurt Frank?"

"I don't know, but everything seems to lead back here."

"There ain't nothing I could tell you that would help."

"Why were you, Frank, and Patrick interrogated by a state trooper in your senior year?"

"Like I said, there ain't nothing I could say that'll help. We're done here." Karl turned around, faced the bar, and drank his beer.

"Listen, Karl, you might be in danger yourself. Someone killed Patrick years ago, and now an attempt was made on Frank's life in the same way, a hit-and-run. If it has anything to do with what happened in high school with you three, you could be next."

"I'm right here if they want me. I expect they know where to find me."

"Who are they?"

"Whoever hurt Frank and killed Patrick. I don't know who they are, but I'm sayin' I'm not running."

"Where did you go during those two years after high school? Were you running then?"

Karl scowled. "That's none of your business." He stood up, removed some cash from his pocket, and laid it on the bar. "If you know what's good for you, you'll stay out of my life!" he shouted and walked out.

CHAPTER 27

The next morning, Tuper and Ringo drove to Clancy to see Amber. Dark clouds formed in the sky, and he expected rain before he got back home. Ringo waited in the car with the windows down. It was nearly nine o'clock, and Tuper found Amber having breakfast. She sat at a table, holding her teddy bear with one hand and eating with the other. Two other women sat at the table with her. One was in a wheel chair; the other, an attractive lady with a perfectly coiffured, white bouffant, had a walker next to her chair.

"Good morning, Amber," Tuper said. "Remember me?"

"No, I'm sorry, should I?"

"I'm a friend of Frank Finnigan. I was here two days ago."

"How is Frank?"

"He's in the hospital, but he's getting better."

"Is he coming to see me?"

"Maybe when he's feeling better."

Tuper hoped he could gain Amber's confidence so she would reveal something helpful, but he had to be careful. He didn't want to hurt her in his quest for the truth.

"How's the food here?" he asked, sitting down.

"Not that bad. Some residents complain, but I think it's all right. They make the bacon nice and crisp, and that works for me. Would you like some breakfast?"

"No, thank you."

While she ate, Tuper asked questions that didn't call for an emotional response. He kept his voice low, hoping the other women wouldn't get involved. Finally, he approached the subject of her son and was surprised at her answers. "Do you have children, Amber?"

"No, I was never blessed with kids."

"I'm sorry to hear that."

"I was never married either, but that's okay. Most everyone I know who got married eventually got a divorce, so I guess I was saved that heartache."

"I guess you were."

The woman with the walker, who sat to Amber's left, rolled her eyes. Then she muttered, "Depends on what day it is."

"What's that?" Tuper asked.

"Depends on what day it is whether or not she has children. Or I should say, a child. She cries for hours sometimes over her little boy. Her *lost* little boy."

Amber either didn't hear or chose to ignore her. "Would you like some milk?" she asked.

"Sure, I'll have a glass."

Amber called the server to the table and asked for milk.

"Can you tell me what Frank was like in high school?" Tuper asked.

"Frank was handsome and so smart." She took a deep, savoring breath. "Do you know my Frankie?"

Tuper explained again that they were good friends.

"How is he?"

"He's in the hospital, but he's okay."

"Is he coming to see me?"

"Soon." Tuper realized his answers didn't really matter, so he might as well give her hope. "He wants to see you, but he can't travel right now."

"Oh, that's nice. What's your name again?"

"Tuper."

A caretaker came up to the table. "It's time for your walk, Amber." The employee turned to Tuper. "I can take her later if you'd like, so you can continue your visit."

"No, go ahead," Tuper said. "I'm about to leave."

The caretaker guided Amber away. Tuper remained in his chair, drinking his milk.

"She can't maintain very long," the woman with the walker said.

"How long have you known her?"

"I've been here ten years, and she was here when I came. We've sat at the same table for the last seven, so I know her pretty well."

"How long has she had the teddy bear?"

"She had it when I came here. She's never without it. In the beginning, she told me her boyfriend gave it to her for her son, but now sometimes she seems to think it's actually her baby."

"Is she a lot worse now than when you first met?"

"She's always had problems drifting in and out of reality, but her coherent moments are shorter and less often than they used to be. She tells some pretty wild stories and sometimes it's hard to know what is real and what isn't."

"What sort of stories?"

"She used to talk about how she and some friends stole a

school bus and had a party. She said all but three students in the high school were there. She always had the same details with that one, so I believed it for a while. Then one day she told me there were about twenty kids at the party."

"That is true. She was involved in that escapade. It happened in Roy, a very small town northeast of here, and the high school only had about twenty students."

"Well, I'll be darned," the woman said. "I grew up in Salt Lake City. We had some small towns in Utah, but I never knew what they were really like. I was a city girl all my life."

"What brought you here?" Tuper didn't really care, but he wanted this woman to talk. She might know something useful.

"My husband had a younger sister in Clancy who's a nurse, and when he got cancer, they took us in. She was a big help that year. After he died, I didn't want to be a burden, so I came to live here. They visit and take me places. It's not so bad."

"That's good." Tuper feigned interest.

"I'm Thelma, by the way."

"Tuper," he said with a nod. "What else can you tell me about Amber? I'm her brother, but we were separated for many years, and I don't know how much she remembers. Sometimes, I just say I'm her friend because I don't want to upset her. I'd rather not go into why we've been apart so long, but honestly, I didn't know where she was until just a few days ago. I'd like to know more about her, but I'm not sure she has the ability."

"Well, I can tell you what she's talked about, but I don't know for certain if any of what she said is true."

"I understand. I can put the pieces together with what I know to be factual."

A caretaker appeared and took the other woman in the

wheelchair away without speaking to anyone. Thelma kept talking. "Like I said before, she cries a lot about her lost son. She calls him Frankie. She blames herself, but she usually does it in the third person. She's always saying 'It was Amber's fault.' Did you know she had a child?"

"I knew she'd been pregnant. That happened in her senior year of high school, but I didn't know if she gave birth, or miscarried, or what exactly happened." Tuper realized he sounded rather detached for a brother. "I was in the military, and my parents wouldn't talk about her pregnancy."

"I'm pretty sure she had the baby and that it was a boy. That part never changes. Amber says she got to hold him for two days."

"Did he die?"

"No, I think she gave him up for adoption, because she always says things like 'they took him away,' and 'he was better off,' or 'they could give him what I couldn't.' Stuff like that. I'm guessing Amber had her first break with reality right after her baby was born. Maybe that's why they took her baby away."

"Why do you say that?"

"Because her life seems to have ended after she gave birth. She seems to be stuck in her high school days. She has no stories after that. Although she did say she lived in Kalispell once and that she had to leave."

"Did she say why?"

"No."

"Does she ever talk about someone named Patrick?"

"She's mentioned him, but Amber always seems uncomfortable when she says his name."

Thelma started to say something else, but another caretaker walked up. "Excuse me, Thelma, you have a visitor."

"I have to go." Thelma stood. "It was nice talking to you."

As he walked outside, the dark clouds let loose. Tuper drove back to Helena, using the one working windshield wiper.

CHAPTER 28

With Bella's new information, plus what Tuper learned, Lana was pretty certain she could trace what happened to baby Frankie. She googled *Thanksgiving Day 1969* and discovered the date for the holiday that year was November 27. She then searched birth certificate records for any child born in Montana around that date. She knew that Amber went into labor either on the 24th or 25th and was back in Roy on the 28th, which meant the baby was likely born on November 25th, but Lana included the 24th and 26th, just to be safe.

She discovered an Asian-American baby born in Great Falls on the 24th, which she immediately eliminated, and two babies born at Central Montana Medical Center in Lewistown during that window of time. One boy arrived at 8:32 p.m. on November 26, which was the date Bella said Amber gave birth. He weighed seven pounds, four ounces and was twenty inches long. Lana continued reading the certificate. The baby's name was Kyle, the mother was listed as Jenny, and the father as Rick Smythe. A girl was born less than five hours later at 1:01 a.m., and her name was Antoinette Marie. The parents were Brenda and Craig Wells.

Lana figured one of those two must have been Amber's baby, most likely the boy. But unless the baby was naked when Bella saw him or unclothed in the photo, she wouldn't really know the sex. And if so much trouble had been taken to hide the identity of the newborn, perhaps Amber had lied about the baby's gender as well.

Lana began a search for Antoinette Marie Wells. She was the third child born to Brenda and Craig of Lewistown. They had two more children afterward, making a total of five. It seemed unlikely they would take in another child right in the middle of the ones they had. A little research showed that Brenda was the mother of the other children as well. There was no indication any of them had been adopted.

Baby girl Antoinette grew up in Lewistown and was still living there. She married when she was twenty-two, had two children of her own, and was currently working as a waitress in a café called Harry's Place.

The story on the other child was far more interesting. First, the parents were not from the area. Their home was in Missoula, so it was odd that they would give birth in a rural hospital five hours away. Lana continued to research, getting more excited with each new fact. Finally, she yelled, "Shazam!"

"What is it?" Tuper asked.

"I found the birth of a boy the same day as Amber's child was supposedly born. The parents are Jenny and Rick Smythe."

"Not Senator Smythe?" Clarice said.

"One and the same."

"That can't be Amber's baby. It doesn't make any sense,"

Clarice said. "Wouldn't we know if the senator had adopted a baby?"

"Probably, but maybe not. They could've kept it a secret somehow. Maybe that's why they wanted a baby so far away from home."

"Wouldn't the birth certificate say Amber on it?"

"No. When people adopt newborn babies, the hospital files a new birth certificate, as if it was the original—to protect the baby's privacy. But you're right; there would be another record somewhere, a sealed file listing the birth parents. That might take a little more effort to find. I'll keep looking, but first I want to check something else."

Lana disappeared into cyber space for nearly an hour, occasionally mumbling to herself. Finally, she said, "There's no record of Amber Carlton ever being in the hospital that year."

"Maybe she used a midwife," Clarice said.

"Or maybe she used a different name when she checked in," Tuper suggested.

"But she would need an ID, wouldn't she?" Lana asked. "Even a small hospital like the one in Lewistown must check to make sure they have the right person. I know it was nearly fifty years ago, but they must've checked something as basic as that. Why would someone come in pregnant and use a different name?"

"Because she wasn't married," Clarice said. "It used to be that people were ashamed of out-of-wedlock births. Things have changed a lot in fifty years."

Lana continued as usual to answer her own questions. "Or, it could be to use another person's insurance, but that would be insurance fraud." She stopped talking and started typing again.

"What are you looking for now?" Clarice asked.

"I'm checking insurance records for the two babies, Kyle and Antoinette."

"But what if Amber used a midwife?"

"Then there wouldn't be a record. But if she used another name to access someone else's insurance, we'll see the evidence."

Lana was deep into her task when Clarice turned to Tuper. "I'm curious enough to want to know what happened to that baby, but how does it really matter? What does it have to do with Squirrely's hit-and-run?"

"That's what I've been sayin'," Tuper muttered. "But Agony goes off on these tangents all the time. 'Following the clues,' she calls it. She's like a dog with a bone when she gets ahold of something. She won't let go."

Both Clarice and Tuper were surprised when Lana looked up and said, "You're the one who's been dogging Amber, hounding an old woman who's not in her right mind. You must think there's something there too."

"I ain't been talkin' to her 'cause of her baby. I've been tryin' to find out what those boys were all hidin'. We may both be barkin' up the wrong tree, but I don't know where else to look."

"Unless there was something else in that newspaper that I missed," Lana said. "I looked at every article, notice, and ad in that paper, and Patrick's obituary was the only thing that had any connection to Squirrely. Another set of eyes would be good though. Do either of you want to read through the paper?" Lana looked directly at Tuper.

"I'll do it," Clarice said quickly. "Where is it?"

"In the duffel bag behind the sofa."

Clarice went to get the paper, and Lana delved back into

her work, keying her way through old hospital and insurance records. Lana discovered which insurance company covered Antoinette Wells and traced the policy. Everything seemed in order. The mother, Brenda Wells, had the same insurance for all of her children. Craig Wells was a classified employee for the local school district, and his insurance covered his wife who appeared to be a stay-at-home mother. There were no apparent improprieties with the claim.

Lana turned her attention to Kyle Smythe and his parents, the couple from Missoula. After checking and double-checking, she spoke up. "Oh my! This is interesting."

"What?" Tuper asked.

She continued to type without saying anything further.

"What did you find?" he asked again.

Lana still didn't answer, just kept typing.

"Dang it, woman, you never stop talking, then you throw something out there that I might actually want to hear, and you clam up. What is it?"

"I'll be darned."

"You'll be worse than that if you don't tell me right now," Tuper said.

"No insurance claim was filed for Baby Kyle."

"So, they didn't have insurance. Big deal. Not everyone has it."

"Oh, they had insurance. They just didn't use it. They paid cash."

CHAPTER 29

"Why would someone pay cash to have a baby delivered if they had insurance?" Clarice asked.

Tuper and Lana looked at each other.

"Amber Carlton didn't have insurance, did she?" Tuper asked.

"No, she did not," Lana said. "So, she delivered the baby under someone else's name, specifically, Jenny Smythe."

"But then the birth certificate would have the wrong name on it," Clarice said. Her mouth dropped open. "That's the point, isn't it? She checked in under a different name, and the baby went home with the Smythes."

"That's my guess," Lana said. "And they paid cash so they could never be charged with insurance fraud."

"You'd think insurance fraud would be the least of their worries," Clarice added.

"You'd think," Tuper said. "But it would also be the easiest to prove."

"It all makes sense now." Lana was still excited. "That's why Amber left town the next day, just like Bella said, because she didn't want to talk about where the baby went. It also explains why Amber keeps saying it was all her fault—and why she still grieves over the loss. But it doesn't tell us why she did it, or what it has to do with Squirrely's accident or Patrick's death. Unless"—she paused—"Squirrely and Patrick knew about the baby transfer. I wonder if the Smythes paid Amber for the baby. And if they did, how much? I'll see if I can find a money trail. Maybe the guys were all paid off and told to leave town. But that doesn't make sense. They left way before the baby was born. No, there must be something else. And how did the Smythes happen to find Amber to buy her baby? I haven't found any connection between the families. I'll research again, but I tried earlier when I was checking out the two babies born in Lewistown. Amber wasn't connected to either Antoinette's parents, nor Kyle's parents. But I'll take a closer look just to make sure."

Lana opened her mouth to say something else, but Tuper cut in. "Agony, you're getting off track again. The baby may not have anything to do with any of this."

"Maybe not, but you have to admit, it's mighty peculiar, especially since Squirrely is probably the father."

Tuper didn't want to admit Lana was onto something, but he figured she probably was. "How does any of this explain why Patrick was killed?"

"Maybe he was trying to extort money from them. Smythe is a big-wig politician, and Patrick had information that could hurt him."

Tuper raised an eyebrow. "You think Squirrely was doing the same?"

"It would explain the money in the bag."

"You know Squirrely. Do you really think he's capable? And why nearly fifty years later?"

"Maybe he was doing it all along," Lana said. "And no one knew it."

Tuper scowled. "Squirrely never had any money. Look how he lives. He doesn't have a pot to pee in or a window to throw it out of. That doesn't make any sense."

"You're right. That part doesn't fit, but I still think there is some connection, and I intend to keep looking."

"You do that. I'm headed to the hospital to see Squirrely. If he'd just wake up, we could get a lot of questions answered."

"How is he?" Clarice asked.

"It's not looking good. The doctors were hoping he'd be awake by now. I'll keep you posted," Tuper nodded and walked out.

Clarice went back to perusing the 1994 newspaper, and Lana left for cyberspace once again. A good hour passed before either of them spoke.

"I just can't find anything that connects Amber or her family with the Smythes," Lana said. "I'm running out of trails to follow. How about you?"

"Nothing different than what you found so far." Clarice glanced down at the section she was reading. "Wait a minute. Here's something. Maybe you saw it, but you never mentioned it. Probably because you didn't know her name when you went through the paper."

"What is it?"

"The personal Mother's Day ad that reads *Happy Mother's Day, Amber.*"

CHAPTER 30

After hours attempting to track the Mother's Day ad to Amber, Lana got nowhere. She couldn't tell if it was meant for Amber Carlton. No names that she recognized were connected to it, but whoever sponsored the ad may have had someone else place it for them. She couldn't see how it could possibly have mattered anyway, except that it might explain why Squirrely had the newspaper. But Lana wasn't convinced Squirrely even knew Amber was pregnant. *Who would know that for sure?*

Frustrated, Lana picked up her cell and called Tuper. "We need to visit Squirrely's mother. She would likely know if her son knew about the pregnancy. She probably knows a lot that might help us."

"She might, but it's not likely she'll tell."

"It's her son, why wouldn't she want to help?"

"You ain't met the woman. I'm not sure she even likes him."

"She can't be that bad," Lana said. "Let's go see her. I'll talk to her."

"She ain't gonna like you any better 'n she likes me. I'll go by myself. I'm sure you have plenty to do on your own."

In spite of the heavy rainfall, Tuper drove to Great Falls to see Norma Finnigan. He didn't expect to be warmly received, but he didn't care. Agony was right, Squirrely's mom likely had information they needed. He parked as close as he could to the front door of the assisted living facility, but he still got plenty wet by the time he made it inside.

"What do you want now?" Norma grumped when she saw Tuper.

"I want answers."

"I ain't got any."

"You may not care about your son, but I do. He's hanging on by a thread, and I'll be damned if I'll let the bastard who did this get away!"

"It don't matter much who killed him if he dies," Norma said. "And there ain't nothing you can do to help him if he lives."

"Maybe I can stop the guy from making another attempt on Squirrely's life."

Norma didn't respond and instead said, "You're getting the floor all wet."

"Why don't you just tell me what I want to know, and I'll get out of here."

"I don't know nothin'."

"Did you know Amber Carlton was pregnant in high school?"

Silence filled the room. Finally, Norma said, "Yeah, I knew."

"Did Frank?"

"Yes."

"Did he know it was his baby?"

Norma frowned. "We didn't know whose baby it was."

"But they were a couple. Was there someone else?"

"Yes."

"Who?"

"A guy named Patrick."

"And you're sure of that?"

"I'm sure Frank believed it." She turned and looked at the wall.

"Because you convinced him?" Tuper asked, but it was as much a statement as a question.

She turned back to Tuper. "It was for his own good. What was he going to do with a baby? He was just a kid himself. No, he needed to go into the service and become a man. He was starting to get all sentimental like his weak father. He even bought Amber a ..." She stopped talking.

"A teddy bear for the baby?"

"Yeah, that's right. The goofy kid even stitched a red heart onto it. He wanted me to take it to her, but I told him no. I'm pretty sure he convinced his father to do it though—the old fool."

And Amber still had the bear, Tuper thought. "How did you convince Frank to leave her?"

"That took some doing, but everyone knew Patrick was with her at least once. It could've been his baby, and once Frank realized that, it was easy to get him to join the military."

Tuper knew Norma was odd, but she gave him a chill. She was so uncaring. It made him feel even sorrier for his friend, Squirrely. "I take it you didn't like Patrick much?"

"That kid was nothing but trouble from the moment he

came to town. Frank was the perfect son until that kid showed up. My boy got good grades, never missed school, always helped me with chores, but when Patrick showed up, everything changed. He started acting out, ruined his chance of going to college, almost ended up in jail."

"What happened that almost put him in jail?"

"I don't want to talk about that."

"I need to know. I think it's the key to Frank getting hit with that car. If that's true, and he survives this, it could happen again."

After a long moment, she finally told the story. "Patrick, Karl, and Frank were out drinking one night. They had gone to a bar in Grass Range where they could get booze. Patrick looked older and had a fake ID. On the way home, they got into an accident, and two people in the other car were killed. The kids left and didn't report it."

People had died! Tuper hadn't expected that. "Who was driving the car the boys were in?"

Norma hesitated for a split second, then said, "Patrick was driving his father's car."

"And there was an investigation?"

"A trooper came to see the boys one day at school. Frank came home and told me. The cops didn't seem to know much, but for some reason they were on the right trail. The boys all denied it."

"And they were never arrested?"

"No, Patrick's father told the boys to deny everything. He promised them nothing would ever come of it, if they just did what he said. It happened a few weeks before graduation, and he told them to leave town right after school was out. They all did. I don't know what strings Mr. Gallagher pulled, but it all went away."

CHAPTER 31

Lana parked her bike on the porch out of the rain, and went inside. When she left for her ride, it was sprinkling. She didn't expect to get caught in a Montana downpour. She soon discovered the rain patterns were very different from California's. One more thing she found so different here, but nothing was as bad as the winter she had just experienced. Spring she could handle.

She removed a clean towel from the linen closet and dried her hair. Her spikes were gone. It stuck to her head like a pixie, making her look about twelve years old. She fluffed it the best she could and decided to leave it until later. She had no one to impress.

Armed with Tuper's new information, Lana began a search for car accidents in Grass Range in May of 1969. She wasn't sure how having the details would help, but she had long ago discovered that the more information she had, the easier it was to figure something out. Before she could get the specifics she needed, she had to determine what kind of car the boys were driving when the accident occurred. She knew the car belonged to Patrick's father, so she checked DMV records to see what was registered to James L. Gallagher that year. She found three cars, a 1965 black Buick Riviera Grand Sport, a red 1960 Chevy C-10 Apache pickup, and a light-blue 1966 Cadillac De Ville.

Lana looked first at newspaper articles reporting vehicular accidents. She was able to narrow the search by the date of the boys' suspension from high school. Although she wasn't sure how long it took deputies to discover the boys were involved, she gave it a month range. If she couldn't find anything, she would expand the search window further. It helped tremendously that she knew the general area where the accident took place—somewhere between Grass Range and Roy. At least she hoped that information from Norma Finnigan was accurate, but it was possible the boys drove somewhere else before coming home. Nevertheless, she had to start somewhere. It didn't take long before she found a fatal accident on highway US 87 just outside of Grass Range at the MT 200 junction. The article read:

2 killed, 1 Injured in Crash, Near Grass Range

Two adults were killed, and one teenager was injured in a car crash involving a white 1962 Ford Fairlane. The deadly accident occurred about 12:45 a.m. on US 87. Of the three passengers in the Fairlane, only one survived. The driver, a forty-one-year-old male, was taken to the hospital in Lewistown but died shortly after his arrival, police said. The thirty-nine-year-old female passenger was pronounced dead at the scene, and the fourteen-year-old boy in the backseat was hospitalized in critical condition.

Investigators indicated that the Ford Fairlane was traveling north on US 87. A red Chevy pickup was seen in the area, but there

were no apparent witnesses. The injured teenager has yet to regain
consciousness or answer questions.

No names were released, which meant she had to look for additional articles regarding the accident. Lana also checked the obituaries, which were challenging to sift through because she was often distracted by something far more interesting. But she found a follow-up article dated two days later with the names of the fatal victims, Sandy and Brian Teller. Their son, Jeremy Teller, was out of the ICU, but he had multiple injuries that would keep him hospitalized for months. No new details were given about the accident. That was the last article she could find about the crash, so she had to assume nothing newsworthy happened on the case after that.

Lana turned her attention to police records. Looking through accident reports was a boring task, but it didn't take too long because she had a specific date, time, and area. However, when she found the report, she was disappointed. James Gorham, a trooper with the Montana Highway Patrol, had filed the paperwork. For some reason, another trooper named Michael Quince conducted the field work. The reporting was sparse, but he'd done follow-up on every red Chevy pickup in the area. Yet even that effort was tenuous. The survivor, Jeremy Teller, claimed he saw the truck try to pass them, and that's all he remembered. He couldn't be certain if the vehicle hit them, ran them off the road, or just passed really fast. They had no other leads, and the case was left unsolved.

Lana searched the names of the investigators in the case and discovered James Gorham retired five years after the accident, then passed away eight years later from lung cancer. Michael Quince remained with the MHP for forty more years and retired ten years ago. He was apparently still alive and well on a small ranch just outside of Great Falls.

She called Tuper. "Are you still in Great Falls?"

"I was just about to leave. Why?"

Lana gave him the information about Michael Quince. "You might want to see him before you come home. I ran his address on Google maps, and he's just on this side of Great Falls." She gave Tuper the phone number she'd found for him as well.

"You ain't nothin' if you ain't thorough," Tuper said.

"Hey, Pops, I think you just paid me a compliment."

"Don't let it go to yer head."

CHAPTER 32

Tuper knocked on the door of Michael Quince's farmhouse. A healthy-looking, seventy-something man with gray hair and mustache greeted Tuper with a friendly smile. "Come in out of the rain."

"Thanks," Tuper said, following him inside.

"Would you like something to drink? I don't get a lot of visitors, so I don't keep too many supplies on hand. But I have some soda pop if you're interested."

"That would be great."

"Orange or cola?"

"Orange, please."

Quince retrieved two orange soda bottles from the refrigerator and handed one to Tuper. "I hope you don't mind the bottle. I can't drink from those cans. They taste like aluminum to me."

"This'll do."

Quince sat down at the kitchen table and gestured for Tuper to do the same. "You said you were interested in a case I was on. I have to tell you, I've been retired for more than ten years. I don't know how much I'll remember, but I'll help if I can."

"This one goes way back. To 1969 to be exact."

"That's expecting a lot from this old brain. What case was it?"

"A fatal car accident near Grass Range. A teenage boy lost both of his parents, but the case was never resolved." Tuper handed him the initial police report, plus the investigative report written by Quince a few days later.

"I remember," Quince said, before he even looked at the paperwork. "We had very little to go on. It was one of my first fatal accident investigations. I was at the scene of the accident with another trooper, but I didn't write the initial report. That was done by ..." He paused, rubbing his forehead. "What was his name?" Then he looked at the report. "That's right. Gorham wrote it. Good guy to work with, but he was swamped with other things, so I was given the case. I did the rest of the fieldwork." He looked at what he'd written. "There was obviously another car involved in the accident, but we never found it. We thought it was a red Chevy pickup, but we weren't even certain of that."

"You said there were other reports. This was the only follow-up I found. Do you remember what investigation was done on the incident?"

"I remember this well. It bothered me my entire career because I was never able to solve the case. Jeremy Teller, the kid in the car, came to me several times over the years to see if we had discovered anything new. But I never had anything to tell him. I thought for a while that I knew who was driving the other vehicle, but I never got the chance to prove it."

"Why is that?"

"I followed up on every red Chevy pickup registered in the

county. Now granted, it could've been someone outside the county or even the state for that matter, but I think it was some locals. I was encouraged early on to stop investigating."

"You were ordered to stop?"

"Not exactly. I was told that the information we had was too flimsy and that I was wasting my time."

"But you thought it was a cover-up of some sort?"

"I'd never go so far as to say that, leastways not then, but it didn't feel exactly right to me either, especially after I talked to those boys in Roy. A couple years later when young Teller came to me for answers, I tried looking into it again and dang near lost my job over it. That's when I let it go."

"What happened?"

"I was told in no uncertain terms to stay out of it."

On his way home, Tuper drove to Clancy. He wanted to talk to Amber again. It was time for the residents' evening meal, and he hoped to catch her in the dining room. But when he arrived, Amber was already in her room. He was told she left the table early because she was tired. He didn't want to bother her while she was resting, so he sat down in Amber's spot at the table.

"Good evening, Thelma."

"Nice to see you again, Tuper. Sorry, but your sister was tired. You just missed her."

"That's what I heard, but I wanted to say hello to you."

She smiled. "Thanks, it's always nice to have a visitor."

Tuper asked Thelma a few questions about herself and chatted for a while before he delved into what he really wanted to know. "Did Amber ever talk about the father of her baby?"

"She talks about Frankie a lot. I always thought she meant her son, but one day I realized she was talking about her boyfriend. I thought she was just mixing things up, so I asked. She was having a good day so she was able to explain. I assumed he was the father since she called the baby Frankie too. But one day she said something strange that made me wonder."

"What did she say?"

"She suddenly blurted, 'What if the baby was Patrick's?' When I questioned her further, she said, 'No, he couldn't be. Frankie had to be the father.' Then she clammed up and wouldn't tell me anything more. It never came up again."

CHAPTER 33

The rain fell lightly as Karl Haberman stumbled out of the bar into the dark parking lot, right after the owner called closing time. He'd been there every night for over a year now. There wasn't much else to do in this one-horse town. He sometimes wondered why he'd returned to Roy, but he wasn't really wanted anywhere else. His wife was dead, and his two sons didn't want him around. His eldest wouldn't even talk to him. Karl felt like neither of them liked him that much anyway. They only tolerated him because their mother made them. He knew things might be a little easier if he didn't drink, but they couldn't blame everything on the alcohol. He had tried to quit several times, but too many ghosts haunted him. The booze helped them go away, at least temporarily.

He thought about the accident all those years ago, like he did almost every day of his life. They were all just kids, drunk and having a ball … until they weren't. They weren't moving fast enough for him, so he dared the driver to go faster. In a reckless split second, all their lives were changed forever. He thought about the next two years that he spent moving from place to place and trying to drown in a bottle. He often wished he had, but he was too much of a coward to ever go that far. Vietnam made things worse, so he spent the rest of his life pretending life was worth living, but he knew better. Anyone looking in from the outside thought his life was okay, but he knew it was never okay. It was far worse.

He turned down the street toward his house. He only had a block and a half to walk. The street was empty. He thought he saw someone come out of the Legion bar and get in a pickup. There were no other signs of movement on the street. He glanced around. Most of the houses were dark with slumber. He heard an engine and looked up. A dark car without lights was headed right toward him. The engine got louder. His first instinct was to get out of the way, but alcohol clouded his mind. He felt like everything was suddenly in slow motion, even the raindrops. The car came closer. The engine grew louder. *It's over*, he thought. *The pain would end.* He closed his eyes and felt the impact, then his body flew through the air. *I deserve this. Finally, no more wondering, or waiting, or suffering. It would all soon be over.*

The rain had finally stopped again, making it easier for Lana to ride her bike to Nickels to open the bar. Clarice wasn't feeling well and had asked Lana to cover for her. Clarice was asleep when Lana left or she would have objected to her early morning bike ride.

Clarice had trained her well, and Lana never said no when she was asked to work, even though she didn't much like bartending. She hated the drunks hitting on her, and she found the smell of the bar and the alcohol nauseating. But

Clarice had been kind to her, and Lana wanted to pay her own way. She didn't mind the morning shift as much because most of the patrons were still sober. This morning was uneventful, and she was glad; but she was even happier when someone came in to relieve her at nine.

Lana rode home, took a quick shower to get the smell off, and sat down with her laptop. She checked several of her email accounts, including Hotmail. She had dozens of message accounts, all of which she used for different purposes. Hotmail was the oldest and the only place she received news from home. She never sent emails from there because she didn't want to be traced. *He could and would trace her if he got the least inkling of her footprint anywhere online.* Lana was good, even better than him now, but he had taught her most of what she knew, and she realized she couldn't get careless or overconfident. The least little mistake, and he would find her.

She opened another message from him:

—*You can't keep hiding. I'll be back in the US in a few days. Get ready.*

She was sure he was phishing, that he didn't really know where she was, but it made her stomach ache anyway. *Why won't he just leave me alone?*

She closed her Hotmail account and opened her Gmail. She used this service primarily to get Google alerts when she needed them. She would add a name to her alert list, and whenever anything about that person was in the news or a blog, or they did anything that put them in the Google search engine, she would be notified by email. All she had to do was click the link, and it would take her to whatever article had been posted. The alerts were a great way to get information without googling someone's name every day. Lana never kept the accounts very long. She would close the Gmail address when she no longer needed it and open another when she did, always with a different username and fake information. As long as she used a Google address, she could get the alerts.

She had received quite a few alerts since she added Senator Rick Smythe to her list. Most of the news was routine political stuff, but she had to spend time sorting through it to make sure. He would be up for re-election soon, and it was evident he planned to run again. Lana didn't think much of most politicians. She didn't trust people in general, but politicians ranked higher than most in that department. Maybe it was because she knew more about them than the general public did. She had never missed an opportunity to vote—until she went into hiding. At first, it bothered her that she couldn't cast her vote, but she soon discovered she had other means of getting her vote counted.

She glanced at her Gmail and saw she had six alerts, all about Smythe. She started with the oldest one, which had come in about six the night before. She deleted each after she read it. The senator had given a speech at a VA conference, spoken out against a bill regarding abortion rights, and had done several other similar things that weren't useful to this case.

Smythe was the only person she had received alerts for since she started working with Tuper on Squirrely's hit-and-run, even though she had listed several names. She had just finished reading Smythe's last notice when an alert appeared for *Karl Haberman*. Followed by another one for *Roy, Montana*. They both were about the same thing. Karl was dead—the victim of a hit-and-run.

CHAPTER 34

"This can't be a coincidence," Lana said. "It must be the same person who hit Squirrely. And probably killed Patrick." She and Tuper were in Clarice's living room, but Lana was too worked up to sit. So she paced. "But why now? Why twenty-five years later? That just doesn't connect for me. Something must've happened that started the cover-up rolling again. I think it has something to do with the cash Squirrely has. It's always about money. Money makes people do crazy things. Do you think Squirrely learned something he could use to extort money from someone?"

"That's pretty iffy," Tuper said.

"It appears that Patrick's father was the one who was able to stop the investigation into those three boys. I wonder how he did that. He didn't seem important enough to have that kind of influence." She glanced around the room. "Where's Ringo?"

"He's at the trailer."

She raised an eyebrow. "So, you stayed at Greta's last night?" He seemed to stay there more than anywhere when he was not in his cabin. She wondered if his "girlfriends" knew about each other.

"That's none of your business."

"Don't get testy, old man."

Tuper shook his head and changed the subject. "Patrick's father did have a lot of money. Maybe he just bribed the right people."

"See? We're back to money again," Lana said. "But he'd still have to know the *right* people in order to bribe them."

"Or he knew someone who knew someone."

"Or he had leverage on someone or made a deal of some kind. So many possible scenarios exist. But they all come back to Patrick's father, James Gallagher. I need to find out who he was connected to." Lana turned her attention to her keyboard.

"How you plan to do that?"

"I'll look at anyone and everyone James Gallagher has ever associated with. It will take time, but I don't know where else to look. We're hitting dead ends everywhere else. This may have started fifty years ago, but people are dying today. Someone has hit a nerve recently."

"What do we know so far?" Tuper asked.

"We know that in 1969, two people were killed in an accident that appeared to involve Squirrely, Karl, and Patrick—and James Gallagher stopped the investigation. Around the same time, Amber gave birth to a boy, and that baby went home with Senator Smythe—who would have influence over people." Lana's pulse jumped. "I bet that's it. There must be a connection between Gallagher and the senator. That's where I'll start."

"But he wasn't a senator yet, was he? He was pretty young."

"Twenty-six to be exact, and no he wasn't a senator yet." Lana buried herself in the internet once again. For fifteen minutes, she was quiet. Then she said, "Senator Smythe was in local politics and probably being groomed for Congress. He was already campaigning." She didn't say anything for nearly five minutes while she continued to search. "But get this."

After a minute or two, Tuper said, "Get what?"

"Senator Smythe's father, Tim Smythe, was attorney general for the state of Montana at that time."

"Now that's a connection."

Lana looked at everything she could find about Gallagher that might lead to either Rick or Tim Smythe. She discovered they were of the same political persuasion as Gallagher. She searched through campaign contributions for both politicians, but the donations were difficult to trace. So many had been made by corporations and businesses that she had to check out who owned them. It was tedious and frustrating. She started to uncover Gallagher's financial records to see if he had made a sizable contribution to either of the Smythes' campaigns, but decided it was too time consuming. She would do that as a last resort.

She went back to researching Gallagher. It was difficult because she needed information from fifty years ago, and internet data was scarce in those days. But she just had to find the tiniest connection, a reason to believe Gallagher and the senator, or his father, knew each other. She was tracing Gallagher's school records when she discovered it. Tim Smythe and James Gallagher both attended the University of Michigan. But Michigan was a large school, and although they were there at the same time, it was possible they never knew each other. The school yearbook showed otherwise. They played on the same baseball team. A little more digging into dorm rosters put it all together—they were not only teammates, they were roommates.

"That's it," Lana said out loud.

"What?"

She shared the information with Tuper, then added, "But I have to check one more thing."

Lana searched the medical records of Jenny Jones Smythe, Tim Smythe's daughter-in-law. "Shazam!"

"What?" Tuper asked.

"That explains it."

"Dang it, Agony," Tuper said when Lana didn't respond right away. "When you have nothing worth hearing, you jabber non-stop, and when you have something I need to hear, I have to pull it out of you. Now just spill it."

"Okay, Pops. Settle down before you have a heart attack," Lana said. "Jenny Smythe couldn't have children. She had already miscarried twice and was told she couldn't carry a baby to term. Tim Smythe must have helped Gallagher make his son's accident go away, and in turn, Gallagher made sure Smythe's son got a baby. That must have been the quid pro quo."

CHAPTER 35

"That still leaves a lot of unanswered questions," Lana said. "Why would Squirrely and Amber give up their kid? Maybe Squirrely did it to stay out of prison, but why Amber? There's still something missing."

"I think I know what that is," Tuper said. "I spoke to Amber's friend at the home, and she said Amber commented once that the baby might be Patrick's."

"Wow! She must've cheated on Squirrely. Maybe she didn't ever tell Squirrely she was pregnant. Maybe she knew it was Patrick's, and giving up the baby was her plan all along."

"Maybe."

"But the threads are still not all connected. Patrick's father knew the attorney general, and between the two, they were able to quash the accident investigation and make a baby switch at the hospital. But why go to all that trouble to get a child? Why couldn't Rick and Jenny just adopt a kid? Even if they wanted this particular baby for some reason, why the cover up?" Lana got up to pace. This puzzle was driving her crazy. "And how much did Squirrely, Patrick, and Karl know?

Did they know about the whole baby thing? They obviously knew about the accident, but did they know how it got resolved? And what does it all have to do with what's going on today? Why was Patrick killed? Why was Karl killed? And why make an attempt on Squirrely's life? Why now? And another thing, where did Squirrely's money come from? We have more questions now than we did when we started."

"Are you done?" Tuper asked.

"No. My point is, we've learned a lot, but none of it answers the question we started with. Who tried to kill Squirrely?" Lana paused. "Now, I'm done."

"Good."

"But what if—?"

Tuper shook his head. "I thought you were done."

"Not quite. You have that friend Brad What's-his-name."

"Bergstad?"

"Yeah," Tuper said reluctantly. "What are you thinking?"

"He still has that DNA lab, right?"

"Yes."

"We should run the DNA on Kyle Smythe, Amber, and Squirrely. Then we can prove we have the right kid. When Squirrely wakes up, you can tell him about his kid, if he doesn't already know."

"And why would I want to do that?"

"Don't you think he'd want to know?" Lana asked.

"If he wanted me buttin' in his business, he would've told me about the kid before."

"Unless he didn't even know that Amber was pregnant. Or he didn't think the baby was his. But something has been going on, and he must know about it or he wouldn't be in the hospital right now. Or at least someone *thinks* he knows something."

"Did it ever occur to you that Squirrely might not want to know he's a father?"

"Then don't tell him. But at least we could confirm that Kyle is Amber's son."

"What good would that do? And how would we get Kyle's DNA?"

Lana ignored the first question. "I haven't figured out exactly how to pull it off, but let me do more research on Kyle and see what I can find. I know he lives in Helena, but I haven't done much follow up yet."

"You do that," Tuper said. "But I think you're getting way off track again." He stood. "Tell Clarice I'll be right back. I'm going to get Ringo." He walked out the door.

Lana dived into the research on Kyle Smythe. Finding information about him was easier than some of the others because he was a senator's son. It was always simpler to find information for famous people and their offspring. And the Smythes were no exception. She already knew that Kyle had been born in 1969 in Lewistown and that his parents were living in Missoula. That's where she concentrated her search.

Lana was still deep into databases when Tuper returned an hour later. Ringo ran up to Lana and she squatted down in front of him and scratched his ears and petted him. When she stood up, he walked away wagging his tail.

"What did you find out?" Tuper asked.

"Kyle lived in Missoula for the first ten years and attended Sussex School, a private institution, from kindergarten through fourth grade. He moved with his family to Helena in 1979 where he spent fifth grade in First Lutheran School. It appears that the school only went to fifth grade, and I couldn't find any other private schools in Helena during that time, which probably explains why he went to public schools after that. He graduated with honors from Capital High School in 1987, then went to Stanford University in California. He was involved in a lot of clubs and organizations, but get this, one was the debate team. Do you think that's inherited? I think certain skills get passed down through your DNA, don't you? I don't mean everything. Lots of things are learned. But some skills, like math or tech skills seem to be innate. What do you think?"

Tuper didn't comment, not that Lana paused long enough to give him the opportunity.

"Shortly after graduation from Stanford, Kyle joined the Peace Corps and was with the first group to go to Zimbabwe, Africa. He came home with a wife, Emma Ray, another volunteer. I saw photos of them. She's a tiny little thing, around five-feet tall with short, curly chestnut-colored hair, blue eyes, and freckles. Very striking in a natural kind of way. Not long after they returned, Kyle went to work for the U.S. Forest Service in Helena. The next year, Emma got a job in a public school teaching fifth grade. They both went back to college and obtained graduate degrees. Their first son, Atlas, was born in 2000. In 2004, Emma gave birth to another son, Kace, and then a daughter, Paisley, in 2006. That's about all I have for now."

Tuper opened his mouth to say something, but Lana cut him off. "Oh, and in all my research, I never found anything that indicated Kyle was adopted or not the biological offspring of the Smythes." She looked at Tuper, who was staring at her. "Now I'm done."

"Did you say his wife's name was Emma?"

"OMG! I did. Do you think that's who Squirrely was talking about when he said 'Give it to Elba'? Maybe he said Emma. But why would he say his son's wife's name, instead of his son's? Wouldn't he tell you to give the money to Kyle? If she's the 'Emma' he was talking about"—Lana used air quotes when she said the name—"then he would have to know about his son. No, something's wrong. I'm going to keep looking for Elba."

"I wonder if Squirrely knows anything about Kyle," Tuper mumbled.

"I don't know. But if those are his grandchildren and they're living right here in Helena, don't you think he'd want to know? I think we should get a DNA test done, just to make sure."

"And how would we do that? We would need a sample from Kyle."

"Or one of his kids."

"No, leave the children out of this."

"Okay, but I bet I could get one from Kyle. I can find out where he is and just pick up something he uses. It wouldn't be that hard. Trust me, I can get a sample. And you could take one easily from Squirrely. He'd never know."

"Drop it, Agony. We're not doing that."

CHAPTER 36

Lana had made up her mind to get a DNA test on Kyle Smythe. Tuper had said to drop it, but he hadn't used a tone that indicated he really meant it, at least that's how she interpreted it. She was certain he wanted to know too. If Squirrely turned out to be Kyle's father, they'd know they were on the right track. And if Squirrely ever woke up, Tuper could decide whether to tell him. Lana had convinced herself, and no one could stop her.

She continued to gather information about Kyle Smythe. She needed to know exactly where he worked and what hours. She found what she could online, and as soon as Tuper left, she made a few phone calls to Kyle's office. She discovered he would be at Vigilante Bike Park that afternoon, a part of Centennial Park in Helena. She studied Kyle's photograph to make sure she could identify him.

Lana changed into hiking boots, wishing she had a decent pair of running shoes, jumped on her bike, and took off. It would take her about twenty-seven minutes to ride to her destination, according to Google maps. Kyle was supposed to arrive at the park around the same time, and Lana had no idea how long he would stay. She was pretty certain she could make up some time. She normally rode faster than the average biker, and today she would make certain.

She picked up speed once she got onto York Road, pedaling as fast as she could. It was only a two-lane road and a little busier than she had hoped, but she managed to keep a good pace until it turned into East Custer. The street was busy and didn't have a bike lane. Cars zoomed past. She turned left when she reached North Sanders Street. A big semi honked at her, and she flipped him off as she made the turn. There were no bike lanes on Sanders either, but it had far less traffic, and she was able to maintain a good speed, until she hit the road construction. She managed to get through, but it set her back a few minutes. She checked her phone and was still ahead of schedule by fourteen minutes—plenty of time if she didn't lose any more ground.

Her GPS told her to turn right on Cedar, which she did. She knew the street turned into North Last Chance Gulch when she crossed North Montana. As she approached the intersection, a car whizzed past and turned right in front of her, forcing her to veer left to avoid slamming into it. She hit a pothole and bounced hard, losing a little control. She tried to compensate and get her balance, but a car was coming toward her. She swerved to the right, overcompensating, and suddenly went down. She slid across the pavement, dragging her bike with her.

Dazed, Lana looked around to assess the situation. She saw a tall, slim man running toward her from a pickup parked across the street.

"Are you okay?" he asked.

Lana stood, picking her bike up with her. "Yeah, I'm fine."

She spat the words out, angry at the driver who ran her off the road and at herself for not being able to keep her balance.

"Excuse me, but you're bleeding."

Lana looked down at her arm and saw it was bloody and dirty. The top of her forearm had a six-inch pavement burn. "I'm okay," she said, a little softer. She glanced down and saw that her front wheel was bent. "But my bike, not so much."

"Can I help you? Maybe take you somewhere?"

"How far is it to Centennial Park?"

"Less than half a mile."

Lana checked the time on her phone. "I have to get to the park, but I can make it on foot."

"What about your bike?" the man asked.

Lana didn't answer. Her head hurt and she felt dazed. She removed her helmet and that relieved a little pressure.

"Please, let me help. I'll put your bike in the back of my truck and drive you where you need to go."

She checked the time again. "Okay. Thanks."

When he lifted her bike, his sleeve pulled up, exposing a bald eagle and flag tattoo on his forearm. He carried the bike across the street with one hand and hoisted it over the side into his pickup. Lana walked beside him, and for the first time noticed he had a cowboy kind of handsomeness, a look she didn't generally find attractive. But there was something different about him. She shook off the thought, blaming it on the blow to her head. The man looked around thirty, stood about six-foot-three in his cowboy boots, and was slender with broad shoulders. His dark, wavy hair was slightly too long, and his vivid blue eyes brightened his sun-weathered face.

"Are you sure you don't want me to take you to get medical attention?"

"No, I'm good. I need to take care of something, and I don't have a lot of time."

"I have a first-aid kit. Please let me clean you up."

Lana looked down at her messy arm.

"I don't know where you're headed," he said. "But do you really want to go looking like that?"

"You're right, but please be quick."

The man retrieved the kit from the cab, opened the tailgate, and set it down.

"That's a big first-aid kit. Do you do this often?"

"What? Rescuing damsels in distress? No, first time. My grandmother gave me the kit. I think she was concerned about me hurting myself and not being able to get help. You know how grandmas are."

No, not really, Lana thought. She'd never had a grandmother around.

He removed a bottle of peroxide and some cotton balls. "Hold your arm out, and I'll dab this on. It may hurt, but you need to clean up the wound."

Lana reached for the bottle. "I can do it." She poured the peroxide over her wound, not even flinching as it bubbled and foamed. She took several cotton balls, wiped it off, then poured more peroxide. When she cleaned it the second time, she noticed several areas were scraped and bleeding.

"I owe you a bottle of peroxide," she said, as she handed him the nearly empty container. She held out her left arm. "There, see, it's not so bad."

"You're a tough little cookie, aren't you?"

"I don't think anyone has ever called me a 'cookie' before, and you may not want to do it again, or you'll see how tough I can be."

He raised both palms. "I get the point. I apologize." He

reached into the kit. "If you don't mind, I'd like to put the bandage on for you. It'll be a lot quicker if I do it, and I know you're in a hurry."

She acquiesced, even though she didn't like taking help from anyone. She had been on her own for so long and had so little trust ... But he was right, the bandage would be quicker and likely stay better if he handled it. She held out her arm without saying anything. He put ointment on the gauze he had readied, laid it carefully on her arm, and taped it with precision.

"Are you a doctor, or something?" Lana asked, factitiously.

"No, but I was a medic in the army. I learned a thing or two. You ready?"

"Yeah." She paused. "Thanks."

The man picked up the kit, stepped quickly toward the passenger side of the truck, and opened Lana's door.

"I'm okay, you know. It's just a little scrape."

"Just being polite, ma'am."

"Ma'am? Really?" Lana started to climb in.

He smiled, then got into the driver's seat. As he started to pull away, he said, "I'm Brock Shero."

"Lana," she said.

"Hello, Lana with no last name. It's nice to meet you."

"Look, I really appreciate you doing this for me. I'm just upset at the idiot who ran me off the road and at myself for not being able to control my bike."

They reached the park and Brock said, "It's a large area; where do you need to go?"

"Vigilante Bike Park. Do you know where it is?"

"You're looking at it." He drove past the baseball diamonds and pointed to the right. "I'm in no hurry. Would you like me to wait and take you and your bike somewhere when you're done?"

"No, thanks. I'll call someone to come get me."

He stopped the truck, stepped out, and walked around to the passenger side. Lana was out before he could open her door.

"You're not from around here, are you?" he asked.

"Nope." She normally couldn't stop talking, but she was never open around strangers. People often thought she was shy when they first met her, but she wasn't. She just never knew who might betray her.

"California?"

Lana was startled for a second. "Why would you ask that?"

"Just a guess."

Lana frowned and wondered if he had been following her.

"Maybe it was your accent."

"I don't have an accent."

"That's right," Brock said. "That's why I thought you were from California. People from California don't have accents."

"People who don't have accents could be from anywhere." She suddenly realized she was wasting time. "I have to go."

"Would you like to get a drink sometime?" When Lana hesitated, he added, "I know it sounds like I'm hitting on you. I guess I am hitting on you. But I enjoyed our four minutes together and would like to get to know you better. Can I at least call you?"

"I'll call you," Lana said, starting to walk away.

"Wait! You don't have my number."

"I'll find you," she called out as she moved across the park carrying her bike. "Thanks for the lift."

CHAPTER 37

When Lana was far enough away, she took out her phone, opened her notes app, and wrote down his license number, which she had committed to memory earlier. She felt compelled to check him out, in case he had been sent to watch her. She parked and locked her bike in a rack. No one could ride it away with the bent wheel, but she didn't want to lose what was left of it.

The first thing she needed to do was find Kyle Smythe. She saw a small group of people gathered about sixty feet away. She walked toward them and spotted the US Forest Service truck parked nearby. She was in the right place. She had no idea how she would get Kyle's DNA, but she was confident she would figure out a way when the time came. She wasn't even sure what Kyle was doing or how long he'd be at the park. All she knew was that some college students were planting trees as part of a conservation program.

Kyle Smythe, dressed in his forestry uniform, was already talking to the crowd when Lana walked up. She stepped into the group, wondering if her spiked flaming-reddish-orange hair made her stand out too much. Then she saw another girl with a purple mohawk. The rest were more conservative looking, but Lana still felt like she blended in enough. She guessed she was ten years older than most of them, but no one ever deduced her age when she met them. She could easily pass for early twenties. Besides, this was college. She could be any age.

Lana listened carefully to Kyle's explanation about the trees they would plant and the reasons for choosing these particular trees. She found it quite fascinating. She was a strong believer in conservation and did her best to do her part whenever she could.

Then Kyle gave detailed instructions on how to do the actual planting. "I have all the equipment you'll need in the truck. I'll open the back and you can pick up what you need, including gloves. As you can see, the spots where you'll plant the trees are marked with a stick and are color-coded. So are the saplings. There are twenty-two sticks in all. Eight right here, six over there near the end of the bike park, and another eight near the baseball diamonds." He pointed toward each area as he spoke. "Please make sure the color on the sapling matches the color on the stick. It's important that we have the right trees in the right places. Any questions?"

"Are we working alone or in pairs?" one student asked.

"You can do it however you want. It's not that difficult, but if you're more comfortable in pairs, that's fine too. As long as we get them all done in the next hour—because that's when I have to leave. I'll work right alongside you, so if you have questions, please feel free to ask. I'll plant the first sapling, and you can watch what I do. The most important thing is to be careful with the roots. And don't eat any worms you find."

Some students laughed; others didn't seem so sure.

When no one else asked a question, he passed out sheets of paper. "Here is your map with the planting spots marked and color-coded. Please get the trees in the right spots. And be sure to wear gloves. You don't need to get a blister, then get it infected, and lose a finger."

Lana thought it was another attempt at humor, but the girl with the purple hair asked, "Really? Is that a thing?"

Smythe smiled. "The state requires you wear gloves, so just wear them please."

Some students formed pairs, but Lana moved apart from the group so no one would ask her to join them. She needed to work alone. The students gathered by the truck, picking out their tools and trees. Lana looked at her map and hung back to see what Kyle would do. When she saw him pick up a blue-tagged tree, she did the same. She didn't have a plan yet, but she had to stay close. Maybe he would discard a water bottle or chewing gum or something, although he wasn't chewing gum or drinking water. She had done her research, so she knew what things were better than others for obtaining DNA.

They all formed a circle around Kyle as he planted his sapling, explaining each step as he went. It was fairly simple, but from the way he explained the process, you could see his love for nature. Lana was impressed. When he finished, she dug her hole and planted her tree alongside Kyle's. He walked by and said, "Good job."

Lana continued to keep an eye on him, staying as close as she could, while trying not to be too obvious. He still hadn't done anything that might give her a DNA sample. She couldn't steal his hoe. It was too big to walk away with, and he wore gloves when he used it.

When he went back to the truck to get another sapling,

several students joined him. Lana slipped in alongside, and that's when she saw her opportunity. Kyle removed an ice chest from the cab and set it on the tail of the truck. *Finally,* Lana thought, *he's going to drink some water.* She would get the bottle one way or another.

Kyle pulled off his gloves, put them next to the ice chest, and opened the lid. "Who wants water? It's pretty warm out here for a spring day, and you need to stay hydrated." He removed several bottles of water as he spoke. Lana let others get their water first, then stepped up. He handed her a bottle. When he turned to pass out another one, Lana slipped one of his gloves into her pocket, pulling her shirt down over it to make sure it was covered.

"Where's the nearest restroom?" Lana asked, when he turned back toward her.

"Over there," he pointed to his right, "by the ballfields."

"Thanks." Lana smiled and left. She had what she came for.

CHAPTER 38

L
ana called Tuper to pick her up. She would have rather
asked Clarice, but her bike wouldn't fit in Clarice's car.
Lana carried it out to the road to wait for him. Tuper arrived
within ten minutes, opened the hatchback, and stuck the bike
in the back atop his tools and other junk.

"What happened?" Tuper asked.

As they drove toward home, she told him the whole story
about the ride and the guy stopping and bandaging her arm.

"Are you sure you're okay?"

"I'm fine. It's just a little scrape."

"What were you doing over there anyway?"

"I'll tell you," Lana said, "but don't get mad, Pops."

"Oh no, what did you do?"

Lana explained how she obtained Kyle's DNA sample.

"You did what?" Tuper sounded irritated.

"I've got his glove." She pulled it out, touching only the tip,
and held it up. "I'm sure Brad can use it to get DNA. Then
we'll know for certain if the switch was made in the hospital.
Right now, we're just speculating. You need to get Squirrely's

DNA. You can swab his cheek. Just take a clean Q-tip, wipe the inside of his mouth with it, and put it in a baggie. He'll never know you did it. It's not like it'll hurt him or anything."

"What if Patrick is the father, not Squirrely? Then we won't know anything more than we know now."

"So, get Amber's DNA too. Then we'll know for certain. Even if the baby was Patrick's, it'll still mean everything we found so far is true. I've spent hours tracking information for the Smythes. I connected them because of this child. If Kyle is not Amber's child, we need to look elsewhere for answers, and we need to do it soon. As it is, it'll take time to get the samples, drive them to the lab, and wait for the results. I say you do it. In the meantime, I'll keep looking. We need to know why Patrick was murdered in 1994. And if the hit-and-runs are connected, which seems likely, we need to know why it took twenty-five years for the killer to come after Squirrely and Karl. And another thing, why did Amber leave Kalispell right around the time Patrick was murdered? I'll keep working on those connections, but if we're looking in the wrong place, we need to find another angle."

"I'll think about it," Tuper said.

Lana smiled to herself. She knew that meant he would do it. He just couldn't come right out and say she was correct. "You do that, Pops."

They were quiet until they reached Clarice's house. Tuper unloaded her bike and said, "I'll see you later."

Lana didn't ask where he was going, but she was pretty certain he would have DNA samples when he returned.

"Wait," she said. "I'll be right back."

Lana dashed into the house, got several Q-tips from Clarice's bathroom, and stuck them in a baggie. She placed a few assorted-size baggies and the Q-tips into a larger bag and ran back outside before Tuper could leave.

"Here." She handed him the bag.

"What's this?"

"It's everything you'll need if you decide to get the samples. Just be careful with the Q-tips. Don't touch the ends and keep them separate from anything you get from Amber. You probably won't be able to get a swab, but grab something she drinks from, like a glass, or even a fork or spoon. I'm sure Brad could use any of those. Again, be careful you don't touch anything more than you have to."

Tuper shook his head and took the bag. "Humpf," he said and got in his car.

~

Tuper drove to the hospital and sat with Squirrely for a few minutes. He spoke to him about the DNA sample, even asking his permission, while knowing full-well he wouldn't get a response. Tuper struggled with the whole thing. Asking himself if he would want to know if he had a child out there. *Heck, I probably have several children I don't know about. It's better that way.* But if he was in Squirrely's position, it might be different. Amber was Squirrely's first love, and from what Tuper knew about him, maybe his only love. He figured Squirrely already knew. Tuper had learned a lot from the investigation that Squirrely had never intended for him to know, but did Squirrely know if Kyle was his son? *I guess if I find out and he wakes up, I can tell him I know, and he can decide whether he wants me to tell him. But Agony's right, we need some answers.*

He swabbed Squirrely's cheek, following Lana's instructions, and left the room.

Tuper checked the time. If he hurried, he could get to Amber's while she was still having supper. He knew this DNA task wouldn't be as easy, and he wasn't even certain he would go through with it. He could make that decision when he got there.

At the rehab center in Clancy, Tuper went directly to the dining area, arriving about halfway through the meal. Amber was at her usual table with her teddy bear on her lap. The woman in the wheelchair was sitting next to her. Tuper nodded when he walked up.

"Hello, Amber. How are you today?" When she didn't answer, he asked, "Where's Thelma?" Still nothing.

Tuper sat down and continued to chat with Amber. She kept eating without saying a word. This was new behavior. He hadn't seen "silent Amber" before. She usually said something, even if it didn't make much sense. But tonight, she kept looking at him, sometimes staring for long periods. Finally, she said, "Daddy?"

Tuper didn't know what to say, but it made his heart feel heavy. This poor woman had suffered all her life, and he wondered how much of it had to do with her experiences in high school, her pregnancy, and whatever else happened to her. Or maybe her mental problems were all genetic, but he had to get whatever answers he could. Maybe it wouldn't do her any good, but maybe it would. For all he knew, she could be in danger too. If the Smythes were trying to squelch any knowledge of the baby's birth, Amber would be in the most danger of all. He had made his decision, but he also thought it wouldn't hurt to answer Amber as if he were her father. It might bring her some comfort, and what harm could it do?

"Yes, Amber."

"I have a new friend. Her name is Tiffany. She has tons of Barbie dolls, and she let me play with them today."

"That's nice"—he hesitated for a second—"sweetie." Tuper felt uncomfortable, but he thought he should use some term of endearment.

"I know," she said.

"Drink your juice now, Amber."

Amber drank the remaining juice in her glass and smiled at him. "There."

"That's a good girl. I'm proud of you."

Tuper reached over and carefully retrieved the glass, not touching the rim. After glancing around, he slipped it into his gallon-size baggie.

CHAPTER 39

L ana woke up in the middle of the night and couldn't get back to sleep. She had too many unanswered questions running through her mind. She was convinced the same person who killed Patrick also killed Karl and had tried to kill Squirrely. There were too many similarities and too many connections between them. But why was Patrick killed in 1994 and then twenty-five years later, the killer came after Karl and Squirrely? And why did Amber bolt from the home in Kalispell a day or two after Patrick was killed?

Lana had a hunch that Patrick had been blackmailing the Smythes. She got up, fired up her laptop, and continued checking bank records for Patrick and the Smythes, which she had been working on for several days. She hit a dead end with Patrick. Either he never had an account, or the bank had destroyed his records because they were too old. She had discovered that most banks kept records for ten years after an account was closed, but some kept them longer. Most of the time, she could at least find a trail of the account even if the contents were empty, but with Patrick she found nothing. She tried every bank within a two-hundred-mile radius.

Rick Smythe's search was different, however. The senator started banking with First Interstate in the early seventies and continued his account with them up to the present. He also banked with Wells Fargo, which had acquired First Interstate Bancorp in 1996. Lana was quite familiar with the banking industry and knew her way around their security systems better than anywhere else. She shuddered when she saw that Smythe had an account with Bank of America. That was the one place she hated to hack. *He* would be there, and *he* would know if she dared to step in. If she had to check anything there, it would have to be quick.

She started with Wells Fargo, checking the withdrawals around the time Patrick was killed in 1994, but found nothing. She did the same with the First Interstate account, and after much research found a withdrawal of $20,000 in cash on April 25, 1994. It wasn't the same amount in the duffel bag, but it was something.

Lana still had the Bank of America account to check out, but she was nervous. It wasn't something she could do that quickly, and she didn't want to be inside the site very long. It was too dangerous, and when she was nervous, she was more likely to make mistakes. She decided to call on her friend Ravic. He could go in and do what she needed. She and Ravic had become cyber friends many years ago when she was a novice. He knew she wasn't a black-hat hacker, so he helped her when he could. They had never met, never had a phone conversation, and never exchanged text messages. Their only connection was in cyberspace. She knew nothing about his life in the real world, and as far as she could tell, he knew nothing about hers. She wasn't even certain of his gender.

They never discussed the world everyone else lived in. It was an unwritten rule that if anyone started asking personal questions, it was time to break away from them. Ravic never asked her anything, and vice-versa.

Lana went to Ravic's hacker account and posted a note.

—*R U busy? I need a favor.*

Ravic got a signal whenever anyone posted there. She had a special hacker account too, but very few people had that information. Ravic was one. He responded within a minute, apologizing for taking so long. She laughed at the absurdity that a minute was a long time in cyberspace.

—*Glad to help, Cricket. What's the job?*

Lana—*B of A again. I need to know if Senator Rick Smythe made any major withdrawals in early 1994, from Jan to mid-May.*

Ravic—*Really? Politics again? R U sure U want to go there?*

Lana—*It's not like that.*

Ravic—*Gotcha. I'll get back to U soon.*

Before she could type "thanks," he was gone. She wrote it anyway.

Lana was so engrossed in the web, she jumped when she heard a knock. It was still fairly dark out. She checked the time: 5:28. She went to the door and peeked out, then opened it. "You're early this morning."

"I saw the light, so I figured Clarice was up," Tuper said. "I didn't expect to see you awake already. Or haven't you gone to bed yet?"

"I woke up around three and couldn't sleep, so I've been working."

"Learn anything?" Tuper asked, as he walked into the kitchen and put tea water on.

She told him about the withdrawal from Smythe's account.

"That could be anything."

"I know. It's not much. I still think Patrick was blackmailing Smythe, and it ended in his demise. Otherwise, why would Smythe wait twenty-five years to kill Patrick? And then another twenty-five to kill Karl and/or Squirrely? What does the senator do, kill someone every twenty-five years whether he needs to or not?" She grimaced. "No, there's something missing, and I just can't put my finger on it. I know the money amount is not the same, but maybe all three men were blackmailing Smythe, and that was the share he gave to Squirrely. Who says it had to be divided equally?"

She paused for a second. Tuper waited.

"Besides, I have another bank account I'm checking. Maybe we'll find something else," Lana said. "Not only that, I learned a little more about Patrick Gallagher. I told you his work history was sporadic, but I discovered he lost at least two jobs for stealing from the company he was working for. Once it was for stealing a mop bucket, which just seems ludicrous. If you're going to steal, why not make it something worthwhile? I guess he figured that out, because the next job he lost was for stealing gas from the station he pumped at, and the third time he moved up to actual cash. He was never charged or convicted, just lost his jobs. It seems the once-handsome, charming Patrick Gallagher was a loser."

Tuper didn't say anything while he made his tea. He carried the cup back to the table and sat down. He stared at Lana for a few seconds.

"I know. I've been babbling, but I'm done now. Do you know anything new? How's Squirrely?"

Lana's computer barked.

Tuper said, "I took—"

Lana raised her hand to stop him from talking. "One sec."

The bark was the sound she had set for when she got a message on her cyber account. She checked to see what it was.

Ravic—*I checked it. Account wasn't opened until 1998. Want me to look anyway?*

Lana—*No, not now. Thanks.*

Ravic—*Always. I'm here to serve.*

When Lana didn't say anything right away, Tuper asked, "Well?"

"Symthe's other bank account was opened four years after Patrick died, so that's no help."

Without any small talk, Tuper said, "I took the DNA samples to my friend Brad. He'll run them in his lab. He said he wasn't that busy right now, so it shouldn't take long."

"You got Squirrely's DNA?"

"And Amber's. I took a juice glass she'd been drinking from. Brad said it should work and the gloves were perfect. He said he always gets good DNA from gloves, unless, of course, too many people have worn them."

"I didn't think about that. They were older gloves, and I assumed they were his personal gear. Who knows? They could be a pair he keeps in the truck that other people wear too, but I don't think so. He took them out of a canvas bag, which I expect was his own. Did Brad give you a time frame?"

"He'll call when they're ready, but it won't be more than a few days."

"Great. I learned something else that might be helpful, but we'll need to do more investigating."

Tuper looked skeptical. He always did when Lana used the word *we.* "What is it?"

"I checked neighbors and friends for Rick and Jenny Smythe, but most of them are not that accessible. Some have died, some moved, others have lived close, but have no apparent connection to the Smythes. A few of them we could go talk to, but that'll take a lot of time. Finding out what people know is a lot harder than checking a document or a record. So, I decided to check the US Census to see if anyone else lived with them over the years. It was very interesting." She paused for effect.

"And?" Tuper asked.

"In the 1970 Census—"

This time Tuper interrupted her. "I thought the Census wasn't public until fifty years after it was done."

"Actually, it's seventy-two years after. I'm not sure why that number, but I could look it up if you'd like. Anyway, you're right, it's not public, but that doesn't mean I can't see the data."

"Of course, it doesn't," Tuper grumbled.

"So, do you want to hear what I learned?"

"Yes," he said in the same tone.

"In 1970, when Kyle was a year old, they had a nanny living with them named Esmeralda Garcia. She was still there in 1980 when he was eleven, and she stayed even after he left home. However, in both the 1990 and 2000 Census, she's listed as a housekeeper. But she was not in the household in 2010."

Lana always stopped whenever she reached a dramatic moment, partly to make sure Tuper was listening. She knew that bugged him more than her incessant chatter, as he called it. He seemed to be getting used to her pauses, or at least he didn't complain as much, but she loved riling him any way she could, so she kept it up.

"Your point?" Tuper finally asked.

"This woman probably knows all the family secrets."

"Do you know where she lives now?"

"No, but I will soon, and then we can go see her if she's local, which I think she is."

"We?"

"Yes, I need a break from this computer, Pops. You don't get to do all the fun stuff."

CHAPTER 40

Tuper pulled into a trailer park with single-wide mobile homes and parked in front of #23. A large dent on the side matched the screen hanging off the front window. The home was old and in serious disrepair, which Tuper noticed made it no different than the others they passed coming into the park.

"What if she won't talk to us?" Tuper asked, not getting out yet.

"She will," Lana said.

"What makes you so sure?"

"Because you're very persuasive. But mostly because this woman was a member of the Smythe household for forty years, and I'm sure she thought she was part of the family. Then one day she suddenly has to leave. I'm betting they got rid of her because the heat was on political figures, you know, the ones who were fighting immigration while they had undocumented workers in their own homes. The senator was one of them. If that's the case, I'm betting Esmeralda is bitter."

"Unless he gave her a handsome payoff."

Lana looked around the neighborhood. "Does it look like she was paid handsomely?"

"Maybe she already spent the money."

"That's possible. But if she's undocumented, he could just turn her in if she said anything. He didn't need to pay her off."

"Let me do the talking," Tuper said, as he finally opened his door. "Better yet, why don't you stay in the car?"

"Right, that's gonna happen." Lana got out.

They carefully walked up the wooden steps, both wondering if they might collapse at any moment. A board on the side was pulled away from the frame, hanging, as if it was about to fall off. Paint was peeling, leaving patches of brown on the dirty-white exterior. Tuper knocked on the door.

A woman of Mexican descent, who appeared to be in her seventies, answered the door.

"Esmeralda?"

"Yes, that's me."

"Do you know Senator Smythe?"

She started to close the door. "Go away and leave me alone."

Lana stepped forward. "Please, ma'am, we need your help. It's for Kyle."

Esmeralda re-opened the partially shut door. "Is he okay?"

"He is now, but worrisome things are going on. Please, may we come in and talk to you for a few minutes?"

"Are you cops?"

"No, we're not," Lana said. "But two people connected to Kyle have been killed, and another one is in serious condition. We're investigating on our own because one of the victims is a dear friend."

Esmeralda opened the screen. "Come in." She invited them to sit on her worn sofa. In contrast to the exterior, although everything was old, the place was sparkling clean and tidy. "I'm not sure I can be of help. I haven't even seen Kyle in quite some time."

"We think the recent events stem from something that happened a long time ago, so you may know more than you realize," Lana said. "And we'd appreciate anything you can tell us."

"I'll do what I can, but if it has anything to do with the senator, I don't want to get involved."

"Why would you think it's about the senator?"

"Because that's who I worked for, and he's not a nice man."

"You worked there for quite a while, right?" Lana asked.

"Over forty years. I was only eighteen when I started."

"Why did you leave?"

"They didn't need me anymore." Esmeralda sighed. "I gave my life to that family, and they just dumped me. Rick really liked me when I was eighteen. I was pretty back then, young and thin too. Now I'm old and used up. I never had my own life. I gave my best years to the senator and to Kyle. I loved Kyle though. He was the best part of my life. When they let me go, I wanted to go help Kyle and his children, but I couldn't."

"Why?"

"The senator didn't want me affiliated with his family in any way. I could've been a big help to Kyle. I didn't want a paycheck, just room and board and incidentals. I don't need much."

"Were you there when Kyle was born?" Lana asked.

"No, I didn't go to work for them until Kyle was a month old. Jenny needed help, and I fell in love with that little boy right from the start. Putting up with Rick, her husband, was another story."

"Why is that?" Lana asked. Tuper just sat there, watching

Lana in motion. He was impressed with how she was able to get Esmeralda to open up. Of course, he'd never tell her that because it would go straight to her head.

"So many things," Esmeralda said, then stopped.

"Did you know Rick's father, Tim Smythe?" Lana decided to call the senator by his first name because Esmeralda had done so. Lana hoped it would open up more personal thoughts.

"He was the worst. All the Smythe men think they own their women, except Kyle. He is very good to his wife. He treats her like an equal—no, better than that. He worships her. But not his father or his grandfather. They are both power-hungry, chauvinistic pigs. You can only imagine how they were with their hired help. Tim Smythe only wanted young girls as housekeepers. They went through a lot of house-keepers over the years. Several left pregnant."

"And you think Tim Smythe was the father?"

"I know he was."

"And Rick didn't treat you well?"

"He did at first," Esmeralda said.

"Why did you stay?"

"I loved Kyle, and I needed the job. And Jenny was always pleasant, even though Rick cheated on her and treated her like scum. Her mother-in-law wasn't a nice person either, but maybe if I had to put up with a husband like hers, I wouldn't have been nice either." She paused. "I'm sorry, I'm ranting. I've tried to get rid of the anger, and most days, I'm okay. But when I think about all the time I gave them and how I have nothing to show for it, the whole thing upsets me again. I'm madder at myself than them. I was never strong enough to stand up to them. And now I'm angry because Kyle's children are growing up, and I can't be there for him."

"Did you ever hear Rick or Jenny say anything about Kyle's birth?"

"Only that he was born in Lewistown because they were traveling when Jenny went into labor. What are you getting at?"

"It's not important," Lana said. "Did you see much of Tim Smythe over the years?"

"Yeah, he came around a lot, and we went to his house too. I usually went along so I could take care of Kyle."

"I want you to think carefully. Did you ever hear either of them mention a woman named Amber?"

Esmeralda shook her head.

"What about Frank or Frankie Finnigan?"

"No."

"Patrick Gallagher?"

"No."

"What about Karl Haberman?"

"No, I'm sorry, but they talked about a lot of people. They could've, and I just don't remember." Her brows drew closer, and her face tightened. "There might be something about when Kyle was a newborn."

"What's that?"

"I was cleaning Rick's office, and Rick and Tim were in there talking. Rick got a call and gave the phone to his father. Tim was loud and giving orders. He said something about a car accident, but I don't think that was the real concern. The reason I remember it at all was because when he hung up, he said, 'Kyle is safe now. We're all good.' I couldn't help myself, so I asked if there was something wrong with Kyle. Rick assured me everything was fine and asked me to leave the room and finish cleaning later. They obviously didn't want me to hear any more, but it really wasn't my business."

"When was that?"

"Early on, not too long after I started working for them. I tried not to hear much after that."

Lana gave an understanding nod, then asked, "Do you have a job now?"

"I clean houses and offices. I'm too old to get a decent job, and I don't have any education. I wanted to help Kyle after I got my citizenship papers, but the senator found out and told me I couldn't."

"But if you had citizenship, he didn't have leverage over you anymore."

"He told me if I wanted to keep breathing, I needed to stay away from his family," Esmeralda said, her voice tight. "He said I'd never know when it was coming. I still wake up sometimes from the nightmares. And when I'm in public and I hear a loud noise, it makes me jump. As long as he's in office, I don't dare cross him. But one thing is for sure."

"What's that?" Lana asked.

"He'll never get my vote."

CHAPTER 41

Tuper and Lana returned to Clarice's house, and Lana immediately took out her computer and sat down to work. Tuper and Clarice sat at the table chatting when Lana shouted, "OMG!"

"What is it?" Clarice asked.

Lana didn't answer. Instead, she dashed over to the sofa, reached behind it, and removed the duffel bag. Lana flipped through the stacks of hundred-dollar bills. "Just as I thought," she mumbled.

"You thought what?" Clarice asked.

"Do you have any idea how long Squirrely has had this money?" Lana asked, looking at Tuper.

"No," Tuper said, "but he's had the duffel bag a long time. I've seen it before, but I never knew what was inside."

"Well, someone has had this money for about a quarter of a century."

"How do you know that?" Tuper asked.

"Because all those hundred-dollar bills were printed before 1996. That's when they made the first major design change since 1929. Look," she said, holding up one of the bills "See the size of Benjamin Franklin? He was smaller on this design. It's actually a different image, but it's hard to tell because he looks just the same. Yet if you look at his clothes, you can see the difference. Watch." Lana brought up an image of a hundred-dollar bill with the 1996 changes on her monitor and turned the screen toward Tuper and Clarice. "See his collar. And look how much bigger his face is. The changes were made to prevent counterfeiting. They added a lot of security measures too, like the watermark with optically variable ink." She pointed to the screen. "Right there to Franklin's right. The ink changes from green to black at different angles. The reserve also added a fine line around Franklin and Independence Hall, but that's hard to see with the naked eye. And also very hard to reproduce. The seal is different too, and they added a letter to the serial number. The first of the 1996 series was produced in October of 1995, so this money was gathered together before that date. What are the chances of having that many hundred-dollar bills with none printed after 1996? Someone put that bunch of cash together a long time ago." Lana sighed.

"You think Squirrely has had it for the past twenty-five years?" Tuper asked.

"That's one possibility. Maybe he got the money long ago from Patrick, or from one of the Smythes, but he felt too guilty to spend it."

"Or maybe someone else had the money all these years, and Squirrely just got his hands on it," Clarice chimed in. "And that's why he got run over."

"Either way, it still seems to lead back to Patrick's death in May of 1994." Lana paused for just a second. "Or to when Amber left Kalispell."

"Or both," Tuper said. "But how can we ever find that out?"

"Why don't you ask Amber?" Lana suggested.

"I'm not sure she could tell us anything, but it's worth a try." Tuper stood. "I'll be back for supper."

Clarice shook her head but smiled. "Of course, you will."

Tuper joined Thelma and Amber at the table. He found it was easier to catch her if he went at mealtime. The woman in the wheelchair wasn't there.

"She's having a really good day," Thelma said.

"Great. She doesn't get that many." He turned to Amber. "Hello, Amber. Do you remember me?"

"Yes, you're my friend, but I'm sorry I don't know your name."

"It's Tuper." He didn't say anything about being her brother, in case she corrected him in front of Thelma. He figured it was easy to explain, but he didn't want to take a chance.

Thelma reached for her walker. Tuper pulled it closer to her, and she pushed herself up. "I'll leave you two alone to visit."

As soon as Thelma left, Tuper asked, "Amber, do you remember living in Kalispell?"

"Yes, it was a nice place. I liked it there."

"Why did you leave?"

Amber's mouth opened, but nothing came out. A blank look covered her face. Then she said softly, "I don't know."

"Do you remember leaving there?"

"Yes, two men came and got me in the night."

"Did they bring you here?"

"No, they took me to a hotel to meet my parents. We traveled around a little. It was nice. Then we came here. I think I've been here ever since."

"Yes, you have." Tuper smiled. "Do you have any idea why they took you out of the home in Kalispell?"

"My parents said it wasn't safe because Patrick was causing trouble again."

"What kind of trouble?"

She shook her head. "I don't remember."

Tuper wanted to ask about her baby, but she was having a good day, and he was afraid it would put her over the edge. She had so few good days, he couldn't ruin it for her. Besides, he had learned what he came for. Patrick had been stirring things up, and as a result he was killed, and Amber moved. Everything led back to the Smythes and Patrick's father and the damage control they did in Roy, Montana.

CHAPTER 42

Tuper left Amber and drove back to Helena, stopping at the hospital to check on Squirrely. He stepped out of the elevator and started down the long hallway toward the ICU. He saw a man at the other end near Squirrely's door. He thought the guy came out of Squirrely's room, but he couldn't be sure. The man walked toward him. They passed about halfway, but neither spoke. Tuper glanced over to see if he recognized him, but he didn't. The man kept his head down and didn't make eye contact.

Just as Tuper reached Squirrely's door, two nurses pushed past him and entered the room. Tuper followed them inside.

"What happened?" Tuper asked.

"Please wait outside."

Tuper stepped out, but before the door closed behind him, he heard someone comment about a machine being unplugged. Tuper ran down the hallway toward the elevator. He pushed the button and waited.

Before the door opened, a security guard approached. "Sir, I need to talk to you."

"We need to catch that guy," Tuper said.

"What guy?"

The elevator door opened, and Tuper stepped inside.

"Sir," the security guard said, moving to block the elevator door from closing. "You need to come with me."

"You need to come with *me*," Tuper argued. "We need to catch the man who just left Squir ..., uh, Frank Finnigan's room."

"That was you."

"I went in after the nurses. Before that, I saw a man come out of his room. We need to catch him before he gets away."

The guard stepped inside the elevator. A young couple tried to get on, but the security guy held up his hand, "Take another elevator, please." He let the door close behind him.

When they reached the first floor, they looked around in the crowd, then hurried out to the parking lot. But Tuper couldn't find him. "He could be anywhere by now."

"Right," the security said, as if he only half believed him.

"I should get back to my friend," Tuper said.

"No, first you need to come with me."

Tuper glared at him.

"We need to ask you some questions, and at the very least, you need to give us a description of the man you saw."

Tuper sat in a little cubicle, answering questions thrown at him by hospital security until the police arrived. Then he answered the same questions all over again. The last line of interrogation came from the detective. By then, they had information from the security tapes. "Do you know anyone who would want to harm your friend?"

"Just Senator Smythe."

"This Frank Finnigan knows the senator?"

"As far as I know, they've never met."

"So why would Senator Smythe want to kill him?"

"You'll have to ask the senator."

"You're a crazy old coot, aren't you?"

"So, I've been told. Can I go now?"

"Get out of here."

Squirrely was resting well with no apparent damage done by the intruder so Tuper left. By the time he got to Clarice's house, she had gone to bed, and Lana was back to work on her computer.

"Where have you been, Pops?"

"It's a long story."

"If you hooked up with one of those ladies at the home, I don't want to hear it."

"You're sick, Agony."

"I never know about you. Although, they are a little old for your taste." She pointed to the kitchen. "Clarice left you a plate. It's in the refrigerator. Get your food and tell me what happened."

When Tuper finished his story, Lana said, "That's not good. Or maybe it is. Maybe they'll put a watch on Squirrely's room so the guy can't come back."

"I spoke with my friend at the sheriff's office. He said they already put someone on it."

"Do you think the attack came from the senator? Do you really think he's been killing people to cover up how he got his child? If that's the case, why hasn't Amber's life been threatened? Maybe it has. Obviously, her parents thought so. They had her secretly moved from Kalispell in the night. And maybe the senator's henchmen haven't been able to find her since. Or maybe because she has dementia, they think no one would believe her anyway. Besides, I checked out the senator's whereabouts when Squirrely was run down. He was in Washington DC at some big meeting, then I thought he could've hired someone to do it. But that would be foolish too, because then more people would know his shady little secrets. But maybe he just has one thug who does his dirty work, and he trusts him."

"Agony," Tuper interrupted. "What's your point?"

"What if it's not the senator?"

"Then who?"

"Maybe it was Jenny, his wife, Kyle's mother."

"Yeah, I know who Jenny is."

"The Smythes own two homes, one in the DC area and one here in Helena where they raised Kyle. But Kyle moved out nearly thirty years ago. Jenny probably stays here so she can be near her grandchildren. And we know her husband is a womanizer, so maybe she doesn't want to be with him anyway. But she has as much, maybe more, at stake in keeping the circumstances of their child's birth a secret. Maybe she's the one who's been running these people down."

Tuper had to admit the thought had crossed his mind as well. "But how can we prove any of that? Whether it was Jenny or the senator, we have no proof."

"But you have cop buddies, like that Johnson guy. Can't you give him the information you have and let them handle it? They could get the feds involved. I bet they already have a file on the senator. Maybe this would get them rolling."

"I can't do that to Squirrely. He either doesn't know about Kyle, or he's spent a lifetime keeping it a secret. I'm not going to out him now."

"But as long as he's alive, he's in danger of someone coming after him again."

"I thought about that, but as long as the cops have a watch on his door, he should be safe. When he comes out of the coma, he can decide what he wants to do."

"What about Amber? She could be at risk too."

"I don't think so. She's so far gone that no one would take her seriously. And I really doubt if anyone, other than her sister, even knows where she is."

"That's true, and it's not like she has any ties to the government." Lana turned to her laptop again. "I've been doing a lot of digging, but there's not much to be found on dear old Amber. She doesn't have a driver's license, nor does she file tax returns. She doesn't get social security or any kind of disability. She's been tucked away most of her life."

"Who pays for the home in Clancy?"

"It's paid by a trust, but I don't know who set it up. I've been working on that, but so far, I can't tell where it comes from. My best guess is that her parents or her sister provide for her, but I can't be sure. Actually, I doubt it's her parents because they didn't have any money back then. Heck, they couldn't even afford insurance. So, unless they hit the lottery or struck gold or something, the money probably doesn't come from them. Which means, I have more searching to do."

CHAPTER 43

B rad Bergstad, a man in his early forties, wearing shorts, a plaid shirt, and a baseball cap, greeted Tuper in the lobby of the DNA lab. Tuper knew Brad was willing to help him in any way he could to pay back what Tuper had done for him and his father decades ago. Tuper and Brad's father had been good friends for many years, and he'd stepped up when Brad's parents got a divorce. He'd given the two men a home for a couple of months and saved Brad from his delinquent self on more than one occasion. Brad's success was payment enough for Tuper, but he appreciated Brad and his DNA lab, which had recently helped him find a missing six-year-old boy. And now he needed his services again.

Brad shook his hand. "You're the only person I know who consistently asks for maternity tests. Most women know when they give birth to a child." Brad gave him a quizzical look. "It's the father who's usually in question."

"Strange circumstances."

Brad handed over two envelopes. "I labeled them *Mother*

and *Father* since you didn't want any names on the documents."

"Thanks, Brad, I appreciate it. And thanks for rushing them."

Tuper chatted with him for a bit, then stuck the envelopes in his front pocket.

"I thought you were anxious to see the results. Aren't you going to read them?"

"There's someone even more anxious. I'll let her be the first to know."

Brad tilted his head and narrowed his eyes. "Was that *your* DNA, Toop?"

"No, not this time." He tipped his hat and left.

Tuper walked into Clarice's house and handed the envelopes to Lana.

"What are these?"

"The DNA test results."

Lana's eyes widened. "You haven't opened them yet? Aren't you dying to know the results? I can't believe you haven't read them already."

"I thought you'd want to be the first," Tuper said. "Go ahead."

"Thanks. I'm opening Amber's first. If it's not her kid, then it sure isn't Squirrely's."

Lana ripped open the envelope and looked over the information. She smiled. "Kyle is Amber's baby boy. We were right. Amber had a child, and the Smythes ended up with it, probably as a payoff for keeping Patrick out of prison."

Tuper nodded. Lana reached for the other envelope.

"I don't want to know who the father is," Tuper said.

"Really? Why not?"

"We know everything we really need to know. It doesn't matter to us whether the father was Patrick or Squirrely."

"It kind of does matter, but only if Squirrely isn't the father. If he is the father, then it's pretty likely they traded the kid for his freedom. If he's not the father, then it was likely Patrick's, and we get the same result. However, we can't really know for sure if it's Patrick's kid because we have no way to test. Maybe it was Karl's. He hung around with them too." Suddenly her eyes opened wide. "Maybe it was Tim Smythe. Esmeralda said he was a real womanizer. Maybe he charmed the poor girl." She sighed. "But there's no way to know that either. And I suppose it would all still come out the same, especially if no one knew who the father was." Lana smiled. "Anyway, aren't you curious? I am."

"You can look, but don't tell me. If Frankie wakes up, I don't want to be keeping a secret from him. If I don't know the truth, I won't have to."

"But what if he wants to know?"

"Then you can tell us both."

"You live a strange kind of truth, Pops."

Lana took her time opening the second envelope. She looked at Tuper with a blank expression, giving no sign of what was inside. "Okay," she said, returning the paternity test to the envelope.

"I also stopped by and saw Squirrely this morning. They're keeping watch and even followed me when I went in."

"They probably still don't trust you."

"Actually, I'm the only person on the approved list to see

him. Anyone else who shows up is considered suspect, and the detective is to be notified. But I don't care if they watch me; it's not like I'll be doing anything wrong."

"You mean like taking more DNA samples from the guy in the coma?"

Tuper scowled. "Have you learned anything new?"

"No, I still haven't busted through on the trust that funds Amber. Although, I've pretty much eliminated her parents as the donor, which was no surprise. They had no assets except the house they owned in Roy, which was worth about $35,000. They sold that and moved to Arizona, then any money they had was used up when her father got cancer."

"What about her sister?"

"She's a possibility but not looking likely either. Her husband worked for the government and has a decent retirement. She worked as a CPA, took off for a while to raise her family, then did seasonal tax-filing gigs. She never went back to work full-time. I haven't found any fantastic real estate investments or anything. Her husband came from a military family, so there was no big trust fund left to him. Even if there had been, someone has been paying for her care for over fifty years. That was long before they would've had money."

"Maybe her support was part of the original deal and came from old man Smythe, the attorney general."

"I thought about that, but he didn't have that much money. Whoever set it up, structured it so the payments came from a non-profit corporation, funded by a trust, that helped people in need with certain mental problems—and she was one of the lucky ones."

"But you don't believe that?"

"No. The non-profit was set up the year after Kyle was

born, and Amber has been the only recipient of the awards. A few little grants have been paid out to others, probably to make it look legit for tax purposes, but the real money goes to Amber's care."

"So that pretty much leaves the senator. Maybe he isn't such a bad guy after all."

CHAPTER 44

Lana had hit so many dead ends that she needed a break. She decided to focus on something more interesting and, hopefully, fruitful—finding her knight in shining armor. Or at least a cowboy in his Silverado. She googled Brock Shero and found no Twitter, Facebook, or other social media accounts for him. Either that wasn't his real name or he didn't do social media. She liked the last thought, although the first was intriguing as well. After all, she had been living incognito for a long time herself. On the other hand, if he was sent to find her, he would have *wrong-named* her too. Now, she had to investigate further.

She checked the DMV site and found his driver's license. The picture matched, so he was real. The license plate number was assigned to his Silverado truck, which was registered in his name. She felt a little better. But just because he was local didn't mean he wasn't hired to find her. No, that didn't make sense. If her stalker hired someone locally, he already knew where she was. And if he knew where she was, he would've approached her by now. *I'm being paranoid.*

She continued her search into Brock Shero. He was a local boy who grew up on a small ranch just outside of Helena. He wrestled in high school, got average grades, and joined the army right after he graduated. He spent four years in the service, then attended Helena College University of Montana for two years, majoring in fire and rescue. He joined the Helena Fire Department after college and had worked there ever since. So, he had a respectable job and wasn't likely corrupt. A little smile tugged on Lana's face.

He had no criminal record, but two speeding tickets, one five years ago and one when he was nineteen. She could find no record of marriage or children, at least not in the state of Montana. He had two older sisters, both married and living away from home, and a younger brother, twenty-five, who still lived on the ranch with his parents. Brock had purchased a home in East Helena two years ago, and it was listed as his residence. He sounded legit. But if *he* hired Brock, he would definitely look legitimate. He was good at what he did, and he was nothing if not thorough.

Lana wanted to see Brock again, at least thank him, but she didn't dare. She had a good thing going here in Helena, and she didn't want to mess that up. Yet she knew if he was sent to find her or taunt her, it was too late anyway. She decided to wait and see if he *coincidentally* showed up again. Her frustration mounted. This was what her life had become, and she wondered how long she would have to look over her shoulder. As she saw it now, it could be forever.

Feeling vulnerable, she checked her Hotmail to see if any new messages had come in. There was nothing. She sighed with relief. A moment later, she wondered about the silence. The lack of emails made her even more suspicious. Was he deliberately not contacting her because he already knew where she was? Lana didn't want to be forced to leave Helena. This was the closest she'd come to having a family in a long time. Even though Pops could be pretty annoying, she liked it here. She slammed her laptop shut with frustration.

"Whoa. What's that all about?" Tuper suddenly came into the room.

"Nothing," she said, "I just need a break. And I'd like to take a bike ride, but I can't do that." She shrugged. "I don't know when I'll be able to get my bike fixed, or if I can. I think it's pretty hopeless, so I guess I'll have to buy another one." She knew that would take a while, since she had very little money. She could easily hack into any account and get money, but that wasn't in her nature. She was not a thief. She would earn the money the old-fashioned way, but she wasn't getting enough hours at Nickels, and she gave most of her pay to Clarice for room and board.

"Let's go," Tuper said.

"Go where?"

"Just come on, Agony, and bring your bike." He walked toward the door. "I know a guy."

They drove to a house in East Helena with a circular drive-way. Tuper pulled in past the house and parked in front of the large metal shop about thirty feet to the left. A large sign hung over the door that read *MacFarlane's*. A fat-tire cruiser leaned against the outside wall.

Tuper opened the hatchback and reached for Lana's bike.

"I got it, Pops," Lana said, grabbing it first.

Once inside, there were bicycles everywhere. Some were standing as if ready to ride, others were taken apart or in stages of being built. A large workbench at the back of the shop was covered with parts. Tools hung on pegs on the wall, and a large tool chest stood next to the workbench. In spite of the overwhelming quantity of bikes and parts, everything seemed to be in order.

A man in his late fifties with short, gray hair and glasses approached them.

"Hello, Toop. I haven't seen you in a while." The man reached out and shook his hand, then looked at the bike. "You haven't been riding, have you?"

"Not a chance. Dave, this is Agony. It's her bike."

"My name is Lana," she said. "I had an accident. The frame is pretty bent. I don't know if it can be fixed."

Dave took the bike and looked it over. "Does it have any sentimental value?"

"No, I just need something to get around."

"Then I wouldn't spend any money to fix it." He pointed to a row of bikes in the back. "I have several similar to, or better than, this one."

"I don't have the cash right now, but I'll look to see what you've got."

Dave glanced at Tuper, who gave him a nod. Dave turned back to Lana. "I can make you a good deal, and you can make payments, if you want."

"I'd better wait until I have the money. Just let me see what it's going to cost." She walked over to the row of bikes.

"Did you see that old Schwinn Firenze road bike when you walked in?"

"The green one against the wall?"

"Yes, I can loan you that until you can afford to get one. It's rare, but it has no real value."

"Really?"

"I'd be glad to."

"Why?" Lana asked, attempting to keep a neutral facial expression.

"Let's just say I owe Tuper a favor, and he'll never need a bike. His horse would be jealous. Keep it as long as you need, and when you get the money, come back and I'll make you a good deal."

As they walked to the car, Lana asked, "Is there anyone in this town who doesn't owe you a favor?"

"A few."

CHAPTER 45

"Whoa!" Lana said with more volume than she intended and without looking up from her laptop.

"What is it?" Tuper asked.

"I was checking the hospital records and guess what I discovered?" As usual she didn't wait for a response. "Squirrely's bill has been paid. Who would do that? It made no sense to me, so I investigated further and found the source." She stopped talking, like she usually did when Tuper actually wanted to hear what she had to say.

"Who?"

"Not a who, but a what."

"Agony, you're not making any sense."

"It was paid by the same non-profit corporation that's been paying for Amber's care all these years. Who would do that? It must be the Smythes, but that doesn't make any sense. Why would they try to kill him, then pay for his care? Something is totally messed up here."

Tuper's phone rang, interrupting her babble. Tuper took the call and stood to go. "I'm headed to the hospital."

"Who was that?" Lana asked. "Is Squirrely awake? Is he worse? He didn't die, did he?"

"Stop, Agony. That was Deputy Johnson. He said the senator's wife is at the hospital to see Squirrely."

Lana jumped up. "Well, let's go."

"I think it might be better if I handle this one alone."

"Really? Who's the one who got Esmeralda to talk?"

Tuper sighed. "All right, but let me take the lead." He paused. "On second thought, you better stay here. I'm going to confront her with the truth, and that might put my life in jeopardy. I don't want you in the same boat."

"I'm not scared," Lana said, walking to the door, thinking this was the safest she had felt in a long time. A little hit-and-run killer was the least of her worries.

"That's the problem," Tuper mumbled. "You should be."

Tuper and Lana walked into Squirrely's room and found Jenny Smythe, an attractive, petite woman with very little makeup sitting next to his bed. Her softly curled, ash brown hair complimented her perfect olive skin. She spoke tenderly to Squirrely. An officer stood near the door, watching. Jenny looked up and gave them a gracious smile. "He's still not awake," she said in a compassionate voice.

Tuper walked over. "We need to talk," he said. "But not here."

She stood. "I could use a cup of coffee."

Very little was said on the walk to the cafeteria. They found a secluded table in a far corner.

"I'll get the drinks," Lana offered. "What would you like?"

"Coffee with a little cream, no sugar," Jenny said.

As Lana left, Tuper introduced himself. "I'm Frank's best friend."

"Nice to meet you. I'm Jenny Smythe, but you already know that, don't you?"

"I do."

"How much do you know?"

"I know about Amber and the baby and the deal that was made." He didn't want to say too much until he knew what Jenny's intentions were.

"How is Amber? I know she isn't well, but is she doing okay?"

"She has some good days and some bad."

Lana returned with coffee for Jenny and herself and a cup of tea for Tuper. She set them on the table. "What did I miss?"

"Not much," Tuper said. "Jenny, this is Lana. She's ..." He didn't know what title to give her.

"I'm his partner. Not life partner, or anything like that." Lana shuddered. "We sort of work together. I'm basically his technical assistant, because he doesn't know anything about technology. I mean nothing. He still has a flip-phone."

"I think she got the point, Agony."

"My name is Lana," she said, extending her hand. "Nice to meet you, Jenny. Are you the one paying for Frank's care?"

"I like you," Jenny said, nodding. "You don't beat around the bush. Yes, I'm the one funding the non-profit."

"So, you've been paying for Amber's care as well?"

A slight rise in her vocal pitch showed her surprise at the question. "You know about that too?" She shrugged slightly. "Yes, she needed the help."

"Does your husband know?" Lana asked.

So much for taking the lead, Tuper thought.

"Yes, but it's my money. I inherited quite a substantial trust."

"Did you try to kill Frank?" Lana asked.

"No! Of course not. Why would I do that? He gave me the greatest gift I could ever have. Kyle is the best thing that ever happened to me. And now I have three beautiful grandchildren. I would have none of them without him and Amber."

"I can think of lots of reasons you might want Frank dead, but we won't go into those right now. Do you know who tried to kill him?"

"No," Jenny said. "I wish I did."

"What about Patrick?"

"What about him?"

"You said Frank gave you Kyle, but how do you know Patrick wasn't the father? Did you have a test done?"

"No, there was never a test. I still don't know for certain who the father was. It doesn't matter anymore."

"Did your husband try to kill Frank?"

"No, he would have no reason to either."

"Unless he was worried about his career," Lana said.

"Rick loves his job, and all the power and prestige that goes with it, but he'd never go that far. There was no need to. I told both of the boys that if they ever needed anything to come to me. Patrick did once. He was pretty down on his luck and needed a car."

"How much did you give him?"

"Twenty thousand. He bought a used car and still had some left. Then he died less than two weeks later."

"And you're sure your husband didn't kill him?" Tuper asked.

"No doubt in my mind, and it's not because I believe in Rick or love him. I don't. That ship sailed a long time ago. We live separate lives, so the marriage is just for appearance." For a moment, she looked wistful. "I don't even like him much anymore, but killing someone is not something he'd do or pay to have done. He's a pig, much like his father, but he's no killer. At the time, I wondered if my father-in-law had gone after Patrick, but when I found out the exact time he was hit, I realized Tim was with us."

"He could have hired someone," Tuper said.

"No, he would never let someone have that kind of leverage over him. I'm sure if Tim wanted Patrick dead, he would've killed him himself. Besides, my father-in-law is dead now, so he couldn't have hit Frank."

"But after Patrick was killed, you were concerned enough to have Amber moved from Kalispell?" Tuper asked, taking over the questioning.

"Yes, I facilitated that," Jenny said, unsurprised by the inquiry. "Amber's parents contacted me because they were worried. I had her removed and brought to them, and they found the place in Clancy. It was a bit of a mess, and it took a while to get the funding transferred."

"Did you know Patrick was in the hospital after that vehicle hit him, and then he disappeared?"

"What do you mean?" Jenny looked startled this time.

"There was a John Doe in the hospital with the same exact injuries as Patrick. He was in no condition to walk out, yet he left the hospital mysteriously, and the next day, Patrick was found dead."

"I know nothing about that. I had no idea what happened to Patrick. All I heard was that he was dead, and his body was pretty beat up."

"I'm confused about one thing," Lana said. "You had

resources and a respectable family. Why didn't you adopt a child instead of going the clandestine route?"

"Impatience, more than anything. I was raised wealthy and used to getting my way. I didn't want to wait two years to get a child, then possibly lose him or her because the parents changed their minds. I didn't want one from another country, and I wanted the world to think he was mine. So, when this opportunity arrived, I jumped on it." Jenny shifted in her chair and seemed to drift back in time. "I wore stomach pillows that made me look pregnant and went through all the motions. My friends all thought I was pregnant. When the baby was due, we traveled to Lewistown and waited until Amber went into labor." She paused and shook her head. "Looking back, I realize what a spoiled brat I was, but still, I wouldn't change a second of my time with Kyle, so I guess I'm not truly sorry. Except for all the pain and suffering Amber has gone through, and I've done what I could to make up for that. I know it's not much, but it's all I know to do." Jenny's chin dropped to her chest. "Amber changed her mind after the baby was born and wanted to keep him. I know that because I overheard my father-in-law talking to my husband. Rick lied about it, and said I misunderstood, but I know what I heard."

"What *did* you hear?"

"Amber called James Gallagher and told him she couldn't give her son up, but Gallagher told her it was too late because all the paperwork had been done. He told her she'd go to prison for fraud, and that her parents would too because they were involved."

"Because when Amber checked into the hospital, she used your name?" Lana asked.

"Yes, my father-in-law made sure she had ID that said she

was Jenny Smythe, with my address. She claimed to not have any insurance, and we paid cash for the hospital stay. We did the same with her prenatal care to keep the insurance companies out of it. Kyle went home with Amber, and the next day, her parents brought him to us as planned." Jenny took a deep breath. "I should've stopped everything when I found out Amber wanted to keep him, but I couldn't, even though I knew it was the right thing to do. But I was so set on starting my life as a mother that I couldn't get myself to say anything. I had seen Kyle at the hospital, and I know it sounds crazy, but I loved him already. And, as I said, I was spoiled and privileged, so it was easy to convince myself that I was a better choice for a mother. If Amber took him, she might change her mind later and not want him, and that wouldn't be good for the baby."

Lana waited to make sure she was done talking and then asked, "What about Karl?"

Jenny's brow furrowed. "Who's Karl?"

"Karl Haberman."

"I don't know him."

"He was the other boy who was in the accident in 1969."

Jenny tilted her head and pursed her lips, looking confused. "What accident? I really don't know what or who you're talking about."

CHAPTER 46

"Do you believe her?" Lana asked, as they drove away from the hospital. "She sure sounds convincing, but we already know she tells lies. She's been living with a big one all her life. But why would she pretend to not know Karl? She fessed up to everything else. What would she have to gain by lying about the accident or Karl? Although, I suppose if you were the one to kill him, it would be best to deny knowing him at all. And if she's telling the truth about not knowing Patrick was in the hospital, then who got him out? I suppose the senator could have arranged that and Jenny didn't know. What do you think?"

"I think she's telling the truth," Tuper said, shaking his head at her incessant babble. "But I'm not convinced she knows her husband as well as she thinks she does." Tuper turned and headed back toward the east side of Helena.

"Here's what I'm having trouble with." Lana shifted to face him. "If Patrick wasn't blackmailing the Smythes, why would the senator kill him at that particular time? I know it coincides with a payoff, but still, it was a mere twenty grand. Then he waited twenty-five years before going after Squirrely and Karl." She shook her head. "Something happened recently to set this in motion. And don't you find it odd that Jenny knew nothing about Karl? I suppose it's possible that her husband never told her about the accident or the cover-up. We know Jenny thought Amber was a young girl who couldn't, or didn't want to, raise a baby and wanted him to have a good home. But why was the accident a bigger issue for the Smythe men than the baby swap? Something else must have happened, or we're missing a piece."

When Lana finally took a breath, Tuper asked, "Are you done prattling on?"

"Almost. What do you suppose happened with the accident that made it so problematic for them? Everything we have on the senator is circumstantial. We have no real evidence. What can we get that would put him away?"

"I dunno."

"So, how are we going to find out? I'm at a dead end here, but we can't just give up. We have to get justice for Squirrely. We've uncovered fraud, manslaughter, bribes, blackmail, and a baby purchase, and we can't do anything with it. We know Senator Smythe is guilty, so how do we prove it?"

Tuper pulled into Clarice's driveway. "I'll go see Quince, the trooper who worked on the Grass Range accident, and you stay here and see if you can work some magic with that machine of yours."

Quince appeared pleasantly surprised to see Tuper. He invited him inside and gave him a bottle of orange soda without asking.

"Thanks," Tuper said and took a drink. "That hits the spot."

"I know this ain't no social call, but I'm glad to have the company just the same. I don't get many visitors. What can I do for you?"

Tuper decided to give him a little more information to see if it might trigger something. "It's about that accident in Grass Range. I think it's connected to something that happened recently, but I can't figure out what would have triggered it. Is there anything else you can tell me about your investigation?"

"I've told you everything I know. Like I said, we had some very likely suspects, but no real hard evidence. We were dealing with too many powerful men."

"Like the attorney general?"

Quince's mouth twisted in a sour expression. "Just like that."

"And perhaps a rich businessman who ran the largest car dealership in town?"

"I see you've done your homework. Yes, Gallagher and the attorney general were friends. I didn't discover that until later, but I'm sure that's why the investigation was stopped. I still snooped around a little but only when young Teller came looking for answers. And that was twenty or thirty years ago."

"Is there anything you can remember from one of those reports you wrote that seemed to have gotten lost?"

Quince thought for a few seconds, then picked up the report Tuper had left the first time he visited. Quince took the time to read through it, while Tuper drank his soda.

"I remember one thing that must've been in the second report because it's not here, and I know I included it. I talked to the witness who saw the red Chevy pickup, and he was sure there was a girl in the vehicle, two or three boys and one girl. The witness claimed the girl was driving. I never was able to identify her, but I was pretty certain who the boys were. They all denied it, of course, and they had alibis for the time of the accident. Witnesses were questioned who supposedly saw them in Grass Range earlier, but I never got the chance to get answers. Other than that, I don't know what to tell you."

∿

When Tuper relayed the information to Lana, she ran with it. "So, Amber was with them when the accident occurred, but no one knew that. She didn't get a referral at school. There's nothing in the records to indicate she was there." Lana's eyes widened. "Maybe we've been looking in the wrong direction. Maybe it's been Amber all along. What if she killed Patrick? And that's why she left Kalispell. What if she killed Karl and tried to kill Squirrely?"

"And just how could she do that? She doesn't even drive, much less have a car."

"Maybe she knows how to drive, and no one knows it. But she steals a car from the facility and takes it back when she's done."

Tuper slapped his hand on his forehead. "That's ridiculous. She's a crazy, old lady who doesn't drive and isn't coherent most days. Besides, what possible motive would she have for killing those boys?"

"You just said it. She's crazy. Maybe she doesn't need another reason. Maybe in her mind they were the reason she lost her baby. Who knows what's going on in that woman's brain?"

Tuper thought about it for a minute. Agony did have one good point. Amber's problems seemed to stem from the loss of her child. Then he shook his head. "Naw. There's no way

Amber could've pulled this off. Even if she could drive, which she can't, and had a car, which she doesn't, she gets too confused to actually find her way to Roy or even Helena, much less back home again. Besides, she's not crazy. That was a poor choice of words. She's mentally ill."

"Or she's faking the whole thing," Lana said. "She's been at this a long time. She should be really good at it by now."

"You're getting way off base here. I don't think Amber's presence in that car, if the fourth person was even her, makes any difference. There must be something else."

"I don't know; sometimes my hunches are right."

"And sometimes they're just wacky. If you saw Amber, you'd know."

"Good idea, Pops. Let's go see her."

CHAPTER 47

L ana and Tuper were headed south on Interstate 15 on
their way to Clancy to see Amber. Tuper made several
turns and drove through areas Lana didn't recognize before
getting back onto the highway.

"What's the matter?" Lana asked.

"I think we're being followed. We picked up that black car
shortly after we left Clarice's, and in spite of my zig-zag, it's
still with us."

Lana glanced around worriedly, then slowly scooted down
in her seat. Tuper looked at her. His eyes narrowed.

"Who are you hidin' from?"

"Whoever's following us."

"I figure it's one of the senator's henchmen, but why would
you hide from them?"

She sat up a little. "I don't want to get shot."

"You're not going to get shot."

"How do you know?"

"Because if it's the senator's men, they won't be that obvious. Besides, if I get shot, I'll probably crash the car, and you won't be in too good a shape anyway."

"Thanks, that makes me feel a lot better."

"This isn't the first time you've done that in the car. Whoever you're running from—"

"Who says I'm running from anyone?" Lana broke in.

"Like I said, whoever you're running from is none of my business, but I'd like to help if I can. So, if you ever want to tell me, I'll do what I can to protect you."

Lana didn't respond right away. Finally, she mumbled, "Thanks."

She kept glancing back at the vehicle.

"What are you doing?" Tuper asked.

"I'm trying to get the license plate number so I can look it up."

"It's eight, four, three, five, five, five," Tuper said.

Lana wrinkled her brow.

"What?" Tuper said. "I saw it back in Helena."

"Why didn't you tell me so I didn't have to keep looking for it?"

"I didn't know you were."

"Okay. I know that in Montana the first number on the plate is the county it's registered in. Do you know what county number eight is?"

"No. But I know it's not Lewis and Clark or Cascade County."

Lana had already opened her laptop and was starting it up. "I'll check." In less than a minute, she said, "It's Fergus County. Isn't that where Roy and Grass Range are?"

"Sure is."

They were nearly to Clancy when Lana spoke again. "Knowing the plate number won't help much."

"Why's that?"

"The license plate was stolen."

"Just the plate? Not the car?"

"The car could've been stolen too, but the plate is not on the correct car. The plate belongs to Gennifer Putnam, who lives in Lewistown and is forty-three years old. She drives a 2009 silver Toyota. That's not what's following us. So, someone stole something. You don't suppose it's Amber, do you? Maybe she stole the car, went to knock someone else off, and is returning to the facility now. You need to let her pass so we can follow her."

"Agony, Agony, Agony, it's *not* Amber. It's a man driving the car, but if he *is* following us, I don't want to lead him to Amber."

Tuper took the first off-ramp when he got to Clancy. The black Honda behind him exited too and stayed on his tail all the way to the fire department.

"Why are you stopping here?" Lana asked.

"Because there's no police department."

The Honda passed slowly, with the driver looking away so they couldn't see his face. Lana had already turned her head so he couldn't see hers.

"You're not sure who he's after, are you?"

Lana shrugged. "Probably not me."

They waited about ten minutes and watched carefully as they drove away. When Tuper was certain he wasn't being followed, he drove to the rehab center where Amber was living.

Amber was in the activity room when they arrived, so Lana

and Tuper joined her there. Two people greeted Tuper when he walked in.

"They think I'm Amber's brother," he said softly.

"Okay, but I'm still calling you Pops."

Tuper stepped past Lana and approached Amber, who sat on a sofa by herself, rocking her teddy bear as if it was a baby.

"Hello, Daddy," Amber said. "I'm glad you're here."

"Hi, Amber. It's nice to see you too." He turned toward Lana. "This is my friend, Lana."

"So nice to see you again," Amber said. "I know you. You live in Roy too, don't you? Did you bring your Barbie dolls?"

Another woman approached in her walker, but she didn't sit down.

"Hi, Thelma," Tuper said. "Are you having a good day?"

"Better than Amber. She's been like that all day. She's living in her young childhood years. She's been talking about playing with Barbies all day, as she sits there rocking her teddy bear. She keeps talking about her mother and father."

"That's too bad. I was hoping she was lucid like yesterday."

"She *did* have a good day yesterday." Thelma took a step with her walker. "I'll leave you to visit with her and hope she's better tomorrow."

Lana and Tuper both tried conversing with Amber, but most of what she said made no sense. After about fifteen minutes, they gave up and left.

"Maybe you're right," Lana said.

"Could you repeat that?" Tuper asked, cupping his ear with his hand. "I don't think I heard you."

"All right, it's not Amber killing people. So, who is it?"

"It's probably the senator, but just repeat the part where you said I was right. Never heard you say that before."

"Not likely you'll hear it again either."

CHAPTER 48

Tuper and Lana were only a few miles north of Clancy when Tuper's phone rang. He handed it to Lana. "See who it is."

"It's a 406 prefix," Lana said.

"Answer it."

She flipped it open. "Hello, Tuper's phone."

"This is Thelma, Amber's friend." She sounded anxious. "Can I speak to Tuper?"

"Hi, Thelma. This is Lana. Tuper's driving, but I'll put him on speaker."

"You can do that?" Tuper asked. Without answering, Lana pushed the button for speaker and held the phone in front of Tuper. He leaned toward it and said, "What's wrong, Thelma?"

"There's a man here talking to Amber. I've never seen him before, but he called her by name, like he knew her."

Tuper slowed down, looking for a place to stop. "And no one told him her name?"

"No, they wouldn't do that out front. And I don't think he is who he says he is."

"Who does he claim to be?"

"He said his name was Patrick Gallagher."

"What?" Lana blurted. "Turn around!"

Tuper checked his rearview mirror and slowed to a crawl. Two cars passed him, then he made a quick U-turn in the middle of the road.

"Thelma, we're coming back. Please stay with them and listen to whatever he says. Don't let her go anywhere with him."

Tuper pressed the accelerator, pushing the old Toyota as fast as she would go. Lana kept checking the time. They were back at the facility in less than five minutes. They both jumped out of the car and ran toward the front, with Lana two steps ahead. Before they reached the door, a black Honda raced directly toward them.

"Look out!" Tuper shouted.

Lana jumped on the hood of a nearby car and rolled. The Honda clipped the side of the car, and Lana flew to the ground. The Honda kept going, tires screeching as it left the parking lot and careened onto the highway. This time, Tuper got a good look at the driver.

He ran over to Lana. "Are you okay?"

She stood slowly, checking to make sure nothing was broken. Her left arm and leg were scraped and bleeding and her shirt was torn, but she could walk and move her arms. "I'm fine," she said, the veins on her neck pulsing. "Let's go after him."

"We'd never catch him, and we need to make sure you're okay."

"I'm fine," she snapped. "That's the same jerk who was following us. I just want to get that idiot."

"We will. It's the same man who was in Squirrely's hospital

room. But for now, let's go see if Amber's okay, then get you cleaned up and report this."

"Do you have to call the cops?" Lana's voice cracked as she asked.

"If we don't, someone here will."

Just then, several people dashed out of the rehabilitation home. Lana looked up at Tuper, her face turning white and her lips trembling. "I'll meet you at the gas station up the road. Pick me up when you're done."

She took off running before the staff members reached them. One was Carey, the director. "What happened?" he asked.

"Someone left here in a hurry. He hit a car and"—Tuper hesitated—"nearly knocked me down. Can you call and report it?"

"Sure," Carey said. He looked at Lana running away. "Who's that?"

"I don't know. Just a jogger, I guess. Please take care of this. I need to check on my sister."

Thelma met Tuper before he got to the activity room. "Amber's still in there on the sofa. I stayed with the man while he was talking to her, but he left pretty quick after I called you."

"Tell me as much of the conversation as you can remember."

"He told her his name was Patrick Gallagher and that he was an old friend from high school. She laughed and said she wasn't in high school yet. He said, 'Don't you remember me?' When she told him no, he asked if she remembered Frank Finnigan. She said, 'Of course, he's my friend.' The guy tried to convince her that he was Frank's friend too and that she knew him. That's when I left to call you because he was kind of badgering her. I didn't like it because Amber always got real agitated when the name Patrick was mentioned, even if she said it herself."

"Patrick is dead, so it couldn't have been him. You did the right thing in calling me."

"I thought so."

Tuper's phone rang. He looked and saw Lana's photo. "Excuse me," he said to Thelma and answered the call.

"When you leave to get me," Lana said, "cross the street and drive up Old Alhambra Road. Do you know where it is?"

"Yes."

"I'll keep going until I get to the fire station, then I'll wait there if you don't see me along the way."

"Okay. Are you sure you don't—"

Lana had hung up. Tuper looked back at Thelma. "When the man asked Amber about Frank Finnigan, did he say Frank or Frankie?"

She thought for a second. "Frank, definitely, not Frankie."

"Did he say anything more after you came back from calling me?"

"Not much, and Amber had stopped talking altogether."

When they reached Amber, Thelma patted Amber on the shoulder. "Are you okay?"

"I'm fine," Amber said. "That man was funny. He thought I was in high school."

"Yes, he was just being funny," Thelma said. "I'm going to leave now, but Tuper will visit with you. I'll see you soon." She walked away.

Amber sat there calmly with her teddy bear tucked under her arm and her hands folded in her lap.

"Hello, Amber. It's Tuper. Are you okay?"

She looked up at him with hollow eyes, then back at her hands. She didn't respond. He sat next to her quietly for a while, then tried again. This time Amber smiled. "Did you bring the dolls?"

Tuper talked to her for a few minutes, but Amber remained in her childhood years. When a uniformed officer came into the room, Tuper left Amber and walked out with him. Tuper told him what had happened, including the part where he thought he was being followed. Tuper gave the license plate number but said nothing about it being stolen. They could figure that part out for themselves.

"Do you know the man who did this?"

"No, we've never met. But I recognized him from the hospital where he tried to kill my friend, Frank Finnigan."

"Why is he following you?"

"I don't know." Tuper was getting impatient. He wanted to get out of there, make sure Lana was okay, and get home. "You need to talk to Helena PD. They can fill you in." Tuper shuffled. "Are we done here?"

"You can go. I'll be in touch."

Tuper drove up Old Alhambra Road, but he didn't see Lana along the way. He continued on until he reached the fire station. When he didn't see her there, he parked and went inside. Lana was standing near a window talking to a firefighter. He noticed a new bandage on her left arm this time and one on her leg.

"Hi, Pops, thanks for coming to get me." She waved as she walked out. "Thanks, everybody."

She held out both bandaged arms. "Look, they match now."

"What did you tell the firemen?" Tuper asked.

"That I crashed my bike and you were coming to get me. One guy offered to go get my bike, but I told them you'd be along real soon. Another one insisted on bandaging my wounds. It's all good."

CHAPTER 49

The next morning when Tuper stopped by, Lana was already working on her computer. "Anything new?" he asked.

Lana looked up. "Nothing new. I got a little sidetracked, but I really don't know where to look next."

"You said something the other day about the accident being a bigger problem than the baby transfer. Maybe that's it. Can you find out anything else about the accident?"

"Like what?"

"I don't know," Tuper said. "I'm grasping at straws here. You're the one with the clever mind."

She thought for a moment. "You mean like Patrick's father knowing the people who were killed? Maybe he sold them the car, and there was something wrong with it. Maybe he was afraid the blame would come back on him. Or, was there something wrong with the pickup the kids were driving that made it unsafe, again making him the one at fault?" She paused for a breath. "Or, maybe it was something that happened recently that scared the senator. I keep wondering, why now? Why after all this time did the people involved in the senator's dirty little secret suddenly start dying?" Lana's eyes widened, like they did when she had her version of a brilliant idea. "OMG, maybe it's all about politics. Maybe Smythe plans to run for president. Every single aspect of his life would be scrutinized. I bet that's it."

"Not exactly where I was going with this, but I suppose it's worth looking into."

Lana went back to her search.

Tuper finished the breakfast Clarice had left for him and stood. "I'm off to the hospital to check on Squirrely."

"Bye." Lana didn't look up. She googled Senator Rick Smythe again and read through every article she could find, looking for a hint that he had presidential aspirations or some other reason why he had to obliterate his past. She dove into the dark web too, but after three hours she finally gave up. She found nothing that gave any indication he would be a candidate. All she discovered was that he appeared to be a moderate on most issues and never took a strong stand on much of anything. He also never supported women's rights. This was no shocker and only made her more determined to find some connection.

Next, she hacked into the car dealership that James Gallagher operated, looking for the history of the car the Tellers were driving when they were killed. She was not surprised to discover no records since they were not computerized back that far. She tried DMV records to see if she could tell where the Tellers purchased the car, but she had the same problem. The information was sparse. Then she remembered the police report Tuper had obtained. She opened the folder and looked at the photographs taken at the scene of the accident. There it was—a sticker in the back window that read: *Imperial Motors, Lewistown, Mt.* So, the car did come from Gallagher's lot. *But so what?* She didn't know when it was purchased or if there was anything wrong with the car, and that still didn't explain why it took so long to do anything about it. Especially, since Patrick's father had been dead for so many years.

She had nowhere else to search so she decided to bag it for the day. Before shutting down, she checked her email accounts. She had another message from *him*.

—*You don't have to keep hiding. I miss you. Please come home.*

Heat ran through Lana's body, and her muscles quivered. She wanted to vomit. It made her sick to her stomach that he was trying to sweet talk her now. That's when he was at his worst. She preferred his threats. They were easier to deal with than his fake concern. Maybe because she so wanted it to be real, but she knew it wasn't.

She slammed her laptop shut, ran outside, and jumped on her bike. She needed to get rid of her pent-up energy. It felt good to be in the sunshine after so many days of rain. She basked in the warmth as she rode, picking up speed, and not really caring about direction.

Lana rode on York Road until she reached East Custer. She turned right and rode all the way to the golf course. She made a left and followed the fairways, admiring the view. After she passed Carrol College, she kept going. She was now in unfamiliar territory, but she intended to make a loop and Centennial Park wasn't far away. She knew her route from there, and if she got off course, she had her phone's GPS to get back on track. Yet she preferred to use her sense of direction when she could.

She was pretty certain she had passed the road that led back to the park when she spotted the Helena Fire Department. Maybe she should stop. She had no idea if Brock would be there, but she decided to take a chance. At least she could find out if he really was a firefighter. It had been three days since she met him, and she hadn't seen him lurking around, so she assumed he probably hadn't been sent to spy on her.

She found herself astride her bike in front of an open overhead door. A shiny, red fire engine sat inside. An attractive African-American man in uniform saw her and asked, "May I help you?"

She started to change her mind, thinking she should just leave, but instead she asked, "Is Brock Shero here?"

"Hey, Minion," the firefighter yelled.

Within seconds, Lana saw a man slide down a large gold pole. She had never been to a real fire station before and was a little surprised they actually had poles. At least this one did, just like in the movies.

Lana removed her helmet as Brock walked toward her. She wasn't sure at first it was him. He looked so different in his uniform.

"Minion?" she said.

"Don't pay any attention to him. Everyone here gets a nickname, and Fire God was taken, so that's what they tagged me with."

"Why Minion?"

"Because they know I hate those little yellow, one-eyed guys. But enough of that." Brock gave her a huge smile. "You did it."

"I did what?"

"You said you'd find me, and you did. I didn't expect to ever see you again. How did you do that, by the way?"

"I'm resourceful."

"Good to know," Brock said. "I don't remember telling you I was a firefighter."

"You didn't."

He gave her a curious look, then let it go. "I see you got a new bike."

"It's a loaner."

"Come on inside. You can park it right there. It'll be fine."

"That's okay, I'd better be going."

"Hey, you rode this far. Come inside, and I'll get you a soda or a bad cup of coffee. Nelson made it today, and it tastes like mud."

Lana started to get off her bike when Brock's pager went off. "Sorry, I have to go. Give me your number, and I'll call you."

"I'll send you a message, then you'll have my number," Lana said. "Go."

He shook his head and started to walk away. "But you don't have my number." Just then his phone beeped. His message read *Yes, I do*. He looked back and smiled, giving her a thumbs-up before he dashed off to put out a fire.

As Lana rode away, her phone rang.

"Squirrely's awake," Tuper said. "Let Clarice and Mary know."

"Will do. Have you talked to him yet? How does he feel? Does he remember anything?"

"Slow down, Agony. I haven't even seen him. I was just informed that he's awake and that I can talk to him in a few minutes."

"Call me as soon as you do."

"I've got to go; they're letting me in." Tuper hung up before Lana could say anything more.

She checked her phone for directions to St. Peter's Hospital. It was less than three miles. She could be there in fifteen minutes. She called Clarice to let her know the good news, then started pedaling.

CHAPTER 50

The guard in front of Squirrely's room nodded when Tuper walked up. He was the same one who'd been there the last three days. They exchanged pleasantries, and Tuper went inside.

A detective was just leaving. "Are you Tuper?" he asked.

"Yes."

"I'm Detective Earl Bass. I'd like to talk to you, but I don't have time now. Would you mind coming to the department when you're done here?"

"I can do that."

"Thanks," the detective said and walked out.

A nurse stood on the left side of the bed. Tuper moved to the right. "Good to see you awake, Squirrely."

"Good to be awake," he said. The nurse started to leave. "Could you get me a mirror?" he called out. "I could use a mirror."

She said, "Sure," and walked out.

"What happened?" Squirrely asked in a more-mellow tone than Tuper was used to.

"That detective was here questioning me, but all I remember is going to Nickels to see you, and the next thing I knew a pickup was headed my way, and bang. That's it. That's all I can remember." He took a deep breath as if trying to muster up more energy. "They say it wasn't an accident and that someone came to my room here and tried to kill me again. Did that really happen?" Squirrely was obviously on medication. He spoke slower and more deliberately than usual.

"So much has happened since you were hit." Tuper didn't know where to start. "I'll tell you all about it, but maybe you could answer a few questions for me first."

"Yeh. Yeh. I can do that."

Tuper was happy to hear that "yeh" clicking sound again.

Without much of a pause, Squirrely asked, "Do you have a mirror?"

"No, but the nurse will bring one. Look, I know all about Patrick Gallagher and Karl Haberman and the accident in Grass Range when you were in your senior year of high school."

"You think that's why I was hit? Why?"

"That, and the circumstances that followed. Don't you?"

"Maybe." Squirrely rubbed his hand over his chin. "Yeh. Yeh. Maybe."

"I opened the duffel bag you gave me with the money, the newspaper, and the gun. I thought it might help me figure out who was trying to kill you. I know that money has been around a long time. Where did it come from?"

Squirrely raised his head a little. "Someone gave it to Patrick a long time ago. He asked me to keep it for him so someone couldn't steal it from him, and then he got killed."

"You've had that money for twenty-five years?"

"Yeh, yeh, but it wasn't mine, so I didn't know what to do with it." He laid his head back on the pillow. "Patrick didn't have any kids for me to give it to. No family. I knew someone who *deserved* it, but I didn't know how to get it to her." Squirrely looked toward the door. "Do you think she'll be back with the mirror?"

"She'll be back," Tuper assured him. "Did the money come from the senator and his wife?"

"How do you know that? About them?"

"I know all about the accident, Amber's baby ..."

Squirrely quickly sat up, then lowered himself back on the pillow, too weak to hold himself upright. "Yeh, you do know a lot. What don't you know?"

The nurse returned and handed Squirrely the mirror.

"I don't look too bad," he said. "Yeh, I could use a shave. You think you could help me shave?"

"Sure, I can do that. I'll bring a razor and even trim your hair, if you'd like."

"That would be good." Squirrely closed his eyes. Tuper didn't say anything, hoping Squirrely could sleep.

Lana walked in, carrying her backpack. "How is—"

Tuper put his finger to his lips. "Shh. He's sleeping." Tuper stood. "Let's step out and let him rest. He's not going anywhere."

They went to the cafeteria to get some drinks while they waited. When they returned an hour later, Squirrely was still sleeping. A nurse was just leaving the room.

"How's he doing?" Lana asked.

"He's good, but he was getting a little agitated so the doctor ordered a sedative," the nurse said. "He'll probably be asleep for a couple of hours."

"Why don't we come back later?" Tuper suggested.

"Okay. I have my bike. Can you give me a ride home?"

"Can do, but I'd like to stop at the police station on the way."

"You know what? I think I'll ride after all. It's not that far, and I could use the exercise."

Tuper wasn't surprised by her change of heart. It happened every time law enforcement was involved. *It's none of my business,* he thought. *She'll tell me when she's ready—or she won't. It didn't matter.* He just hoped she wasn't in trouble, and he wanted to be able to help her if he could.

Tuper walked into the Helena Police Department, asked for Detective Bass, and was led to where the detective was working.

"Thanks for coming in," Bass said. "Have a seat."

"Anything for Frank."

The detective asked about Squirrely's living arrangements, his family, and general background information. Tuper had been over this ground when they questioned him after the hit-and-run. He cooperated again, but he didn't volunteer anything extra. He needed to talk to Squirrely first. He didn't want to say anything that might get his friend in trouble, and he certainly didn't want to reveal anything about Kyle. That was Squirrely's story to tell.

"Do you know who might want to kill Frank?" the detective asked.

"I've known him for fifteen years or so, and in that time, I never knew him to have an enemy. He's a good guy, a little hyper, and he gets distracted easily, but he'd never harm anyone."

"You saw someone leave his room on Saturday around 7:15 p.m., is that correct?"

"Yes, I went after the guy and tried to get the security guard to help, but he just delayed me. By the time we got outside, he was gone."

"What did the man look like?"

"About five-ten with brown hair and a little gray on the sides. Sixty-five or so and kind of stocky with a smooth round face. He was wearing a black t-shirt with a flag on it, jeans, and old tennis shoes."

"That's pretty specific. Did you talk to him?"

"No, just saw him pass me in the hallway. I tend to remember stuff I see."

"And you saw him again after that?"

"Monday morning. He followed me to Clancy and to the Elkhorn rehab center where I was visiting a friend."

"Who's the friend?" the detective asked.

"Her name is Thelma."

"Last name?"

"I don't know."

"She's a good enough friend for you to visit, yet you don't know her last name?" Bass raised an eyebrow.

"She's old, like me, and has no one. She can't drive. I can, so I visit her from time to time."

"Have you ever heard her last name?"

"I heard it." Tuper removed his hat and ran his hand through his hair. "Don't remember it."

"I thought you had a good memory."

"Never saw the name. I remember things I see, not so much what I hear."

"And you're sure it was the same guy at Elkhorn that was at St. Peter's Hospital?"

"I got a pretty close look at him when he tried to plow me down with his black Honda. It was him."

"We got the information from the sheriff in Clancy, but the car was stolen and so were the plates."

"You don't say?"

"I'd like you to work with a sketch artist if you wouldn't mind."

"If you think it'll help."

CHAPTER 51

Tuper spent the next couple of hours with the sketch artist until he was satisfied the picture looked exactly like the man he saw. Then he picked up Lana, and they drove to see Squirrely. He was awake and eating supper when they arrived.

"Did you get some rest?" Tuper asked.

"Yeh, yeh, I did," Squirrely said. "Do you know what happened to me?"

"I can tell you what I think happened. You can fill in the blanks or correct me if I'm wrong."

"Yeh, I can do that." He turned to Lana. "Do you have a mirror?"

"Not on me, but we brought the razor and clippers, and we'll clean you up a bit."

"Are you sure you're up to this right now?" Tuper asked.

"Yeh, I'm good."

"I know you and Karl Haberman were best friends from the time you were very young. You and Amber Carlton were high school sweethearts. You all hung around together.

Patrick Gallagher came to Roy in your junior year and joined your group. Patrick was a city boy and a little more daring than the rest of you, so you started getting in more trouble. How am I doing so far?"

"Yeh, all true."

"One night in your senior year, you all went out partying and ended up at a bar in Grass Range. You had a car accident, and two people were killed."

A strained look crossed Squirrely's face. "That still haunts me. Yeh, we never meant to hurt anyone. We were young and stupid and didn't think."

"When you had the car accident, Patrick's father stepped in and covered it up. He was friends with the attorney general, Tim Smythe, and was able to quash the investigation. But Smythe wanted something in exchange. As it turned out, sometime that spring, Amber got pregnant and, although she was your girlfriend, there was the possibility that it was Patrick's baby."

Squirrely's jaw tightened, but he didn't speak.

Tuper continued. "The attorney general's daughter-in-law, Jenny Smythe, couldn't have children, and in exchange for keeping Amber and you boys out of trouble, you had to give up the baby."

"Yeh, almost right, except Amber wasn't with us in Grass Range, and Patrick never had sex with Amber."

"A witness thought they saw a girl behind the wheel." Tuper decided to handle one issue at a time.

"No. No. That was me." Squirrely said no with a clicking sound too. "There was no girl with us. I had long hair at the time. Yeh, I suppose that's why they pegged me for a girl."

"So why did Amber give up her baby?"

"For me, I suppose. I would've been in the most trouble,

probably would've gone to prison. She couldn't bear that. She wanted her baby, but she didn't want to start a family so young, and her parents put a lot of pressure on her to give it up. Yeh. They were concerned about her mental health. We decided that I'd join the Marines and after a few years, we'd get married and then have children."

"But that didn't work?"

"No. No. Amber was fragile, and she had a breakdown right after the baby was born. Yeh. I guess it was more than she could handle. Yeh. Another thing I've had to live with all my life."

"So, if Patrick wasn't driving, why did his father go to that extreme to save you boys? His son wouldn't have been in that much trouble. Probably the most they would've got him for was underage drinking and leaving the scene of an accident."

"There were lots of reasons." Squirrely turned to Lana. "Are you sure you don't have a mirror?"

"Where's the one the nurse brought you earlier?" Tuper asked.

Lana had already started looking in the drawers and pulled out the mirror. "Here it is, Squirrely." She handed it to him. "You're looking quite handsome."

Squirrely looked in the mirror. "Not too bad," he said, staring at his swollen, bruised face.

"You're looking great," Tuper said. "You were telling us why Patrick's father helped you after the car accident."

"Yeh. Yeh. I'm sure Patrick's father didn't want it known that it was his pickup in the hit-and-run. He didn't want the stigma of his son getting in trouble, but mostly I don't think he believed us when we told him who was driving. Yeh. Maybe he was afraid if it went to court, Patrick would be convicted even if he wasn't the driver. Or that since it was his vehicle, a jury might not believe it wasn't Patrick. He had already been in a lot of trouble." Squirrely picked up the mirror again. "Kind of a mess."

"You think that's why Mr. Gallagher helped you boys?"

Squirrely lowered the mirror but held on to it. "Yeh. And when he found out about Amber's pregnancy, he wanted to make a deal. In order to ensure the deal, Patrick told him he was probably the father."

"But he wasn't?"

"No. No. Patrick stepped up for that one. He and Amber had never been together. I'm sure of that. His dad wanted a paternity test, but Amber refused. Yeh. We knew that as long as he thought Patrick might be the father, we'd all get off the hook for the accident. Patrick was wild and loved living on the edge, but he was a true friend."

Squirrely was still holding the mirror. He raised it to his face again but made no comment.

"Have you ever seen your son?" Tuper asked.

"No, and he doesn't know who I am. It's better that way. Jenny has been a wonderful mother, and he's had a good life. I used to talk to Jenny once in a while, but it's been a long time."

"She was here to see you a few days ago."

"That's like her."

"So, you don't think she's the one who tried to kill you?"

"No. No." More clicking. "Sure don't."

"What about her husband, the senator?"

"No." Squirrely shook his head. "I don't think so. He'd have no reason to. He's kind of a jerk, but I don't think he's a killer."

"Any idea who it was?"

"No. I'm afraid not."

Tuper told him what had happened to Karl.

"Oh no. I haven't seen Karl since we left Roy. The last I heard, he had joined the Marines too."

"But you knew Patrick was killed in 1994. Is that why you had the old newspaper with his obituary?"

"Yeh. Yeh. That's why I had it."

"When I opened your duffel I was pretty surprised to find the cash. Do you want to tell me where it came from?"

"Yeh. I can tell you. It was Patrick's. He got it from Jenny. His car had broken down and he needed transportation. That was the first time he ever asked her for money. Yeh. Patrick was a funny guy. He drank too much and never could stay out of trouble, but he was a man of honor in his own way."

"When she gave him the money, he bought a car?"

"Yeh, a used one, nothing fancy, then he planned to keep the rest to live on. He also said someone was after him. That's why he gave me the cash to hold. He thought it was one of his street cronies who were trying to get his money."

"Why didn't he put the rest in the bank?"

"He didn't have an account. Never wanted one. He asked me to keep it safe for him, so I did. Shortly after that, he was killed. No. No. They never found who did it. Probably a drunk driver."

"I think it was the same person who killed Karl and hit you. That's why we thought it was the senator. It all looks like one giant conspiracy and cover-up for the accident and baby's birth."

"No. No. I don't think that's it."

Tuper glanced at Lana, who'd stayed remarkably quiet, then locked eyes with Squirrely. "You gotta help me here, friend. I'm running out of ideas."

"Don't know what to tell you."

"Was there anyone else who knew about the baby? Anyone who might have known what happened?"

Squirrely frowned. "Maybe. Yeh. Maybe."

"Who?"

"A woman, a few years older than us, was having an affair with Patrick's father."

"You think she might have known?"

"They were pretty tight. He could've told her, I suppose."

"What's her name?"

Squirrely rubbed his forehead. "Ah, ah…" Suddenly, he said, "Belle. Her name was Belle. No, Bella. Bella something."

"Bella Younger?"

"No, don't think so. Some Youngers lived in town, but she wasn't one of them. But it was definitely Bella."

CHAPTER 52

Lana was more than willing to help Clarice, who was still not at her best and wanted to get a little extra sleep. When she asked Lana to open Nickels for her, Lana jumped at the chance. Even though she was tired, she was glad to make the money and start paying for her new bike. She had spent many hours the night before researching Bella. Now she was hustling around getting things set up for the early morning customers who would arrive soon. Lana checked her phone: 7:59. She unlocked the front door and turned on the Open sign. Clarice would relieve her in half an hour, and Tuper would arrive around the same time to drive her to Roy. She only had to deal with customers for thirty minutes. She could handle that.

Two men in their mid-sixties, both regulars, soon entered the bar. Lana recognized them but hadn't learned their names. She said hello and served them their drinks. She didn't understand drinking that early in the morning, but these two were there almost every day, according to Clarice. They didn't stay long, but they had to have their drink before they went for breakfast. She tried not to judge. Who knew what their lives were like? After all, no one knew what she had gone through, and she didn't want anyone judging her for what she had done.

Another customer came in soon after, and Clarice walked in right behind him. Before Lana could get his order, Clarice said, "I've got it. Tuper's outside waiting for you. I told him I'd send you out."

"Thanks."

"Thank you for letting me sleep in. I needed the rest."

When Lana got in the car, she said, "Good morning, Pops. You didn't come in for breakfast this morning. Did you stay with Louise, or is the new honey cooking for you now?"

"None of your business."

Lana gave him a knowing smile and changed the subject. "Want to know what I learned about Bella last night?"

"I'm sure you're going to tell me one way or the other."

"Well, you do want to know. First, we have the right Bella. She was born Bella Matthews, right there in Roy, by the way. Can you imagine living in a small town like that all your life? How do you grow if nothing ever changes? I'd go stir-crazy." Lana shuddered. "Anyway, she married Herb Younger in 1975. Seven years later they were divorced, but Bella kept the name Younger. They both continued to live in Roy and neither remarried. I couldn't find anything that connected Bella to either of the Gallaghers, but that doesn't mean the affair didn't happen. That kind of thing wouldn't be recorded. Well, it could be today, with all the social media sites. People post the most personal things. Why would you want to share your shady crap for everyone to see? Anyway, back then, they didn't document gossip. You know, in your time, Pops, back in the good old days."

"There's a lot to be said for those old days before all the technology," Tuper grumbled.

"So, I'm thinking if Bella doesn't want to tell us what went down, maybe her ex, Herb Younger, would. Or maybe I should talk to Bella, and you can go see old Herb. He's apparently still alive. I got an address for him, although I'm sure all we'd have to do is ask where Herb lives and everyone would know. Of course, he was ten years older than Bella when they got married, so he might not remember much. She seemed to like those older guys. James Gallagher was twice her age. But anyway, what do you think?"

Tuper waited a few seconds to make sure she was actually done jabbering. "That's a good idea."

"What part?"

"You go see Bella. I'll try talking to Herb."

"Or we can go together to do both," Lana said. "Maybe we'll get more information if we go together."

"Or not. We'll go separately, then I don't have to listen to you."

"Aw, Pops, you know you love me."

"Don't you have something to do on that machine that'll keep you quiet?"

"Not really."

For the next four hours, Tuper listened to Lana babble. He regretted bringing her along, but the truth was she was darn good at getting information out of people.

CHAPTER 53

It was already afternoon when they arrived in Roy. Lana directed Tuper to Herb's house so he would know where to go. They drove past it, then went back to the Legion bar, which Bella frequented on a daily basis.

"Uh, oh," Lana said.

"What?" Tuper asked.

"It's Wednesday."

"Yep. So what?"

"So, that's the day Bella gets her hair colored. Not every Wednesday, only about every six weeks, but she was almost due when we saw her last time. I hope she's not at the beauty parlor. I don't know what time she goes. It could be—"

"Agony! Just go inside and see if she's here. I'll wait a few minutes. If you don't come out, I'll leave." Then he mumbled, "Or maybe I'll leave anyway."

"No, you won't, Pops. Okay, if I get done before you, I'll just walk over to Herb's house. If you get done, come back here and get me, or join me, or whatever."

"Go."

"Want me to get you something to eat?"

"Just go, please."

Lana got out, walked up to the bar, and opened the door. She could see Bella sitting at her usual table. She turned and gave Tuper a thumbs-up, then joined Bella.

"Hi Bella," Lana said. "Remember me?"

"Of course. What are you doing back here?"

"I came to talk to you."

"Well, ain't I special?"

A young server came over with a drink for Bella and took Lana's order.

"I'll have a cheeseburger and fries to eat here and a cheeseburger to go. Everything on the burger for here, but no lettuce or tomato on the to-go burger, just cheese and onion. Pickles are okay too. And I'll have a Coke or Pepsi for here, and an orange soda to go, but I don't want the other burger or orange soda until I leave."

"Got it," the waitress said.

"You're high maintenance, aren't you?"

"Never thought about it."

"So, why did you come to see me again?" Bella took a good swig of her drink.

"To get right to the point, Patrick Gallagher was killed, Karl Haberman was killed, two attempts were made on Frank Finnigan's life, and now Amber Carlton is in danger. I think, no, actually I'm sure you know more than what you're telling me."

"I don't care what you think I might know; I'm sure I don't."

"Do you really want to risk someone's life because of something that happened so long ago?" Lana asked.

"How would I know anything?"

"Because whatever went down was orchestrated by James Gallagher, Patrick's father, and you two were very close."

Bella started to object, but must have realized it would do no good. Instead, she downed her drink and signaled the waitress for another. "I was twenty-two when Patrick came to town. He was only seventeen but very worldly and seemed so much older. He wooed me until I slept with him, and then he moved on. A month later, I discovered I was pregnant. When I told Patrick, he said he would take care of everything. I foolishly thought that meant we'd be together, but instead he went to his father. James helped me get an abortion. He was very kind and stayed with me through everything. I never even told my parents. No one else ever knew."

Bella stopped talking when the server brought their drinks and Lana's food. When she left, Bella took another good gulp, then continued her story. Lana picked at her fries as she listened. This was not exactly what she had expected to hear.

"James paid for everything and drove me to Great Falls to have the abortion so no one locally would know. He was doing it all for Patrick, but we grew close and continued to see each other after it was over. We fell in love. We had to keep it a secret, of course, because he was married. He wanted to leave her, but he was just too nice a man to hurt his wife and child."

Yeah, really nice guy. Lana did all she could to keep from rolling her eyes. She wanted to blurt out: *He didn't seem to mind hurting you, though, as long as he was happy.* She took a bite of her hamburger to stop herself, then asked, "How long were you together?"

"Three and a half years."

Lana chose her words carefully so she wouldn't give anything away. "And you knew about Amber's baby?"

Bella nodded. "I knew Patrick and Amber had slept together. At least, that's what he told his father. I was shocked because Amber was so in love with Frankie. It's hard to believe she would've cheated on him. I could see Patrick bragging about that sort of thing to his friends, but he had no reason to tell his father unless it was true." She took another slug of her drink, a pained expression on her face. "James went to work on Amber, but she wouldn't abort, and it was getting late in the game anyway. Then one afternoon when we were out together, he told me he had a better solution. He had already spoken to Amber and to her parents, and they were all in agreement."

"What was that plan?" Lana had heard one version, but she wanted to know if there was a new detail that might help them find the killer.

"He had a friend whose daughter-in-law couldn't have children, and he had convinced Amber to give up the baby to them. At first, I thought they planned to adopt the child, but as it turned out, I don't think they filed any legal documents. But Amber had the baby and gave it to the family." She hesitated.

"What?" Lana asked.

"I think Amber changed her mind the day she brought the baby home."

"Why? What happened?"

"Because I saw her at the phone booth on Main Street that night. When she came out of the booth she was crying. I tried consoling her without telling her what I knew, but she couldn't stop crying. She said that 'it was no use' and 'it was too late to do anything.' Then she kept saying, 'if only Frankie was here.' I felt so sorry for her, but there wasn't anything I could do. I couldn't betray James."

"Do you know who the family was that got the baby?" Lana wolfed her burger while Bella talked.

"No, I had a hunch, but James never confirmed it. I know money changed hands and the paperwork was set up to look like the baby was born into that family. James asked me to watch Amber after the birth and let him know if there was any sign she might renege on the deal. That's why I'm the only one who ever saw the child."

"And you're the only one who knew Amber had changed her mind about giving him up?"

"I don't think she ever really wanted to let him go, but her parents were adamant about it. And the night at the phone booth, she told me she snuck out to use the phone because her parents wouldn't understand. She didn't tell me what that meant, but I already knew."

"Did you tell James?"

"Of course, but he already knew. I think it was him she had called."

"The night James told you about the plan to keep Amber's child, was that before or after the accident?"

"What accident?"

"There was an accident that spring in Grass Range, and a couple of people were killed. Do you remember that?"

"Not really." She took another sip. "I vaguely remember it. I know the cops came and questioned some people, but nothing ever came of it. As far as anyone knew, they were just trying to find a witness to the accident."

"James never said anything to you about it?"

"Not that I recall. Why? What does the accident have to do with anything?"

"It's not important."

The waitress came back with Lana's to-go order just as she

finished her fries. Lana thanked her, then looked at Bella. "Thank you for talking to me. You clarified some things." She hesitated. "Bella, I don't want to scare you, but everyone who was even remotely involved with that baby swap has had their life threatened or worse. You need to be careful."

"What are you saying?" She looked shocked. "The Gallaghers are gone. They can't be killing people to cover this up."

"No, but the family who got the child is very much alive. They may not even know about your small part, but you might want to watch your back just in case."

CHAPTER 54

Tuper knocked on Herb Younger's door. A thin man in his mid-eighties opened the screen.

"Are you Herb Younger?"

"Yes, sir. What can I do for ya?"

"My name is Tuper."

Before he could say anything else, Herb said, "You're the guy who's been asking questions around town about Frankie Finnigan."

"That's me."

"Come sit." He pointed to chairs on the porch. "Always glad to help a fellow Marine." Herb kept talking as they sat down. "I enlisted when I was eighteen to avoid the draft. One way or the other, I was going. By joining, I got to choose which branch I'd be in. My boot camp was at MCRD in South Carolina. From there, I was sent to Camp Pendleton in California for my amphibious tractor and fighting training. My next stop was Korea. I had been home for about ten years when Frankie joined. I didn't even know he was a fellow jarhead until you came here. But I wasn't surprised 'cuz he had talked about it for quite a while. You boys had it harder in some ways than we did. No one appreciated your service in Vietnam. That was a real shame." Herb paused. "Sorry, you didn't come here to listen to me carry on."

"That's quite all right. I thank you for your service." Tuper wanted to tell Herb the truth about not actually being a veteran, but he needed information, and protecting Squirrely was more important than his own guilt. Besides, he would have joined the Marine Corps if he could have. It wasn't for lack of trying, but he hadn't qualified.

Herb spent the next fifteen or twenty minutes telling war stories. Tuper listened patiently. He even enjoyed hearing them, but was anxious to see if Herb had any other information. When he finished the next story, Tuper said, "I don't know if you heard, but someone hit Frankie with a car, and he's in the hospital."

"Yes, that's what I was told. How's he doin'?"

"Much better. He has regained consciousness. But we still don't know who tried to kill him. That's why I'm here. I'm convinced the attack has something to do with Karl's death and events that took place in Roy over fifty years ago."

"Really?"

"Yup. How well did you know Patrick Gallagher and his family?"

"They were only here for a short time, yet they caused more of a ruckus than anyone else ever has. Roy was very peaceful before the Gallaghers came to town. Both Patrick and his father disrupted the quiet living here, turned this place upside down."

"What do you mean?"

"They came to town like a tornado and swept through, leaving destruction in their path. That Patrick was a wild buck, charming all the ladies, and then breaking hearts. Before the Gallaghers left, they got two women pregnant, corrupted half the young boys in town, and who knows what else."

"Two women?"

"Yes, my ex-wife, Bella, was one, but that was before we were married. The elder Gallagher, James, took care of it. He got her an abortion and cleaned up after the kid like he always did. That wasn't enough for young Patrick. He had to go and get Frankie's girl pregnant before he left town. Frankie split too. I suppose it was because he knew about Patrick. The girl moved away right after the baby was born. Don't know what happened to her." Herb stared at Tuper. "But both the Gallagher men, Patrick and his father, are dead, right?"

"Right."

"So, how can they be involved?"

Tuper looked up and saw Lana walking down the street toward them. He stayed focused on Herb. "I was hoping you'd know. Is there anything else that happened that involved Patrick, Karl, and Frankie?"

"They stole a school bus and had a party, but the whole student body joined in and no one got hurt. Most of us thought it was pretty funny." Herb stopped talking when Lana approached, carrying a to-go bag. He smiled at her. "Hello, young lady."

"Hello," Lana said, handing Tuper the bag, then shaking Herb's hand. "I'm Lana. I'm here with Pops." She nodded toward Tuper, then spoke sweetly to the old man "I'm sorry. I should've brought you something to eat or drink."

"I have everything I need in the house." Herb started to stand. "Here, take my seat."

Lana boosted herself onto the porch railing. "No, this is fine."

Herb sat back down.

"We were just finishing up here," Tuper said.

"Did you ask about the accident?" Lana asked.

"What accident?" Herb scowled.

"In 1969, near Grass Range, two people were killed," Lana said. "Do you remember?"

"Sure do. I knew George and Grace Teller. What a shame dying so young. I worked with George on a ranch out there. He was good people. Their teenage son, Jeremy, took it pretty hard. I tried keeping in touch with him for a while, but then I dropped the ball."

"Do you have any idea who was driving the car that caused the accident?"

He shook his head. "No, never heard."

"We'd better get going," Lana said.

Tuper stood. "It was a real pleasure talking to you, Herb."

"You too. If you're ever back in Roy, stop in and say hello. But don't take too long. I'm running short on healthy years."

CHAPTER 55

Immediately after they got in the car, Lana fired up her laptop. "Please drive over near the school because I can get a good internet connection there."

Tuper started to question her and then acquiesced. He drove the few blocks and parked in front of the school.

"Why don't you eat while I check something? We may need to make another stop."

"What are you up to now?" Tuper asked.

"Just eat. I'll tell you in a second." While she waited for the internet to load, she asked, "Did you learn anything new?"

"Just that Bella got pregnant by Patrick."

Lana waved her hand. "Yeah, I know that. Bella had an abortion, funded by James Gallagher. Then she had an affair with James and kept an eye on Amber to make sure the baby was delivered to the adopting family. But she didn't know it was the Smythes. She just knew they were important and powerful. That's about all I got out of Bella."

"So, you got more than me."

"Not really," she said. "But I think we've been looking in the wrong direction. I'll be able to tell you more in a minute."

Tuper ate his hamburger. Lana was deep into her machine. He wanted to ask her more questions about what she was researching, but the peace and quiet was a stronger attraction than his curiosity. And she would tell him shortly anyway.

The quiet didn't last long before Lana said, "We need to head to Grass Range."

"What?"

"All this time, we've been concentrating on the senator when we should've been looking at the accident victims."

"The couple who was killed?"

"No, the child who survived. It was something Herb said that got me wondering. Then I started thinking about Karl. It bothered me that Karl got killed because he didn't really have anything to do with the baby swap. I know he was involved in the cover-up because he was in the pickup when they caused the accident, so he probably knew about the whole transaction. And Jenny Smythe didn't know anything about the car accident or Karl, so I started thinking maybe Karl didn't know anything about the baby. So why was he run down? I should've seen it all along, but I was too hung up on finding out if that baby belonged to Squirrely, so I kept thinking the attack on him was about the baby. But what if it wasn't? What if the hit-and-runs were about the accident?" In her usual fashion, Lana didn't wait for an answer. "What if they had nothing to do with the Smythes and everything to do with the Tellers? Herb said he personally knew the victims and that the teenage survivor was pretty upset. What if Jeremy Teller, who would be in his sixties now, decided to get revenge?"

Tuper shifted his thinking now too. "He did go back to the

cops several times, trying to get them to do something on the case."

"I think that when he couldn't get justice for his parents, he finally decided to take it upon himself." She checked her computer again. "If this information is correct, Jeremy still lives in Grass Range. I think we should pay him a visit."

"Are you crazy?"

"We're real close. Let's at least go there and ask a few questions. We can take the 191 to Grass Range, then take the 87 back to Helena."

"I know the route; I just don't like the idea."

"Come on, Pops. It's not that far out of the way. Let's at least drive by his house."

"What good will that do?" Tuper asked, but he wanted to get a glimpse of this guy too. It was all starting to make sense.

Tuper started the car and headed toward Grass Range, while Lana tried to find photos of Jeremy Teller online.

"Here's one," Lana said. "But I think it's about ten years old. I don't suppose he's changed too much in that time. Pull over and I'll show you."

Tuper stopped at the first place he could, a dirt road leading up to a farmhouse. Lana turned the laptop screen toward him.

"That's the guy I saw coming out of Squirrely's room, the same guy who tried to run us over at Elkhorn."

"That's what I thought," Lana said.

When they reached Grass Range, Lana gave Tuper directions to Jeremy's house, which was not much more than a dilapidated shack. They drove past it slowly but saw no evidence of anyone home.

"Let's stop," Lana said.

"And do what?"

"We'll knock, and if he's there, I'll think of something."

"If he's not?" Tuper asked, but kept driving.

"Then I'll sneak inside somehow. The place doesn't look that secure."

"Are you crazy? You think this guy may have been killing people and yet you want to break into his house?"

"Well, when you put it that way ..." Lana typed something on her keyboard. "Maybe we can find him. It's a small town, and where do people go in a small town? They either go out to worship, eat, or drink. My guess is Jeremy's not at church. There are three places to eat, and two are also bars. I suggest we try the bars."

"What's our plan if we find him?"

"Let's just find him first," Lana said. "Turn right. There's a bar up here a couple of blocks."

Tuper followed her directions to the Fox Den Bar & Grill, but there were no cars in the lot.

"It's closed," Tuper said.

"So, that leaves one bar. It's not far from here." Lana looked around, then pointed to a nearby building. "That's it right there."

Tuper drove across the lot to the Wrangler Bar and Café. It sat not far off the highway, with most of the town behind it to the west and miles of open space to the east and north. Lana opened the door to get out.

"Where you going?" Tuper asked.

"To see if he's in here."

"Wait, I'm going with you."

They went inside and waited a few minutes for their eyes to adjust to the darkness. The bar was about a quarter full, and several of the tables had patrons. About half the slot machines were occupied.

"There's quite a few people in here for a Wednesday evening, don't you think?" Lana said. "Nickels gets like this, but Helena is a much bigger town. I suppose when you're the only bar, you get the business. Right?"

"Right." Tuper only heard half of what she said. He was looking around the bar for Jeremy Teller. "That's him."

"Where?"

"Over at that high table by the wall, sitting alone," Tuper said without pointing.

"You spotted him quick."

"Already seen him twice before, at the hospital and at Amber's place," Tuper said. "Let's go."

"We should talk to him."

"No, we shouldn't." He said it sternly, putting his arm around her to turn her toward the door. "Let's go before he sees us."

At first, Lana started to pull away, but then she relaxed and walked out with him. "Good idea. Let's go have a look at his house."

"I'm not sure that's a *good* idea."

"Either that or I'm going back in there to talk to him."

"Now, that's just crazy."

They drove to Jeremy's house, walked up to the front door and knocked, just in case someone else was there. No one answered. They knocked again. Still nothing. Lana tried the handle. It was unlocked.

"What are you doing?" Tuper asked.

"I'm going inside. You can wait here, if you want."

Tuper removed his gun from his hip holster and followed her inside. The place reeked of spoiled food and body odor. No one was in the main space, which consisted of a living room, dining room, and kitchen area. Lana waited while

Tuper checked the rest of the house. He approached the bedroom and stepped through the open door. Empty. He did the same with the bathroom.

"All clear," he said to Lana, who stood near a small corner table.

"Look at this," she said.

The table held an eight-by-ten photograph of a man and woman in wedding attire. "I'll bet that's his parents," Lana said, while snapping a photo of the photo and then one of the whole table.

"What's that for?"

"I don't know yet, Pops, but we might need it. Just look at this setup. There's a bible, a candle, a man's handkerchief, and a necklace with a cloisonné heart" She suddenly reached toward an old newspaper clipping. "And what's that?"

"Don't touch anything," Tuper warned. "That's so old, it's likely to fall apart."

Lana bent over and looked more closely, using the light on her phone to see it better. "It's the obituary for his parents." She pointed to another article. "That's the news story about the crash. And a photo of the accident scene." She looked up. "This is a shrine to his parents."

They drove in silence for the next three hours, except for the occasional expression of delight from Lana, which Tuper had come to realize meant she had succeeded in accessing a site she was hacking.

About a half hour before they reached Helena, Lana yelled, "Bingo!"

"Okay, what have you got?"

"Here's what I think. Jeremy dwelled on the death of his parents and tried for years to get justice for them. When he couldn't, he went after Patrick first because that's who the pickup belonged to. Well, it belonged to his father, but Jeremy probably assumed Patrick was driving his dad's vehicle."

"According to Quince, that was about the time Jeremy stopped asking the cops to solve the case. If you're right, he probably figured the only way to get justice was to kill Patrick himself." Tuper paused. "But why did he wait so long to go after anyone else?"

"That didn't make sense to me either. At first, I thought maybe he was satisfied because he got the driver. At least, he thought he had. Then I started looking at what he'd been up to all his life. He didn't have it so good. He went into foster care after the accident, jumping from home to home before he turned eighteen. He graduated from high school, but he didn't go to college. For a year or so, he worked on the same ranch in Grass Range, where his father had been employed. Then he got laid off." Lana made air quotes around the words *laid off.* "I think he was fired for stealing from them."

"Why do you think he was stealing?"

"Because he was arrested for stealing."

"Okay, that makes sense."

"He stole a saddle from the ranch. He didn't even have a horse, so he was probably going to sell it. The family didn't want to press charges, and I'm guessing they felt sorry for him because of his dead parents, but I can't know that for sure. Two weeks later, they laid him off. After that, he had several arrests for theft, mostly minor stuff, and did some jail time. Until 1994. He stole a car in Lewistown in April and drove it for almost two months, before he was caught. The car was pretty dented up when they caught him. He was convicted and sent to prison for six years."

"So, he had the car when Patrick was killed in May."

"Yes, and he probably used it to kill him, but the two crimes were never connected, so he got away with that one. He got out of prison just before Christmas 1999. By March of 2000, he was back inside for car theft again, along with a couple of other minor theft charges, plus a burglary. This time, he stayed there until 2008. He lasted almost a year before he got caught the third time. He was released three months ago, which explains why so much time elapsed between Patrick's death and the hit on Squirrely."

"Then he found Squirrely and went after him," Tuper said. "And then Karl. Now that he's out of prison, he seems to be picking his victims off one-by-one, and wasting no time doing it."

"Probably because he knows he'll get caught stealing cars and go back to prison," Lana said. "But what do we do now? This is all speculation, and there's so much we can't tell the cops because it could send Squirrely to prison too."

"We need to let him decide."

CHAPTER 56

S quirrely was more alert than he had been the day before. He was sitting up, eating breakfast, and for the first time he looked like he could hold his head up.

"Good morning, Squirrely," Tuper said.

"Top of the morning to ya.'"

"You're chipper this mornin'. Did you get good news from the doctor?"

"Yeh, yeh, I'll be gettin' out of here soon. Sean came by to see me last night. He said I can stay in the back room of the bar as long as I need to."

"That's good," Tuper said. "Squirrely, I think I know who killed Patrick and Karl and ran you down."

"Who?"

"I think it was Jeremy Teller."

"Who's that?"

"He's the kid who was in the car accident in Grass Range. He survived the crash, but his parents did not."

"Yeh," was all he said for several seconds. He stroked his beard. "Do you think I need another trim?"

"No, we just trimmed it. It looks fine, Squirrely."

"If you're sure." He paused again, then said, "Poor kid. I don't blame him, but why'd he have to kill Patrick and Karl? I'm the one who was driving."

"I'm sure he didn't know that, and no one else needs to know either. There were no real witnesses back then, and there'd be even fewer today. But Jeremy needs to be stopped."

"Yeh. Yeh." He paused. "No." He paused for another second. "I don't know. There's just me left, and then he's got no reason to kill anyone else."

"He'll go after Amber if he thinks she was in the car."

"No. No. We can't have that."

"The cops already have a sketch of him. They'll find him before long, but if I give them his name and tell them where he is, they should find him pretty quick. But that decision is yours."

"We can't let him get Amber," Squirrely said. "Yeh. Yeh. You tell them, Toop."

"I'll do that right now." Tuper started to walk away, then turned back. He didn't want to see his friend go to prison. He'd never survive. Besides, he had paid all his life for that one night of fun. It obviously still haunted him. "Squirrely, when Jeremy is picked up, he'll tell them why he tried to kill you. But there's no way a prosecutor could possibly have enough evidence to convict you for that accident. Even if they know you were there, they wouldn't know you were the driver. In fact, they would probably go after Amber. And there's no way they would ever convict her, or even file charges. So, if I were you, I'd stick to your original story—the one you told back then. Deny it all."

"Sure don't want to get Amber in more trouble. Do you think she'd want to see me?"

Tuper nodded. "I think she'd like that. When you're out of here and feeling a little better, I'll take you myself."

∾

Lana sat in front of her laptop in Clarice's dining room, but with a sense of worthlessness. She always felt down when she finished a big project, successful or not. Now there wasn't anything more to do on the case. She was in her element when she was using her skills to solve a problem. Working with Tuper had been good for her, even though she didn't usually make much money, or even *any* money, she felt needed. Then she realized there was still something she could do.

Senator Rick Smythe was up for re-election in just over a year. Even though he hadn't been involved in the killings, he wasn't a nice person, and the voters had a right to know. She had the ability to let them know, and she had time to get a lot of information leaked before the election.

She spent the next couple of hours setting up an elaborate plan to thwart his next campaign. Then she set it in motion by hacking into some Twitter accounts and posting little tidbits about his affairs. Instead of using the actual victims, Lana used fake accounts of women who called him names and told of sexual assaults. The facts were real; the victims were fictitious. She did the same on Facebook but with more detail, and she posted any photos she could find of him with young women. She found a connection to Jeffery Epstein, the alleged sexual trafficker, and sent it viral. She chose not to say anything about Kyle's birth because she didn't want to hurt him or his mother, so she concentrated on the senator's philandering. As it turned out, with a little digging, she was able to come up with a lot of specifics.

This kind of hacking was so easy. Social media had opened up a whole new world for disseminating information, true or not. That bothered her, and she really didn't like people getting false information. But she told herself she wasn't doing that. She was getting the truth out there so people could make their own decisions. Besides, this was kind of fun. She really didn't like the man. She knew she could affect his election results, and once he wasn't a senator any longer, Esmeralda might be able to see Kyle again, maybe even take care of his children. Kyle was luckier than most; he had three mothers who loved and sacrificed so much for him. Amber, who gave up her child and her whole life for him; Jenny, who put up with a horrible marriage for him; and Esmeralda, who was still doing what she thought was best for him.

Lana had to keep Smythe from being re-elected and she could. This was right in her wheelhouse. After all, this was what she was trained for, and a senator was small potatoes.

When she finished, she checked her Hotmail account, always hoping to find nothing. Her stomach churned with fear and disgust when she saw the email.

—*Come on, Baby. I need you to come home.*

Lana felt herself holding her breath. She had to tell herself to breathe. He didn't know where she was, or he would make his move. He would take her by force if he had to. She was worth a lot to him. Needing fresh air before she suffocated, Lana closed her email account and then her browser. She shut the laptop, went outside, and jumped on her bike. *I'll think about that tomorrow. Today, I'm going for a ride.*

She pedaled hard and fast, not paying attention to her destination. She soon found herself back at the fire station, but she rode past. She didn't feel like explaining why she was upset, and she sure couldn't tell Brock the truth.

Lana was only a few blocks past the station when her phone rang, and she saw the name *Brock* flash across her screen. Had he seen her ride by? She felt both nervous and excited. Would he think she was some kind of stalker? She wanted to answer the call, but she didn't know what to say. She wanted to get to know him better, but she was reluctant. She was still not a hundred percent sure he was on the level. Worst of all, she didn't want to get involved, then have to leave. She knew that meant she couldn't get attached to anyone. She also wasn't interested in casual hookups right now. She remembered what he looked like and how hot he was and started to rethink the whole thing. *Maybe having a quick fling wouldn't be so bad.*

She reached for her phone and swiped the screen, but it was too late. He was already going to voice mail. She waited for the beep and listened to the message.

Hi Lana, this is Brock Shero, your knight in shining armor. Okay, maybe my armor doesn't exactly shine, but my fire truck does. I'd love to get together with you. Maybe take you out to eat, or drinks, or dancing, or all of the above. If that's too much, we can just go for coffee. But please call me. We'll figure it out.

Lana liked the sound of his voice and decided she would call him back as soon as she got home. She headed in that direction, moving faster each time she thought about her mission. She had made up her mind and was excited by the prospect. She put any thoughts that might deter her out of her mind.

Hot, sweaty, and exhausted, she parked her bike on the porch of Clarice's house, hoping to be alone for a while so she could make her call. Instead, Tuper greeted her at the door.

"Come on, I want you to go somewhere with me," he said.

"I need to shower."

"You can do that when you get back."

"Where we going?" Lana asked.

"To see someone."

"Who?"

"You'll see. Let's go."

CHAPTER 57

"Thanks for seeing me again, Esmeralda," Lana said as she walked inside.

"Of course."

"I have something for you that might help make life a little easier." She handed her the bag of money from Squirrely, which she had put in a clean, new knapsack.

Esmeralda opened it, and her eyes widened. "What is this? Where did it come from?"

"It's legally obtained. You don't know the donor, but he knew of you and wanted you to have it."

"Who is it?" Tears rolled down her cheeks. "I need to thank him."

"He needs to remain anonymous. He just wants your life to be a little better. Although you're not aware of it, and have never met him, you've done something for him that has made his life a little more bearable. He wants to repay you, and this is the only way he knows how."

"Gracias a Dios," she said, making the sign of the cross. Esmeralda sat there, shaking her head in disbelief, while Lana reassured her again that it was all legitimate. Finally, Esmeralda asked, "Are you sure it's not from Kyle?"

"No, it is not," Lana said.

"Have you seen him? Kyle, I mean."

"Not since the last time we talked, and I probably won't, but there's someone you can ask yourself. His mother is here, and she'd like to see you. She knows nothing about the money, so please don't say anything to her about it."

Lana called Tuper, who waited outside, to see if Jenny had arrived. She had, so he brought her into the house. Esmeralda kept apologizing for her humble surroundings. Jenny tried to assure her that everything was beautiful, but the nanny was obviously beyond embarrassed.

"How is Kyle? I really miss him."

"He would love to see you."

"No, I couldn't do that. The senator wouldn't like it."

"Oh, pooh on the senator. Besides, he won't be a senator for long. He's really struggling in the polls, maybe enough that he'll drop out of the race. A lot of scandals have surfaced, some I was aware of, but many I was not. He becomes more like his father every day. I filed for divorce, and when that news hits the public, it'll probably be enough to put him over the edge."

"It won't hurt you or Kyle if I see him?" Esmeralda asked. "The senator always said it would."

"He lied. He lied about a lot of things. I know Kyle would love to see you. He still talks about you to this day. He has three wonderful children, my grandchildren, who could benefit from knowing a woman like you."

"You are so kind, Mrs. Smythe."

"Please call me Jenny. I've never been fond of the name Smythe."

When they all walked toward the door, Jenny stopped and gave Esmeralda a hug. "*I* miss you too, Elda."

Tuper and Lana glanced at each other, and in unison said, "Elda?"

Jenny and Esmeralda both laughed, and Jenny explained that was what Kyle called her when he was a toddler. It had stuck for years. Lana had a quick flash of all the wasted time she'd spent trying to find Elba in her research.

"Are you working?" Jenny asked Esmeralda.

"I'm cleaning office buildings, but it's only part time now, and getting less all the time. They want younger men and woman, so I don't get as many jobs."

"I sure could use a housekeeper, just for the light stuff, if you're interested. You could live-in, now that I'm all by myself in that huge house."

Esmeralda hugged her again, fighting back tears with little success.

Tuper drove Lana home and went inside to see Clarice and Mary. He told them about Squirrely's recovery, while Lana sat down with her laptop. When Tuper's phone rang, he stepped away, and Lana finished the story he'd started without giving all the details. "The cops have a sketch of the guy who did it. They're after him for the attack on Squirrely and for killing two other people."

Tuper walked back to the dining room where they were sitting. "Thanks, Johnson," he said, and closed his flip phone. He looked across the table at Lana. "They arrested Jeremy. He's been charged with two counts of murder, attempted murder, grand theft auto, and several minor charges. He's going away for a long time."

"Does Montana have a death penalty?" Lana asked, researching it even while she asked.

"Yep, but I don't think they've executed anyone in a while," Tuper said.

"You're right." Lana read from her monitor. "They have it, but the state of Montana hasn't handed down a death sentence since 1996. Capital punishment in this state was resumed in 1976, but only three people have been executed since then. Eww."

"What?"

"The first execution was in 1995, and the victim's name was Lana. That's creepy. Enough of this." She closed the lid. "So, Jeremy *could* get the death penalty, but probably won't. I wonder if he'll take a plea deal. That would sure make it easier on Squirrely. But why should he take a deal? He'll get life in prison no matter what; even a twenty-year sentence is likely to be the rest of his life. He really has nothing to lose by fighting it. What do you think?"

"I dunno."

"I would fight it. He's too old to ever get out of prison if he loses. What can they offer him that gets him to plead? I suppose he could make a deal to guarantee he wouldn't get the death penalty, but if they haven't given anyone a death sentence since 1996, what are the chances they would do that? No, if I was him, I would be fighting it. That could really make it hard on Squirrely though, and maybe even Amber. Gee, I wonder if Amber would even understand any of this. I feel sorry for her. I don't know if I told you, but she had some mental illness problems when she was very young. That's probably why her parents were so adamant about her not having a child. That's also likely why she gave up her child in the first place. She made the ultimate sacrifice. Either that, or she really loved Squirrely and didn't want him to go to prison. Either way, she sacrificed her life for someone else's. I don't know if I could do that. Of course, I've never loved anyone that—"

"Agony!" Tuper interrupted. "Please stop. You're wearing me out."

CHAPTER 58

When Lana was alone again, she picked up her phone and returned Brock's call.

"Well, hello," he said.

"This is Lana."

"I see that. Thanks for calling me back. I was beginning to think you wrong-numbered me. Then I remembered you had texted me from your phone, so you couldn't have done that."

"I've been busy." She didn't offer any further explanation.

"Did you get your bike fixed yet?"

"I don't think it's fixable, but I still have the loaner until I can get what I want."

"I couldn't help noticing that you weren't wearing a ring. Is it safe to assume you're not taken?"

Lana smiled at his choice of words. "No, I'm not *taken*, or given, or any of those words that mean I'm attached. Hmm, attached, that's another word that has an interesting meaning." Without a pause, she added, "I think I'd better stop talking."

They chatted for a minute, then Brock asked, "Could I interest you in dining out this weekend?"

"Maybe we should just try coffee first." She wished she hadn't said *first*. That implied there would be a *second*. And she didn't want to think that far ahead. She hoped he didn't pick up on it. "Do you drink coffee?"

"Every day. And I'm fine with coffee *first*. Then when you see what a nice guy I am, maybe I can convince you to let me buy you lunch or go for drinks."

"We'll see."

"I'll be off work shortly. How's this afternoon sound?"

"Okay," she said, a little reluctantly. It was happening so fast.

"Three o'clock?"

"Yes."

"I'll bet you don't want me to pick you up, so how about we meet at Firetower Coffee? They have specialty coffee and the whole lot. Have you ever been?"

"No."

"Unless I'm wrong," Brock added, "and you'd rather I pick you up, I'd be glad to."

"No, you're right. I'll meet you there."

"It's on Last Chance Gulch."

"I'll find it."

Lana hung up before she could change her mind or say something else she didn't want to say. She had a sudden urge to run. What had she done? It had been so long since she'd had a date or any kind of love interest. She was excited at the thought, yet unnerved by the idea that it might not be real. *What if it was a set-up?*

~

Lana took a shower and a little extra time with her hair. She didn't wear makeup except for a little eyeliner and mascara. She applied it carefully, nervous and excited about seeing Brock again. It had been a long time since anyone had piqued her interest—or she dared take a chance. Suddenly, she felt a heaviness in her stomach and almost changed her mind. She turned her thoughts to what she knew about him. Everything she'd learned from her research was rock solid. She had no evidence or reason to believe he was corrupt, but a paper trail did not always give a full and accurate picture. She knew that better than anyone. Sometimes, people were desperate, but that didn't seem to be the case with Brock. Financially, he was sound. She knew exactly what he had in his bank accounts.

Lana was still fighting with herself when she got on her bike and started toward the Firetower Coffee House. On three occasions during the ride, she almost turned around, but something kept her going forward until she found herself in the parking lot. She recognized his truck parked in front and took a deep breath. *I can do this,* she thought. *I have to do this. I'll be careful, but I have to know if he's after me.* If he was, she would have to leave Helena and start over. The thought disturbed her. She had finally found a place that was starting to feel like home, where people cared about her. Even Pops, though he'd never admit it. *I'll keep Brock close and figure it out. If he's not what he seems, I'll know soon enough and move on.* Then her mind flip-flopped again. *But it's an awfully big risk. Maybe I should just watch from afar.* She rode back and forth near the side of the building, trying to decide. Finally, she took a deep breath, parked her bike, and walked into the coffee house. He sat alone at a table just inside, looking even more handsome than she remembered.

"Hello, Brock."

"I was afraid you would stand me up."

She smiled. *You have no idea. Or do you?*

CHAPTER 59

Tuper pushed Squirrely's wheelchair out to the parking lot and helped him into his car. It would be a while before he was rehabilitated from the accident, but surgery on his basal skull fracture was no longer a concern. His broken wrist would have to heal, but his internal injuries were on the mend and his head back to normal—as normal as Squirrely ever was.

"Sean has your room ready for you. He even fixed it up a bit. He put in a microwave and a refrigerator for you."

"Yeh. That was nice of him," Squirrely said, but his mind seemed elsewhere.

"You okay, Squirrely?"

"Yeh. Yeh. A lawyer came to see me this morning at the hospital. Jenny sent him."

"Good. She said she was going to. What did he have to say?"

"He said I didn't have to worry. Yeh. 'Don't worry,' he said. But I'm worried."

"Did you tell him what happened?"

"He didn't want to know what happened. He said he looked at all the evidence and there was no way they could prove I was there. Yeh. 'Don't worry,' he said. He thinks Jeremy will take a plea deal because he has already confessed. He even admitted to stealing Patrick from the hospital and dumping him on the roadside."

"Did you tell the lawyer anything about the baby?"

"No. No. Not going to. I told Jenny I wouldn't, so I won't. Yeh. 'Don't worry,' he said."

"I think that's good advice. It sounds like it will all work out. Jenny wouldn't have sent a lawyer who didn't know what he was doing. Besides, I have it on good authority that they aren't going to file any charges on you."

"How do you know that?"

"Don't worry, Squirrely. I know a guy."

ABOUT THE AUTHOR

Teresa Burrell has dedicated her life to helping children and their families. Her first career was spent teaching elementary school in the San Bernardino City School District. As an attorney, Ms. Burrell has spent countless hours working pro bono in the family court system. For twelve years she practiced law in San Diego Superior Court, Juvenile Division. She continues to advocate children's issues and write novels, many of which are inspired by actual legal cases.

If you liked Tuper, you can find him in The Advocate's Felony, book #6 of Teresa Burrell's THE ADVOCATE SERIES.

Teresa Burrell is available at www.teresaburrell.com

Keep in touch with her on Facebook at
www.facebook.com/theadvocateseries

What did you think about FINDING FRANKIE?
Please send an email to Teresa and let her know. She loves to hear from readers. She can be reached at: teresa@teresaburrell.com

If you like this author's writing, the best way to compliment her is by writing a review and telling your friends.

facebook.com/theadvocateseries

twitter.com/teresaburrell

bookbub.com/profile/teresa-burrell

goodreads.com/teresaburrell

pinterest.com/teresaburrell